# MARK OF THE GLADIATOR

 WARRIORS OF ROME

HEIDI BELLEAU
VIOLETTA VANE

Riptide Publishing
PO Box 6652
Hillsborough, NJ 08844
http://www.riptidepublishing.com

This is a work of fiction. Names, characters, places, and incidents are either the product of the authors' imagination or are used fictitiously. Any resemblance to actual persons living or dead, business establishments, events, or locales is entirely coincidental.

Mark of the Gladiator
Copyright © 2012 by Heidi Belleau and Violetta Vane

Cover Art by Petite-Madame VonApple, bit.ly/v6FsKa
Editor: Sarah Frantz
Layout: L.C. Chase, http://lcchase.com/design.htm

All rights reserved. No part of this book may be reproduced or transmitted in any form or by any means, electronic or mechanical, including photocopying, recording, or by any information storage and retrieval system without the written permission of the publisher, and where permitted by law. Reviewers may quote brief passages in a review. To request permission and all other inquiries, contact Riptide Publishing at the mailing address above, at Riptidepublishing.com, or at marketing@riptidepublishing.com.

ISBN: 978-1-937551-60-5

First edition
November, 2012

Also available in ebook:
ISBN: 978-1-937551-59-9

# MARK OF THE GLADIATOR

 WARRIORS OF ROME

HEIDI BELLEAU
VIOLETTA VANE

*To my mother, who passed on her love of history and her empathy for all the people in it.*
  *—Heidi*

*To my favorite writers of wonderful classical historical fiction—Mary Renault, Robert Graves, Gore Vidal, Steven Saylor—and to Fellini for Fellini Satyricon.*
  *—Violetta*

# TABLE OF CONTENTS

| | |
|---|---:|
| Chapter 1 | 1 |
| Chapter 2 | 13 |
| Chapter 3 | 23 |
| Chapter 4 | 31 |
| Chapter 5 | 41 |
| Chapter 6 | 57 |
| Chapter 7 | 73 |
| Chapter 8 | 91 |
| Chapter 9 | 105 |
| Chapter 10 | 115 |
| Chapter 11 | 125 |
| Chapter 12 | 143 |
| Chapter 13 | 157 |
| Chapter 14 | 167 |
| Chapter 15 | 177 |
| Chapter 16 | 185 |
| Chapter 17 | 195 |
| Epilogue | 207 |
| Glossary | 211 |
| Authors' Note | 217 |

 CHAPTER 1

## The month of Aprilis. Emperor and Son of the Divine Caesar Augustus and Titus Statilius Taurus being consuls. Year 728 from the Founding of the City.

Anazâr welcomed the first lick of the lash. The pain reminded him, in its primal way, that he wanted to live. Or at least that he *didn't* want to die.

It was always like this. Anazâr would walk into the arena, blinking back the sun, and he would think, *Dying today, that would be fitting; that would be the pleasing fulfillment of an incomplete pattern.* And then he would press the edge of his left thumb against his blade, letting the little cut bloom into pain, awakening his animal self, and death was no longer abstract, no longer a concept, and then he would *have* to fight, have to live. That thing they called Cyrenaicus would emerge to fight in Anazâr's place.

And Cyrenaicus *lived*. He'd lived long enough for Anazâr's left thumb to be etched with faint silvery scars.

The whip brought him to that same threshold of transformation, but left him at it in unconsummated agony, because here, against the post, there was nothing to fight but himself.

A warning breath sounded as the whip cut the air, followed by a line of fiery pain along his back. A moment later, the pain overran the line. Pain—ripping deep down into his straining body while his skin itched at the sensation of blood crawling down his back. Pain. That was all. He could summon up neither hate nor outrage, and he'd lost his fear of this thin leather lash the day he'd seen a nailed flagrum lay open a man's ribs and send him howling and broken to the afterworld.

The time for hate and outrage had passed. Even the bitterest seeds of resentment and despair, sown the day of his capture and watered ever since with an endless string of humiliations and degradations and *pain*, had dissolved into something else, something there wasn't a name for. Not in any victor's tongue, anyway, and that was all that mattered here.

"Ten lashes for laziness, ten for cowardice, and now another ten for disobedience," shouted the lanista's right-hand man. Degis was known for his mastery of the whip. For the evenness of his strokes. The assembled gladiators stood silently, observing the familiar lesson.

Anazâr counted the last ten strokes under his breath, even though it made them more painful, because at least then they couldn't become infinite.

Ten for despondence, ten for scruples, ten for passive rebellion.

When it was over, Degis untied him from the whipping post. "Come on, Cyrenaicus," he said, his voice neither angry nor particularly sympathetic. "You know better than this. You do. So turn it around by the next match, eh? That's if the lanista doesn't sell you first." That last bit was conversational, almost light, but the threat was real.

Anazâr tried to answer, but the pain didn't leave any space to even start to form the words. He twitched his lips and fell to his knees.

"Gaius! Achilleus! Take him to his cell, get him water, and see him bandaged. The rest of you, learn this well. I don't care if there's no glory in it—stick to the script! Don't piss around when it comes to these mythologicals. You *will* be noticed. You *will* be punished. Dismissed!"

They half marched or maybe mostly dragged Anazâr to his cell, then laid him out face-down on the thin bedroll. He heard Gaius sending Achilleus away, and he couldn't help the treacherous relief that seized him, however short-lived it would be, knowing that his dishonorable behavior had at least stolen them a moment of privacy— or what passed as privacy for slaves, anyway.

Someone had left the bandages and salve already, but Gaius didn't turn to the doctoring just yet. Instead, Anazâr felt his hand cup the back of his neck and squeeze. "I should let these fester," Gaius scolded without venom. "Really. I know what you were doing out there. I know it wasn't cowardice. But if you can't go along with what—" *I*, he didn't say, although it was there "—we, *all of us*, do, why don't you just fall on your sword? Why live to make me watch you get whipped like that?"

Never blame for the lanista, who'd ordered the whipping, but then, there never was. No point to it. Blaming what you couldn't control? Might as well spit in the ocean or defy a god by pissing against his temple wall.

"I'm sorry," Anazâr said between the subsiding waves of pain as Gaius carefully wiped his wounds clean and applied the salve. "I'm sorry, but I don't love you nearly well enough to spare you the embarrassment."

"If I didn't know you better, I'd curse you for a cold man. *I* love you well enough."

"As well as you can. And I in return, equally." Gaius began laying the light linen strips over his back—a welcome cool pressure to quell the burning ache. "Thank you," he said, and didn't know whether he meant it for the treatment or the affection. Maybe they were one and the same, here.

"You've done this for me before. The lashing is nothing. Your mood, though, that's what concerns me. You're so close, Cyren. Stay in good standing for another year and you'll almost certainly have enough prize money to buy your freedom. You're still a young man. Still handsome, even if . . ." Gaius trailed off at that. The slave tattoo blazing on Anazâr's forehead lurked after the *if*. "It can be covered. Even scarred out, I've heard," Gaius murmured, somewhat apologetically, as if he were sorry for his own unmarred face.

Anazâr tried to picture himself with a web of shiny scar tissue instead of the dark blue letters that followed the line of his left brow nearly to his hairline. TMQF: *tene me quia fugio*. In his language, *halt me, for I am a runaway*. A hideously practical preemptive measure against a repeat attempt at escape, as if such a thing were inevitable. As if he'd *ever* be so stupid as to try that again. But no. If eventually this life became too much to bear, he'd rather die in combat, where his cowardice could at least mean a fellow slave's glory.

But Gaius's kind words deserved better than Anazâr's sullen silence. Best to lighten the mood. "Am I still handsome? I don't make a habit of seeking out mirrors."

Gaius's knuckles brushed down his cheek, and though unseen, he felt the warmth of the cocky yet fond smile Gaius so often granted him. "The best looking man here, except for me."

With the utmost care, Anazâr pushed upward onto one elbow, twisting his pain-streaked body until he and Gaius were looking into one another's eyes. They were of a kind. Gaius was the only one who could speak his language. Not of his people, no—they had all died, down to the last man, along the harsh journey from Africa Proconsularis to Rome—but close. Very close. They had the same tawny skin, the same close-cropped dark curly hair, the same lean horseman's build that had led the lanista to train them for light-armored fighting. Even a similar network of scars on their bodies, a combination of injuries sustained in matches and those handed down here in the ludus, the ones you couldn't fight back against. No tattoo on Gaius, though; his face was a mirror, perfected. Strong-boned, square-jawed, eyes set deep and wide and guarded. Anazâr liked to think that *his* eyes weren't quite so cold.

They'd known yesterday's games would include a re-enactment of the slaughter of the suitors of Penelope. Anazâr had heard of the story—an old Greek one, called the *Odyssey*—before he was ordered to play the part of Telemachus that morning, but he'd never heard the story in full, and he'd assumed the slaughter was partly symbolic. The Romans did love their symbolism. When the gates opened, the entirely *literal* reality had hit him like a hammer blow: he, Gaius, and two archers would kill these twenty men. Twenty men who were unarmed, unarmored, too old or too young, and all sick, either with disease or fear.

Anazâr had held back. Hence, the lashing. Gaius hadn't.

So when Gaius's thumb brushed over Anazâr's lower lip, seeking entry, Anazâr pushed his hand away. He didn't feel superior—not with his own hands soaked in so much blood, and as much a slave's—but maybe they weren't so alike after all.

Gaius didn't press matters, didn't take offense, just nodded and said plainly, "When you're healed, let me know when to come to you."

Anazâr offered Gaius a noncommittal smile. Perhaps, in a few days, this mood would pass, and they'd fuck, negotiating a brief pleasure all the more tender for being hard-won.

Perhaps, in a few months, they'd face each other across the sand, lay whatever they had aside and fight to the death for a different kind of pleasure: that of the cheering crowd.

For now, he didn't want Gaius. He didn't want anyone. He wanted to want *life* again, instead of merely groping toward it out of an animal abhorrence of death . . . but maybe he didn't want that either.

His wounds hadn't even healed enough to allow for the removal of his bandages, and the lanista had already come for him.

"Ungrateful spawn of a desert whore. I should feed you to something."

Anazâr kept his eyes on the ground, on the lanista's fine black sandals stitched with yellow cord. They both knew the threat was empty. Iunius was a practical man. He wouldn't throw such an expensive slave to the beasts. Sell him off at a profit and be rid of him, though, that was a distinct possibility.

He seemed to sense Anazâr's prediction. "I already tried to sell you. The other lanistae aren't buying. Last week, I could have gotten top price. You were known as a solid thraex. Today, you're known as a half-mad bastard who can't, or won't, follow the simplest of choreography. Speak. State your case."

It was a dire situation. Refusal would be seen as insolence, but any explanation Anazâr offered, whether truth or lie, wouldn't be satisfactory, either.

He seized some Latin words and set them into the air, not even knowing yet what he meant to argue. "I'm not sure, myself, Dominus. A curse. Maybe it was a curse. I meant to follow orders. I can fight. Match me again, Dominus, and I'll show you."

"Idiot barbarian, you don't know shit about curses." Iunius shifted his weight, and the shuffling noise of his sandal soles carried his irritation, Anazâr's dread. "Actually, you're not stupid, but you *are* unpredictable, and that's worse. I could take a loss on you. Sell you to the mines; they'd get a good year's work out of you before you die. Luckily for you, I have something more creative in mind."

A strange, sweet pain shook itself loose inside his chest. *Something. Anything.*

"Thank you, Dominus."

"I've contracted you to another lanista for a period of two months. A very unusual, accidental sort of lanista. You won't be fighting. You'll be training others. It just so happens you're exactly what is needed there."

"Numidians?" Anazâr blurted out. Hope swelled in his chest at the thought of being reunited with more of his people, even for such a short time, even to such gruesome ends.

"Worse. Women! *Gladiatrices*. A perversion of the games. But there's an audience demand for it, so of course the consul will have them fight. The lanista is desperate for a new trainer. The old one couldn't keep his prick out of the stock, so I got a good price for your time there by assuring him you aren't inclined to do the same. I hope your lack of appetite for women is testament to your tastes in general and not the attractiveness of my kitchen slaves."

Was he supposed to respond to that? "I, ah—"

"I don't care *why* you are the way you are. Train them, don't fuck them. Simple, eh? Do the job right, and I'll take you back in good standing. And the lanista is a younger, wealthy man, politically connected, the son of a wealthy plebeian who raised his house to equites status, and that's as close to a senator as quim to ass, or duck to goose. Impress him and I wouldn't be averse to selling you to him and making the position permanent."

*And freed*, Anazâr dared to imagine. Many trainers were freedmen.

"If he's unhappy with your performance, I'll have you sold to the mines or maybe just scourged to death as a morale-booster for the other men, depending on the economy and my mood that day. Is that sufficient motivation?"

"Yes, Dominus. Thank you, Dominus." Anazâr carefully raised his eyes while keeping his neck bent downward. Iunius was thin, gaunt, silver-haired, and a full head shorter, but his presence filled the hall so completely he might as well have been a titan of old. There was a faint smile on his face; Anazâr read it as an expression of self-satisfaction. Iunius had seized financial victory, after all.

After that, things moved quickly, the way they always did when masters made up their minds. There was no use in wasting the trainer's time with the usual schedule of drills and exercises, not on Anazâr, not when he was leaving so soon, so he was made to sit aside and watch the proceedings, his itchy back baking in the sun. He studied the forms, the blows, the equipment, all as if they were new to him. And they were, because for the first time, he was looking at them with a trainer's eye. How best to explain them, to model them, when to introduce them and to whom? Some men spent more time lifting weights than others. Some struck wooden posts, while others sparred together. By which logic were they paired?

He had most of the answers already. It was common practice to second-guess the trainers whenever gladiators gathered. These were matters of life and death, after all, so he and his brothers talked of little else. But then, perhaps to call them brothers was no longer appropriate. All day, they were as focused on the task of training as they'd ever been, but not so focused that they didn't find time to spare him resentful glances. Here, as they took a moment to exchange weapons. There, as they paused for water. Did they think he was being rewarded? They must despise him for breaking their blood bond with his cowardice. For breaking that bond for *anything* other than death.

Even Gaius, who usually smiled like a madman and flirted like a fiend no matter their circumstances, avoided his gaze. Anazâr should have felt relieved that at least he wasn't glowering like the others, but it was a cold comfort.

That night, like the night before, he was barred from the common dinner and sent alone to his cell with food and drink: the same bland but hearty beans as always, but all he could picture as he ate was that his brothers were probably imagining him dining on meat and good wine.

"Dominus told me to give you this new tunic," the kitchen slave who'd brought his dinner said, laying it down beside the bowls. "But you'd better not put it on yet. You're still bleeding a little."

"Am I?" His back was such a mess of pain and itching and scabbing, he couldn't tell one discomfort from another.

"Are you—" She looked ashamed, for a moment, but continued on. "Are you afraid of going? I haven't changed hands for five years now. I don't know if I could bear it again. What if your new master is cruel?"

"Iunius remains my master. This new man is just paying for my services. Anyway, no, I'm not afraid. Iunius isn't exactly kind himself, and anything's better than the mines, don't you think?"

She didn't reply.

He slept on his stomach again and dreamed of riding to war with his kinsmen across the western desert. But the sand beneath their horses' hooves turned to seafoam, and one by one, they foundered and were lost. The water closed above him and stole his last breath.

In the morning, he woke gasping and realized with new dread that he hadn't even gotten the chance to say good-bye to Gaius. Maybe never would, depending on how well Gaius fought over the coming months. So he did what he always did: prayed to the Romans' god Mars and his own goddess Ifri that Gaius would win through safely. He couldn't ask for more than that. Didn't dare. Praying for freedom? Well.

Iunius and two guards escorted him to the house of Marianus.

He'd only ever walked the streets of Rome shackled and heavily guarded on his way to and from matches. This time, Iunius didn't bother shackling him. Walking without the weight of his irons felt close to flying.

He worked hard to keep his exhilaration and terror in check. There were too many strangers crossing his path. He caught himself calculating how best to kill them. Then he would blink his eyes and remind himself that this wasn't the training ground or the arena.

*They're fruit sellers. That's a slave girl carrying water for her old mistress. A group of musicians. Bricklayers. Children.* The world outside was so complicated, so rich and beautiful. The colors and the noises and the smells, oh gods, the smells: woodsmoke, roasting sausages, perfumed oil, spilled wine.

No one looked at him twice. Once, for sure, because few stood above him. But little else caught their eye. There were other tattooed slaves walking these crowded streets. Even a yellow-haired man, likely a Gaul, with TMQF emblazoned on his forehead. Wearing street clothes, unarmed, without the paint of blood or glisten of oil on his skin, Anazâr was no different from any of them.

Soon, the streets grew less crowded, the smells less pungent, the buildings lower, wider, richer.

From the outside, the house of Marianus was an immaculately maintained domus, walls scrubbed free of the graffiti and stains that marred some of their neighbors'. The heavy, red front door was so well-polished, Anazâr probably could have seen his reflection in it, had he the time. As it was, the door immediately swung open, like they'd been expected with some measure of impatience or anxiety. Anazâr thought he'd be sent to a slave's door, but Iunius beckoned him impatiently through the main entrance. He flinched as he passed the threshold, as though some invisible barrier would hold him back, or maybe it was a trick and he'd be punished for being so presumptuous, but nothing happened.

He bent his head so as not to gape at his surroundings. They were standing in a vestibule, and even though they hadn't yet been greeted or invited into the main area of the house, what he could see just here was extravagantly, ridiculously beautiful, as if he'd walked into a giant treasure chest, not a house inhabited by flesh and blood people. Pastoral mosaics assembled from pieces no larger than his smallest fingernail, the shining eyes of shepherds crafted from rare glittering minerals. A marble statue of a goddess, painted delicate pink and draped in gossamer indigo fabric. Gleaming candelabras—no doubt solid silver—flanked the entrance.

"Marianus will see you now," announced a well-groomed slave woman, opening the door to the inner house. When Anazâr caught her eye, he was momentarily stunned by how composed she was, the plaits of her hair speaking of delicate labor. Not like a slave at all, at least not the hardy kitchen women he'd grown to know and respect at the ludus. As beautiful as the house that kept her . . . and just as ornamental.

Well, no fear of Anazâr coming to such a fate: with his grim face, so rough-hewn and perverted by the tattoo, he'd probably never see the inside of this house of beautiful things again. He was already anxious to leave.

She led them through the atrium past a line of waiting men—*lesser* men, Anazâr understood at once—here to feed off of Marianus's wealth, their presence as telling of that wealth as the lavishness of the house they stood in.

Iunius, too, had his own clients, according to Roman custom. Hyenas, more like. Hangers-on. But then, here those roles were reversed and now Iunius himself played the client seeking nobler patronage, come to offer a prize gladiator as tribute.

At least Iunius didn't have to wait. They bypassed the line altogether and followed the beautiful slave into her master's study, an open room that commanded both the atrium and an indoor garden beyond. Anazâr caught glimpses of green vines, fresh blooms, and more statues, before his gaze was arrested by Marianus.

Eyes the same color and luster as the silver candelabras. That was the first thing Anazâr noticed, and also the last, because he forced himself to look down lest he cause offense. The floor tiles were immaculately clean; above, the sweep of Marianus's toga included a narrow crimson-purple stripe that Iunius's toga lacked.

Anazâr barely followed their conversation, an elaborate Latin duel of formal greetings and pleasantries, other than to notice that Iunius took great care with the titles he gave Marianus.

"So this is your man?"

His cue. Anazâr lifted his head and pushed back his shoulders, staring off into that familiar middle distance. Not looking down like a wounded animal, not looking directly at his betters like he thought himself an equal.

"Cyrenaicus," said Iunius. "From Numidia, one of Antonius's men in the Battle of Actium." And now, following the usual script, he gestured to the tattoo. "Once a runaway, until he found his purpose on the sands. Every gladiator he's met has begged submission or died under his sword. Now the glory of battle is all he lives for."

"Is it true?" asked Marianus with mild curiosity. Was it true that he'd killed many men, survived many battles he should have lost? Was it true that he moved like a bird of prey, striking and falling back, fighting with brutal grace? Was it true that now he'd tasted blood and heard the cheers of the audience, he would never deign to return to his rootless barbarian existence? "Is it true what your master says about you? You've no appetite for women?"

"Speak," Iunius ordered.

Shame at the intimacy of the question made Anazâr's throat close off, but he couldn't let it go unanswered. "I will not touch your slaves," he said, keeping his voice gruff and straightforward.

Marianus smiled at that. His mouth was soft, its curve guarded, but not cruel. His lips had a color like they'd been stained by wine. He turned his attentions to Iunius, Fortune granting Anazâr a moment to compose himself. "And he's not—"

Iunius's tone was defensive, quick-snap: "He's virile, I assure you. A powerful fighter and a powerful man. Would a demonstration comfort you?"

"Not necessary!" Marianus replied with an easy laugh. "Do you have a wife where you come from, slave? Is that it?"

A wife, yes. Was that 'it'? Not really. But Anazâr took Marianus's question for what it was: a mercy, maybe even in some wild daydream an acknowledgment of his humanity. "Yes, Dominus," he replied.

"There, see? An honorable man. Sorely needed in certain parts of my household."

Again, not really, but Marianus's kindness was a welcome thing. Anazâr had left without giving his wife sons, failing as a husband in the most basic way, but his final act had been to put her in the care of his brother, should he not return. He hoped *that* match had proven more fruitful for her, that he had at least succeeded for her in one single measurable way. In the end, it really didn't matter: it was just a left-behind thing, an inconsequential concern from another man's life.

"He's seasoned and trustworthy, despite the tattoo. Or perhaps because of it. Can I answer any other question regarding his abilities?"

"I would try him in one of the most important regards: language. Cyrenaicus, speak a greeting and a comment on the weather in every language your master claims you know." Marianus seemed more merchant than patrician in that moment, and Anazâr respected that.

"Hello," he said, "the sun shines brightly," in his best Latin, then his poor Greek, then his strong but rough Egyptian. He swallowed uncomfortably before he repeated the words in the last language, though it was his first: his mother tongue.

"So it is settled, then?" Iunius tried, a tinge of timid hesitance in his tone. So strange, to hear the all-powerful master in a place of inferiority. When his two months were over, could Anazâr go back, having seen it? Not worth thinking about. Two months was a long way away. A lifetime for a gladiator who saw regular combat.

"I'll take him. We can register the contract tomorrow."

# CHAPTER 2

He slept in the house of Marianus that night, deeply and without dreams, on a pallet on the cool cellar floor next to another slave. A Greek, he seemed to be, and Anazâr would have welcomed the chance to practice the language and discover more about the household, but the man was obviously scared of him. So Anazâr left him alone. There was always a sharp line separating gladiators from other slaves. His life was, paradoxically, valued much higher than theirs—more than many freedmen, even—and gladiators were known for violence both in and out of the arena.

He wondered, as he rose in the morning, what it would be like for women to cross that line. What it would be like to show them how to cross it.

The majordomo slave—another Greek, but elderly and without fear—allowed them out of the cellar and saw him fed. A pale, oblique morning light filtered down into the atrium as he sat by the wall and ate from a generous bowl of porridge. He was nervous surrounded by so much treasure, and the walls were crowded with painted scenes from epic stories that taunted him with hidden meaning, so he had little appetite, though he forced himself to eat anyway. A useful habit he'd learned in the auxiliary legion; it had stood him well as a gladiator.

The majordomo led someone toward Anazâr. A large man, almost his own height, with a thick neck like a bull. "Lucius Marianus Ursus," he announced. "A freedman of this house. Cyrenaicus, you will be under his escort."

"So you're the Numidian. I'm taking you to the so-called ludus this morning." Ursus spoke Latin like a native Roman, but his tunic was nowhere near as fine as the one the majordomo wore.

"I'm ready," Anazâr announced, for lack of anything else to say.

The majordomo smiled, tilting a disbelieving eyebrow at him. "I don't think you are," he replied, but then shrugged and continued on before Anazâr had a chance to reply. "Ursus will walk you through the streets. Once there, you will have full authority, and direct him as your assistant. You will report to the dominus every evening. If this arrangement results in any squabbling, it will go badly for both of you. Best to resolve any disagreements before they reach the dominus."

Anazâr was taken aback, at first, that the majordomo would think he needed such a warning, but then Ursus snorted derisively and he understood.

"Don't step too far from my side," warned Ursus as they walked through the red doors onto the quiet street. "You get stopped, you'll need me to vouch for you. And I'll follow your lead at the ludus, but don't you forget I'm a free man. I'll be going home every night to a wife I bought with my own damn money while you'll be sleeping like a dog on the warehouse floor."

"Understood," said Anazâr. As much time as he might spend trying to stay on Marianus's good side, as much time as he might spend training the gladiatrices, he would spend the same tending to Ursus's ego, tiptoeing around the shifting boundaries of freedman and slave. "I hope *you* won't forget that I could kill you within two heartbeats, armed or not, and would do just that at the command of the dominus. Watch me as I train, and you'll learn a thing or two yourself."

"Fair enough. I won't cause problems. The house of Marianus has my full loyalty. They're riding high on Fortune's wheel, and I along with them. The old master won favor with Augustus in the war, got into the equestrian order, and married his son to a senator's daughter before he died. The new master is just as good as a born eques and keeps a tight hand on the business, too. They say he has eyes like a wolf, you know, for the color, and because no one fools him. He's a strong man."

"He struck me as such. But . . ."

"But *what*? Don't talk shit about your betters."

"But he's over there, throwing up behind that pillar."

Ursus jerked his head in the direction Anazâr pointed, anger giving way to disgust. "By Hercules. That's a Lucius Marianus all right, but not the master. It's his brother Felix."

The same toga, but smudged with dirt and wine stains and a few other spots of more questionable origins. The same dark hair, short, but with an undeniable curl. Eyes of a wolf—of a very *drunk* wolf. But yes, now that Ursus had pointed it out, the man currently clutching at the pillar for support and wiping his mouth was younger, maybe even a decade or so, than the master. His face ruddy with drink but soft, with a fresher complexion uncarved by frown lines. Handsome, but without even an ounce of his brother's dignity.

"Should we help him home?"

"We're on important business, and the fool hasn't seen us yet. Keep moving. He'll stumble back there eventually."

No point in arguing. Anazâr cast one last look over his shoulder, saw that Felix was indeed already weaving his way in the general direction of the Marianus house, and resumed his pace.

They walked down the Palatine Hill until the buildings grew higher and jostled each other chaotically. Vendors readied their carts for the day's commerce and called to each other in a stew of languages.

"What place is this?" Anazâr asked.

"The southern Aventine Hill. Marianus owns a few warehouses here. Half of one of them was turned into the ludus." Anazâr must have paused, or shown surprise, because Ursus waved a hand in circles, the gesture of a man looking for words of explanation. "He didn't set out to do this. They were all left to him in a will. Personally, I don't understand the appeal. I've seen women fight naked in a whorehouse, and that's a shitload of fun, but the idea is for them to be *serious* at it. Perhaps even fight men and hope to win. Waste of good snatch, that's what I think. The old trainer—contracted from a real ludus, like you—did what he could, but . . . well, you'll see."

"Where were they bought?"

"A batch from Gallia, all Gaul women except for three Germans. Two from a Bithynian trader: an Aethiopian and a Sarmatian. The last being the most expensive, for obvious reasons."

*A Sarmatian.* Maybe this wouldn't be a lost cause, after all. "Good. But will she take orders? I've heard they—"

"Eat testicles for breakfast, eh? Well, that's your problem. Sometimes she will, sometimes she won't. But if she was as savage as the rest, she wouldn't have been taken alive. Anyway, that's . . ." He looked down at his fingers, curling and straightening them seemingly at random. "Thirteen together. No, fourteen. That's right. There's one more, who wasn't bought at all. A real Roman citizen who killed her husband. The evil bitch should have been thrown to the beasts for a crime like that, but the magistrate sentenced her to slavery instead."

And now she was Anazâr's problem.

*No.* It would do him no good thinking like that. She was his ticket to freedom. They all were.

They walked in silence for a while, until the acrid smells wafting from dye vats announced their arrival in the textile district.

"It's here," said Ursus. "This warehouse. And that's Quintus, the night guard. Wake up, Quintus, you lazy whoreson, the new trainer's here!"

"Go fuck yourself. I wasn't sleeping. Was I sleeping?" Quintus, a man of massive build with a stubble of sandy hair and puffy eyes, shrugged his shoulders, then gestured at Anazâr. "Wait, he's a slave."

Ursus spat to one side. "You figured it out! What possibly could have given him away? Of course he's a slave, you fool, just like the old one. Unbar the door."

"Cyrenaicus the Numidian," Anazâr said by way of introduction. Quintus grunted as he drew back the two massive black iron bolts that barred the warehouse door.

"I've seen you fight before. A thraex—I remember now. Well, good luck." Door unbarred, Quintus made as if to hand a key to Ursus, but jerked back at the last moment to slap it into Anazâr's hand instead.

It might be useful to remember that Ursus had poor reflexes, Anazâr decided as he closed his fist around the heavy, three-pronged key.

Time slowed—doorways often had that magic about them. Ursus snarled. The thud as Quintus kicked the door open spurred Anazâr into action, and he stalked into the warehouse with no hesitation, leaving Ursus no choice but to bob along in his wake. The threshold: a fulcrum across which their balance of power tipped.

In fact, the whole world seemed to go careening off balance.

He bent one knee almost to the bricks while leaning aside. The missile went hurtling over his shoulder to clatter against the wall behind him.

"What the fuck?" Ursus roared, forgetting himself and rushing forward while Anazâr took stock of the situation.

"Good aim," remarked Anazâr. His mind had caught up with the movement of his body. Someone in the darkness beyond had thrown a jagged chunk of wood at him.

"That was the Sarmatian, masters, and no one else! And she's out of things to throw, I promise!" Whoever shouted had excellent Latin; better than his own but still not quite Roman. A hint of *please don't punish us all* hung in the desperation of the plea. That she'd sell out one of her own was very telling of the work Anazâr had ahead of him.

His eyes adjusted to the dimness. They were shackled along the length of a single chain—had apparently lain shackled all night on rough blankets next to reeking latrine buckets. His old cell at the ludus was palatial in comparison. Bile rose in his throat at the thought of women kept this way, but he pushed it back. His wife was a woman— *these* were gladiators, and he'd need to treat them as such if they were to have any chance of survival.

"There's the Sarmatian bitch," shouted Ursus, pointing at one who was crouching in a corner like an animal, but not in fear. Long dark hair matted in filthy tangles obscured her face, and she *laughed*. "Should I throw that bucket of piss on her to teach her a lesson?"

"No," Anazâr said. "Stand back. Who among you speaks Latin?"

Shadowy forms stirred. A woman with skin much darker than his own raised her hand. "I, Amanikhabale, was the one who warned you, Dominus."

*Dominus.* He quelled the urge to look behind him. *I am he.* "You sell out your sisters so easily?" Anazar chided.

Her bold face fell for a moment, but she recovered quickly. "My people are known for learning, Dominus, a quality which could be of great advantage to you. Provided with tablet and stylus, I would quickly write you a detailed report of the food supplies, physical condition, and fighting ability of our motley group of—"

"I don't read, and I'll form my own impressions. Step back. Who else?"

"I am the Roman," said another, as large and broad-shouldered as the Aethiopian—thank the gods they all appeared to have been chosen for size—but shrinking in on herself, barely standing. She didn't even say her name.

"I am Venatrix, the Gaul." Her name meant *huntress*, but she looked more like a shepherdess, stolid and accustomed to patient waiting. Hair that if clean might be that golden color common among her people.

More women raised their hands after her and repeated their names, all mythological or warrior names no doubt assigned earlier that year. A Diana, a Penthesilea, an Atalanta. Some of them spoke in such a heavy Gallic accent that their Latin would be minimal, at best. Venatrix could translate, in that case.

"Those are the Germans," said Ursus, gesturing to the right of Amanikhabale the Aethiopian. "I keep them chained apart. They don't mix well, and they don't speak Latin. Nobody knows their jabbering." The three didn't look different from the Gauls, except they stood closely together and looked directly toward him, not downward, eyes steely and lips tight.

Anazâr imagined that the Aethiopian would have learned much of their "jabbering" by now, if she was as clever as she claimed. But she stayed silent. Holding back in hopes of a more beneficial opportunity?

"I will speak slowly, and I will wait for this to be translated, and then I will speak it again," Anazâr said, beginning his breath from deep in his chest so that his words exploded into the air and echoed from the high brick walls. "My name is Cyrenaicus the Numidian. I am here on the order of Marianus to train you as gladiatrices. Everything I do will serve that purpose. *Everything*. I am not here to punish you or rape you. I've fought in the arena and I will teach you to do the same. To fight, to kill, *to win*. What I teach you in these months will save your lives and those of your sisters. Since your lives are in the balance, I will not be lax in matters of discipline. But I will *not* be needlessly cruel."

One of the Gauls raised her hand again, and Anazâr nodded curtly at her. "If my fighting bad, the master sell me?" she asked.

Ursus moved closer to whisper harshly into his ear. "The old trainer already checked that. Rule is, they go to the arena either way:

gladiatrices or lion bait. Otherwise they'll all fight like shit so they'll get sold for whores and live."

Anazâr had already figured as much. "Nothing has changed," he proclaimed, and then tried to disguise the sympathy in his voice with savage finality: "You have no choice."

*Just as I have no choice.*

"A question from Rhakshna Roxolania, oh master-who-is-slave," shouted the Sarmatian in a strange, guttural Greek. "When can I kill some fucking Romans?"

"Two months," said Anazâr. "Next question?"

The scant light from the few high windows obscured the sun's passage, leaving the cavernous interior of the warehouse in perpetual rank-smelling twilight. *I am a master in Hades*, thought Anazâr more than once that day.

He could do little training. After unchaining the women, he and Ursus saw to their breakfast, and then there was the unavoidable matter of the buckets. He'd tried to organize a line passing to the sewer outside, only to have it break down into a German-Gaul shoving match where filth spilled across the floor as the Sarmatian paced and howled curses.

By the time the sun went down, he'd memorized all their names, judged their strength by having them lift stone weights, checked them for wounds and sores, and taken each alone (save Rhakshna) for a walk around the warehouse in the fresh air, for which they were all probably grateful, even if not all of them were quick to show it.

The Aethiopian was the last. She linked her arm around his elbow and walked as if they were lovers, smiling to passersby. "Can you even read the letters across your forehead?" she asked.

"I know enough," he growled back at her. "I know what they mean."

"That's not the same as being able to read, but fine. What was it like, running away? Being captured again?"

"The first was easy. I'm a horseman. I stole a horse and rode far. But it was winter, and I couldn't keep it alive, so they found me starving on the road." He'd been so far gone with the hunger and the cold and the lashing that the pain of the tattoo had barely registered, until he woke up the next morning and scratched and scratched until he bled all over again and screamed and scratched at his bloody forehead some more. Details, details.

The weather now was a perfectly fresh Roman spring. Cool breeze, but no need for a cloak.

"I could teach you to read, you know. That could increase your value to your master. I'd ask for nothing in return, in the beginning."

*In the beginning.* He could find no fault in her quest for advantage, of course, and perhaps they could establish an allegiance along the way. "We'll speak at breakfast tomorrow. I'd like to know everything you can tell me about the reign of the old trainer—what he did that worked, and didn't. I'll try to bring a tablet and stylus." He wrinkled his nose. "And most definitely soap and oil. Ursus should not have neglected that so badly."

"He's a pig. No better than your pig predecessor. You'd do well to be rid of him, if you hope to change things here."

"You overstep your boundaries," Anazâr warned.

"I'll act more deferentially around the other women, but I propose we establish our relationship upon the most pragmatic of foundations. You're in over your head. You need me. The only one of us who can fight is the Sarmatian, and she'll vault the wall and start killing the audience if given half the chance. Examine your options from the outside, all of them, as wisely as possible, and I'll keep you informed from the inside."

They'd made a full circuit. As he led Amanikhabale back into the warehouse, he saw that the sun had fully sunk behind the row of warehouses to the left. It was time to return for his report.

"Tuck the ladies in for the night?" asked Ursus, rattling the long chain he would thread through their shackles. *The ladies.* Two words, but they were filled with a giant weight of sarcasm and contempt.

"Yes," he hissed through clenched teeth. Amanikhabale may have spoken out of turn, but she was right about Ursus. Not that Anazâr could do anything about it. He addressed himself to the women. "*Vale, gladiatrices.*"

"*Vale,*" they murmured in a hesitant chorus of discordant accents.

"*Vale* my tits and ass," yelled the Sarmatian. Amanikhabale, who obviously counted Greek among her languages, fought back a crooked smile.

 CHAPTER 3

"Marianus is finishing his dinner," said the majordomo, whose name was Alexandros. "But he left word that you were to be sent in immediately. Ursus can wait outside."

Finally free of his unwelcome shadow, Anazâr stepped into the atrium. The candelabras were all lit up now, and warm flickers of light played across the murals on the walls.

"Is he alone?" he asked Alexandros.

"The domina, Aelia, is with him. She takes a keen interest in business and he keeps no secrets from her, so speak freely in your report. They have a young son, but he's staying at his grandfather's house this week."

Alexandros led him through the study that linked the atrium to the interior garden. The stone columns along the edges had white-flowering vines growing halfway up their length, as if the plants were trying to escape through the open roof into the night sky.

Anazâr tried not to stare at the garden, although it impressed him even more than any of the house's other artful treasures. He'd been born and raised in the dusty westlands, where oasis water was too precious to use on anything save crops.

Marianus and his wife had retired for the evening to a doorless room on the right side of the garden. Aelia was a beautiful woman, as the Romans judged beauty; Anazâr had lived here long enough to understand that instantly, to feel it down to his bones. Pale skin, softly curling honey-colored hair, a heart-shaped face with wide, long-lashed eyes set almost too far apart. On the couch where she reclined, the folds of her rose-pink stola draped over her delicate form, which was womanly but near child-sized, though perhaps his judgment in that regard was clouded by his day spent among the gladiatrices.

The slave woman from the other night sat beside Aelia, painting her nails with pigment from a cluster of miniature glass bottles tied together with golden wire, a little treasure in itself. The slave did not look up from her task for a single moment, but Aelia smiled to Anazâr and acknowledged his presence with a friendly, regal wave of her free hand. "So this is Cyrenaicus," she said. "I like his manner."

Alexandros dipped his head and melted away.

Marianus paced into view, sipping from a glass of wine. He nodded to Anazâr and stepped next to Aelia, reaching down idly to stroke one of her curls. Something about the scene made Anazâr's breath catch. Perhaps it was the ease with which they occupied the heart of this sprawling house, or the invisible bond of affection that linked dominus and domina.

"Report," said Marianus. "And speak freely. Recommend what you see fit; ask what needs to be asked."

"Physically, they're well-chosen. All are healthy. But there's a matter of hygiene. I see shackle sores developing, and living in their filth as they are is bad for morale. They'll be of no use to you in the arena, not like this. Other than the Sarmatian, that is—she'd fight in a fountain of piss, if you let her. I understand you might want their hair to be long, to show that they're women when they fight, otherwise I'd recommend shaving, since they're tormented with lice; the first battle will be against *those*. I request a visit from a barber and doctor, better daily access to water, a weekly trip to the baths"—he began ticking items off on his hand—"fourteen standing wooden posts for use in training, more stone weights, twenty buckets of sand—"

"Alexandros, are you making note of this?" asked Marianus.

"Yes, Dominus," came a voice from around the corner. That he could disappear so fully until needed was a sign of his skill and worth as a man and a slave, but also a sign of Marianus's exacting standards.

Anazâr finished all his items. He'd memorized them over and over again every step of the way to the house of Marianus. *One day, maybe I will have a better way . . .* Amanikhabale's lure.

"This all sounds reasonable," said Marianus. "I'm new to this business, but I'm willing to make an investment based on your suggestions and expertise. Alexandros will arrange everything. Thank you, Cyrenaicus."

"Will that be all then, Dominus?"

"Y—"

"No," Aelia interrupted, some spark of inspiration in her eyes. "We should thank him more. Perhaps he would like a glass of wine, or the remains of your dinner, Lucius."

Marianus's eyebrows rose just slightly in surprise, then fell again, his face resuming its expression of perfectly schooled control. "Would you?"

Anazâr shifted from foot to foot, uneasy at this sudden blurring of boundaries. Domestic slaves would know what was proper—would he need to sit on the ground to eat in their presence?—but Alexandros staying out of sight meant Anazâr couldn't look to him for guidance; he had no choice but to take Marianus and Aelia at their word and treat the question as one honestly asked, with no trick answer.

"No, thank you, Dominus. I had porridge and beans with the women at the warehouse. A gladiator's diet must be strictly followed. But I'm grateful for the offer. I'm not used to . . . to household service. But I stand ready to fulfill any of your commands, of course." He hoped his answer would suffice, but if it didn't, he was prepared to take his punishment.

"You'll find that discipline here is quite relaxed compared to your old master," said Marianus, smiling. "Efficiency, honesty, obedience, and loyalty are all I ask for, and you've proved the first three while seeming likely to prove the fourth." He left off touching Aelia's hair, drained his glass, put it aside, and began to pace, full of nervous energy.

Anazâr shifted his glance to Aelia, wondering if she would give him the signal to leave. She didn't notice him; her eyes were on her husband, and a small pout of displeasure settled onto her lips. Anazâr felt invisible, intangible, but not unwelcome. "I wish you would settle down, Lucius."

"You in my bed is what I need for that," said Marianus. His eyes narrowed.

Aelia sighed. "I'd like nothing better myself, but the moon forbids."

Anazâr's stomach lurched in a strange combination of arousal and fear. He shouldn't be here. But he *was*, and so was the slave woman, who continued to paint lines onto Aelia's fingers. She didn't show any trace of discomfort, but then, as a body slave she'd be used to witnessing these things, and likely more than just the *discussion* of them.

Graceful discretion—another skill he would do well to learn, along with Alexandros's trick at disappearing and Amanikhabale's letters. He stayed very quiet and tried to clear his mind. All he had to do was wait for a command, he reminded himself.

"I'd offer you the pleasure of Cosmeta's mouth if she weren't otherwise occupied," Aelia said, and the slave Cosmeta didn't flinch or even pause, just laid down her brush and picked up another one to apply a different color. Anazâr realized she was painting stylized suns onto Aelia's nails. The spark returned to Aelia's eyes. "Cyrenaicus, then! He doesn't have anything pressing to attend to."

Marianus, who'd been preoccupied with his wife thus far, suddenly turned that cagey, hungry gaze on Anazâr, and the regard brought a mix of arousal and fear roiling in his stomach, then diffusing, sinking lower, transmuting into heat and hardness. Not bodily fear—Anazâr had been used for release by masters before, and ones much crueler and less physically appealing than Marianus—but fear of causing displeasure, of being valued lower, of having his place in this household irrevocably changed.

Anazâr thought his hesitance would earn him punishment, but Marianus's face was sympathetic. "I'll give you the choice of refusing, and Alexandros will bring me a kitchen slave instead. No?" Anazâr stood frozen, barely able to breathe. Marianus stepped closer. "On your knees, then. No, not the tile, you can move to the rug. Don't look so surprised. I know some masters take pleasure in the pain of their slaves, but I'm not one of them. I'd have you comfortable."

"Dominus," Anazâr acknowledged, allowing himself to be led to the rug. Marianus didn't grip him, just barely brushed his elegant fingertips across Anazâr's skin with the faith that Anazâr would not let that touch be broken. Marianus's power: the ability to command without threat, to have his expectations fulfilled without voicing them.

That same touch guided Anazâr to his knees.

The fabric of Marianus's tunic was eggshell white and smooth and fine, and the man himself smelled of expensive perfumed oil and faint musk. Anazâr carried the day's sweat and exertion on his back, despite his efforts to sponge himself clean before he'd come to make his report.

He was fortunate to be so close to this man, this nobleman in his prime, everything a Roman man aspired to be. *I will please him. He will lift me as he rises, at his side or at his feet, it matters not.* His cock rose to strain against the rough fabric of his own tunic. He would not dare to touch himself, of course; this act was for his master's pleasure, not his own.

"Cyrenaicus quite likes you," said Aelia. "I can see clearly from here."

Humiliating to have it pointed out. By Roman custom, it was one thing to serve another man as his station required. Quite another to visibly *enjoy* that servitude. To be so affected . . . it was one step away from presenting his ass and begging to be fucked like a woman.

"Interesting," said Marianus, mercifully with no judgment, as he pulled up his tunic to reveal an impressive length of shaft. "I won't hold that as a mark against his virility. He's eager to please, after all. *Begin.*"

Anazâr lowered his head and followed the command. No coy teasing, as he would have with Gaius. He took as much of Marianus as he could without gagging. The tight skin of that hot, heavy prick dragged against his tongue, crushing it. He pulled back and went down again, forcing a little farther this time, and again, and again. Eager to please. *Oh yes.*

"Good man," said Marianus.

The words plucked at a string wound tight somewhere deep inside him. He redoubled his effort, his whole body humming with desire. Every inch he took, every thrust, every wet noise that arose from him—they all conspired to make him painfully hard, so hard he had to lace his hands behind his back to keep from touching himself.

*Later.*

Marianus's gentle hands cupped his shoulders, mapping the muscle and sinew under his skin. "So powerful, and yet you submit to me. The gods must favor my house."

Perhaps that was why Anazâr's body had responded with such unexpected intensity. Fate, the gods, the genii of this house, *ruled* him. He twisted his fingers and bobbed his head rapidly, sucking hard on the upstroke. Marianus groaned, hands flying to grip Anazâr's head, and he knew it wouldn't be long until the completion of his duty. He tilted his chin and did his best to relax his throat, letting Marianus fuck into his mouth with long, punishing strokes.

Still some measure of composure, even then, but not for long. Soon Marianus pounded hard and fast, chasing his pleasure, and all Anazâr had to do was not struggle, not fight, just breathe through his nose and hope he didn't choke too much. Performing these acts, that was expected of him; crying at them—even just as a purely physical response to gagging—*that* would be shameful.

Marianus pulled Anazâr close, the soft white tunic folds soothing his burning eyes. And then, with a satisfied shudder, Marianus released deep into Anazâr's throat.

He swallowed, and when it was over and Marianus had withdrawn, focused his mind on taking slow, deep breaths to still the frantic beating of his heart and the expectant pulsing of both cock and hole.

"*Very* good."

"Thank you, Dominus," Anazâr replied, his voice husky with strain. He leaned back on his heels, brushing his wet mouth and chin with the back of his hand and wrist, but not so enthusiastically as to be read as disgust.

Marianus let his tunic fall. "Alexandros, see him out. And give him a flask of wine for the walk."

"One from the middle amphora," added Aelia sweetly.

Anazâr was about to rise again when Marianus's hand fell, distracted, on the top of his head.

"Well, this is a novel proof of fighting ability." A mocking voice floated in from beyond the doorway. "Perhaps you haven't quite grasped the fact that cocksucking and sword fighting are two entirely different talents?"

A hot flush hit Anazâr's face and he stared hard at the floor to keep himself from rising in anger. Back at the ludus, such words could end in fistfights. But not here. There was no room for pride here. He forced himself not to ball his hands into fists. He wouldn't betray his emotions. He *wouldn't*.

Aelia made a clicking, dismissive noise, and followed it with a sigh of annoyance.

"Move on, Felix," said Marianus. "Don't you have an appointment somewhere to sully my name some more?"

Felix, the drunken wolf.

"Yes, it's off to sully I go. What a pompous prat you are. I hope my brother's spunk doesn't curdle your gut, gladiator. Aelia hasn't been the same since he inflicted it on her."

As Marianus exhaled, his anger seemed to fill the room, filling Anazâr as well and crowding out the shame. The insult to a Roman matron...

"Lucius, ignore him, *please*," she begged. No question she was often in the middle of these disputes, but despite her tone of womanly distress, Anazâr had the sense that she secretly found them more tiring than anything else.

Her words triggered a flurry of movement. Marianus hastened to her side and touched her hair again in a gesture of respect and reassurance. Felix departed swiftly; by the time Anazâr rose to his feet, all he saw was the trailing end of Felix's toga. Finally, Alexandros stepped into the doorway and beckoned, his elderly face composed into an unreadable mask.

An urge burned in him to say something, anything, to reassert his loyalty to the house and to Marianus in particular. If he had any hope of freedom, it would come through perfect service as a slave—the same service which Felix, in his prattling, vicious arrogance, mocked. There was no dishonor, nothing worth disdain, in what Marianus and Anazâr had done. Anazâr's body was Marianus's to use, and Anazâr, for his part, respected and understood that.

There was no time left to form the proper words, so he tried to put all of that into the bow of his head toward the couch. Perhaps it was his imagination, but even though the dominus and domina's eyes were full of each other, they still seemed to spare some attention to acknowledge his leaving.

He held on to that, and silently thanked them for it.

Back at the warehouse, in a lamp-lit storage room cluttered with giant skeins of thread like a strange, thick, cotton forest, Anazâr thanked the house of Marianus again as he drank the wine. It was very good.

He set most of it aside, though, out of determination to rise early and well. He would prove his worth, and help the women who slept below prove theirs. What had happened earlier was disturbing to his image of the house, but ultimately, the younger brother was of no account. Marianus held all power by Roman right, merely tolerating his brother's obnoxious presence.

Anazâr extinguished the lamp and lay back on his pallet.

*Begin.*

The sense of relief flooded him with twice as much warmth as the wine. Servicing the dominus without touching himself, then being forced to walk in silence with the surly Ursus back to the warehouse, had stretched his self-control to the limit, and it had been so long since he'd known privacy, lain down to sleep without the accompanying snores and shifting of other men, that to lie here now alone with his desire and his willing body seemed a gift from the gods.

Fresh in his memory, the touch of Marianus guided him downward.

*Good man.*

He stroked slowly, wanting to draw it out, but gave that up after mere agonizing moments. No more need for control, thank the gods. He tightened his fist around the length of his swollen prick, pumped hard, recalled the heat and the taste of Marianus and pumped even harder, enough for a little pain and then a much greater sweetness. It overcame him, dragging him spilling and shivering and gasping over the edge.

*Thank you, Dominus.*

Nothing of his own on hand to clean himself with, so he used his fingers, wiping them across his skin and then licking away the evidence.

He shouldn't have enjoyed it. But then, he was a foreigner. A barbarian. Roman honor didn't matter here.

Another sip of wine.

Sleep.

 CHAPTER 4

As Anazâr extended the wooden sword to Rhakshna, he tightened his grip on his own. They were blunt but still capable weapons with a core of iron wrapped cunningly in oak, and he'd seen them ruin mouths and destroy eyeballs.

She smiled happily, twirled away from him in a half circle, and swung it to test the weight.

They'd both stripped to loincloths, the better to illustrate proper fighting stance to the watching women. Anazâr had offered her a band of cloth to tie over her breasts, as he'd heard was the custom for women athletes, but she'd shrugged it off. Her breasts were small, high, tattooed with faded blue chevrons, and quite unburnt, disproving the Amazon legend. With her matted hair tied back, he could finally see her face, her knifelike cheekbones, her dark, narrowed eyes.

"Attend," he said in Latin. "She stands well: feet apart and planted beneath her hips, knees slightly bent." And then, to Rhakshna, in Greek, "Do your people fight with straight swords?"

"No."

"Begin by using it as you would a—"

She stabbed at his groin, a rapid but powerless stroke, and he knocked her sword off course with a defensive sweep.

"*Listen*, damn you!"

She hopped out of range and stepped back in with a slashing attack, again easily blocked, but as he thought hard on how to regain control, how to turn this back into a lesson, some crucial little area of space slipped his vision and the ball of her foot struck hard on the inside of his left knee, sending him sprawling off balance.

Gods.

Someone laughed, the sound starting unguarded, but quickly turning nervous and ashamed when Anazâr resumed his stance. Rhakshna pressed her advantage, slashing at his throat. With undivided attention, he blocked once more, seized her wrist with his free hand, then fell on her, bearing her to the ground with superior weight.

Her spasming muscles, her hissing shriek—no, this had gone too far. He realized he had no way to keep her pinned without exposing some part of his body to her teeth, and she was prepared to use them. Instead, he pushed off her and pounced to his feet again, extending his sword to her throat.

"I would have had my knife in your gut, you Roman shit," she cursed, glaring.

"I would have had armor and a shield. Get up. Listen next time, or you'll watch the rest of the day shackled." He spoke to the women. "Most men you fight will have greater weight, longer reach. You must use better judgment and strike more quickly. Rhakshna has the speed, but her technique . . . her technique . . ."

He'd been counting the women as he spoke, the eight Gauls, Amanikhabale, the three Germans trying to look as though they understood (he'd have to find a translator soon), surly Rhakshna scrambling to her feet, the Roman Cassia—

Cassia was gone.

The third storage room on the second level held skeins of cord so thick they might as well have been ropes, and that was where he found Cassia attempting to escape her servitude.

She had a slave brand on her right cheek. And she might have been beautiful—more so than Aelia, even—if not for the subtle asymmetry of nose and jawline that spoke of old healed beatings.

"Where did you think to tie the other end?" asked Anazâr as he lifted the noose from her neck. He hoped to see something in her eyes, some spark of anger or defiance, but her face held no expression but mild frustration.

After Actium, when the shattered remains of Marcus Antonius's Numidian auxiliaries were enslaved by the victors and shackled to the galleys, he'd seen many men lose their will to live. The last of the soldiers of his tribe, an older cousin, had simply stopped rowing the second day. He'd ignored the lashing, ignored Anazâr's pleas to resume, so they'd unshackled him and pushed him over the side. Anazâr still saw it sometimes when he closed his eyes, or when he looked up at a dark ceiling: his cousin's head, bobbing in the waves before it disappeared forever.

"You don't want to die like this," Anazâr told her, economically tugging the knots from the noose until it was straight again. "I have no way to stop you, if you're determined enough. But do you want to know what I think? I think the gods have shown you mercy, that you haven't been thrown to the beasts to be executed. Maybe your fate is to *live*."

It was a terrible, cloying lie, but a necessary one. If he was going to be successful at his task, he had to convince her—convince them *all*—that there was honor and value and meaning in fighting.

"Fated to live," she repeated in a shaky, throaty whisper. "Well, well."

"Come, now. You can tell the other women you had a sudden ailment, if you care."

"I was a Roman citizen. They're foreigners. I don't care."

"They're your sisters now. The lot of a slave is lonely enough without maintaining the distinctions of a life that will never be yours again." He took her by the forearm and guided her away from the cord, from the temptation of the massive skeins that held enough rope for a legion of nooses.

A stubborn, sullen look overtook her features. "I may never have my old life again, but those barbarian cunts will never be my—"

"Cyrenaicus," came Amanikhabale's shout from below. "Chaos erupts! Your presence grows increasingly indispensable!"

A scream sounded, as well, and a familiar laugh.

He hurried, half sliding, down the stone ramp that linked the levels, jostling Cassia along the inside wall.

Ursus lay splayed like a frog, ass up, in the center of the circle of women. The Sarmatian's foot pinned down the back of his neck.

"Touch one of my women again," she snarled in her guttural Greek, "And I'll rip off your withered little testicles and feed them to you raw, like a fucking *goat's*. Aethiopian! *Translate*."

"She says she'll stop immediately now that Cyrenaicus is here, and gives profuse apologies for inconveniencing you," said Amanikhabale.

Ursus sputtered wetly through his mashed-down lips.

Anazâr stalked up to Rhakshna, prepared to strike, but she hopped backward from her perch on Ursus and skittered away, tossing her wooden sword to the side and brandishing her empty hands in hyperbolic surrender.

"He was feeling up Atalanta while you were gone," said Amanikhabale in Greek. "He always frots against the women who move too slowly. It's not as if I haven't been raped by worse, but still, the indignity does tend to accumulate."

Ursus rose carefully, clutching at his midsection. His lower lip was purple and swollen fat with blood. Atalanta, one of the youngest Gaul women, edged farther away from him.

"Get out," ordered Anazâr. He only wished it could be so easy, but he remembered the majordomo's advice well. *If this arrangement results in any squabbling, it will go badly for both of you.* "You're on water-carrying duty for the rest of the day. I don't want to see you until it's time to—" *escort me across the city again* "—report to the dominus."

The paradoxical reality of their relationship: Anazâr the superior in the warehouse-cum-ludus, but outside its walls, once again a slave.

"You . . ." muttered Ursus. He dabbed at his bruised mouth, thought better of speech, and turned and headed for the door. Anazâr knew that expression: he'd suffer for this later, somehow.

"Rhakshna," called Anazâr, pointing so that his arm formed one long line with his sword. Pointing to her throat. "*I* mete out the discipline here. You will return to your shackles, *now*, and forgo the afternoon outing."

She tilted her jaw, sniffing as imperiously as an empress. "It was worth it."

Anazâr didn't miss the tentative softening of Atalanta's face at that—brief and lovely before giving way to guarded hardness again.

"You do not have her lashed," Cassia said in confusion. "Even though she struck her master."

"*You do not have her lashed*," mocked Amanikhabale, plucking at her filthy tunic in perfect imitation of a fastidious matron. "How the fuck did your people ever carve out an empire? You stupid, snivelling, worthless—"

Anazâr saw one of his half-formed plans dissolve before formation, and cursed silently. Gods, *nothing* in his previous life had prepared him for this. "Quiet, Aethiopian. And I'm charging you to speak to Cassia at length tonight. In the morning, I expect a full report on her history and circumstances, or neither of you will have your outing. And Cassia, I am not as averse to lashing as you might believe."

Any bond created—even that of hate—might tie Cassia to this world longer.

"Thank you," said Venatrix. The other Gaul women echoed her words, speaking in the direction of the Sarmatian as well.

The inscrutable Germans bobbed their heads.

Damn, but he needed a translator.

"Look, a big man," said Lucullus. "Hi!"

Aelia ruffled her son's hair and wiped a stain of grape juice from his chin. Anazâr nodded to the little boy, then leaned back, edging his shoulder blades uncomfortably against the dining room wall in an effort to return to invisibility.

Easy enough for an unremarkable Greek like Alexandros the majordomo; nigh impossible for a six-foot gladiator like Anazâr.

Two other slaves stood next to him, poised to clear the dessert plates. They looked vaguely Egyptian and consummately efficient. The flow of food and drink around the Marianus dining table ran smooth as an aqueduct, making the tangle of conflicts at the warehouse seem even more disappointing by contrast.

He wished he had a better report to make, but lying would only exacerbate the problem. He'd have to hope for Marianus's patience, hope that Marianus recognized that even if Anazâr didn't live up to his impeccable standards now, he would in time.

*Give me time, Dominus,* he inwardly rehearsed, but no, it sounded like an excuse. Better to make no apology at all.

Aelia sat at a chair with little Lucullus on her lap; the Marianus men reclined. Their resemblance was striking on the surface, only to fracture as soon they moved, like a reflection in a rain-struck pool.

Marianus, reserved in his gestures, relaxed, laid natural claim to the space at the head couch. Felix, sprawling ungracefully, full of nervous energy, played with a chicken bone. Anazâr had the sense he was waiting for an opportunity to act . . . but on what impulse?

"Give me!" shouted Lucullus, stretching his pudgy arms in the air. He seemed a healthy, happy boy except for an odd darkness under his Marianus-gray eyes, as if from lack of sleep.

Felix prepared to toss the chicken bone.

"I think not," said Aelia, standing up and shifting Lucullus from her lap to her hip. "We'll retire to the garden." She walked away without another word, soothing Lucullus's mild sobs as she went.

Anazâr felt a twitch in his chest as the soft noises stole, unwelcome, into the land of his memory and called forth the lullabies of his native tongue.

"Cyrenaicus," Marianus announced, snapping Anazâr to attention again and dispersing the bittersweet memories. "Report."

"Dominus," Anazâr acknowledged, giving himself a moment to gather his thoughts. He'd planned an entire speech, but with Marianus's eyes on him now, suddenly the troubles of the gladiatrices were the farthest thing from his mind. *Marianus's hand—no.* "The Sarmatian shows promise."

*No, no, no. Save the good news for last.*

*Too late.*

"Her people are good fighters, and she is no exception." He worked his jaw, Marianus's steady gaze never leaving his face. "I imagine that's why you acquired her, Dominus."

A smile.

Bolstered, Anazâr continued: "She should be trained as a thraex with a scimitar. The other women *will* rally around her . . . eventually. Morale is still low among them, and it leads them to turn on one another."

A stitch in his perfectly groomed brow.

"Their physical training goes well. They are strong, and will only become stronger. But to accomplish that, I must break down the barriers between them. Unify them. I need a translator, Dominus, for the Germans. They speak a language called Cimbrian." He forced himself not to wince. He wasn't afraid of rejection, although it would make his task monumentally more difficult, but what if Marianus chose to punish him for his presumption? "You've given so much already, Dominus, please don't mistake my asking for lack of gratitude."

Felix, who'd been silently toying with his chicken bone thus far, suddenly sat up. "*Grovel, grovel, grovel!*" he taunted. "Don't you kill for your supper? And yet you stand here—a barbarian champion of the arena, who bathes in blood—quaking at the sight of my fucking *brother*. He's a jumped-up rug merchant, not a thundering demigod."

*Don't respond.* Anazâr let his eyes fall on that middle distance, standing stock still. Marianus might despise his younger brother, but that didn't mean he'd let a slave disrespect him.

"I treat my younger brother as an exercise in mental forbearance. A living dumbbell, if you will." Marianus's tone was even. The two slaves, seeing some invisible signal that Anazâr missed, stepped forward, quietly gathered up the empty serving dishes, and departed.

"Oh, that's a good one." Felix cast his sardonic gaze over one shoulder toward Anazâr now, narrating casually, "He stole it from a friend of mine, a comic actor. Though I can't place too much blame on Lucius, since I'm an even greater magpie of words. We're all hopeless thieves, save for Lucullus, perhaps. By the way, I speak Cimbrian. I learned it from a charming whore at the Carmentalian House. He taught me how to play the flute, too. I mean, really play the flute, not the metaphor, although—"

"Enough. Cyrenaicus, a translator will be found and assigned to you by Alexandros. As for you, Felix—I already have a job for you. An incredibly easy, not very consequential job, so you should be able to perform it. I would consider reinstating your allowance, if so."

Felix threw the chicken bone behind the couch and clapped. "Lovely, *lovely* money! Well, ever since Alexandros started locking up the silverware at night, my purse is as empty as the deserts of Libya from which your pet gladiator hails. I would gladly replenish it. What is this *job*. Job-thing. Work. *Ugh*."

When he said "pet," Felix's eyes flickered to Anazâr. Looking to see if his hit had landed, perhaps. Anazâr let nothing show.

Neither did Marianus. "The largest wool wholesaler in Pompeii has sent his son to Rome for the summer to study the markets here.

He arrives tomorrow. I cannot greet him; I'll be meeting with one of the patrician aediles to discuss an awning contract for the games. I've composed a short speech. All you'll have to do is greet him at the door of the Aventine shop, apologize for my absence, and read the speech."

Alexandros glided into the room and extended a scroll to Felix, then retreated just as smoothly.

Felix took up the scroll and struck a pose reminiscent of a forum news reader. "All right, let me practice. *Ahem.* Greetings!" So far so good, but Marianus didn't look optimistic. "'I hope that you, your father, and your house are all in the best of health.' What a tedious, formulaic opening. I should replace it with something more creative and specific, like 'I hope your balls are still attached to your penis.' Sorry, I'll continue. 'The presence of my much more handsome and talented brother shows the regard I have for your family and our business relationship, which started many years ago at a sheep-fucking contest in the hills of—'"

"A mistake, I see. I'll strike out the brother line and send a client to read it. Return the scroll."

"No, no, no! You need me to fix this. You'll embarrass yourself with this as it is. Now where was I . . ." Felix focused on the scroll, running a hand through his hair as if in concentration.

"The scroll. Return it." Marianus's left eyelid twitched markedly as he rose from the couch and extended an expectant hand.

Anazâr prayed silently for invisibility, though he had nothing at all to offer any god. Some of the word-sparks that Felix spat out had come close to making him smile, but by this point, he wanted Felix *gone*, dead even, no longer a weight on Marianus, no longer goading and capering like the frivolous imp that he was.

Felix didn't hand over the scroll. In fact, he purposefully held it back, clenching his fist to crumple it. Gods help him, Anazâr knew exactly where this was going. At first he'd been happy not to be dismissed immediately, hoping for another chance to be of service to Marianus, to prove his worth and find a scrap of pleasure, but now he'd give anything to be shooed from the room. No, from the domus entirely. Let him return to the warehouse alone and unscathed.

"Cyrenaicus. Retrieve the scroll."

No more thoughts of escape. He launched off the wall and into the task. He'd trained for rapid striking all his life. Move fast, pluck the scroll, retreat, and finish the sordid fray with as little loss of dignity as possible. *Obedience. Loyalty. Efficiency.*

Felix danced backward with an entirely unanticipated agility. The dinner table now served as his shield.

Anazâr could close the distance in so many ways. Crash through or over the table, pick up a silver grape bowl like a discus and send it spinning into Felix's smirking face, slide under to knock Felix's feet out from under him...

Of course not. Violence against a citizen was unthinkable. He edged around the table, arms spread wide, feeling much like an unfortunate ape of the type sometimes imported from the far south to be slaughtered by hunters in the arena.

"You'll never take me alive!" shouted Felix, and snatched up a wooden ladle as he circled. Laughing, he brandished it like a sword, reciting, "Neptune rushes where the combat burns, while to his tent the Cretan king returns. From thence, two javelins glittering in his hand and clad in bronze that brightened all the strand, fierce on the foe the daring hero drove, like lightning bursting from the arm of Jove—Oww! You're hampering my Homer!"

Anazâr, reversing swiftly, had grabbed his wrist. "Give your brother the scroll," he growled.

Felix ripped off a corner of it with his teeth, flung himself away from the table, and tripped backward over a chair. Anazâr meant to let him go, but Felix's surprisingly strong grip had closed around his own wrist, so down to the floor together they fell.

For just a moment, everything was still: Felix, limp and pliant with shock, body pinned by Anazâr's. Staring up at Anazâr with those pale, otherworldly eyes gone startled and questioning. His mouth open, caught between expressions. Panting.

And then he bucked, body arching uselessly under Anazâr's greater weight, and cried out in breathless mimicry of an overenthusiastic whore, "Oh, *gladiator!* Your strength overwhelms me!" His eyes rolled in false ecstasy and Anazâr, taken aback at first, felt his stomach tighten with disgust. He snatched the scroll, Felix giving it up easily now that he had a new game to play, and disengaged as best he could, considering Felix's pawing.

Anazâr straightened his spine and pushed back his shoulders, walking calmly to Marianus, where he lowered himself formally to one knee and presented the scroll.

"Brother," Felix whined from the floor behind him. "Your gladiator likes you better than he likes me!"

"Leave," Marianus ordered Anazâr as he took up the scroll and clenched it so hard his knuckles went white. Anazâr did not imagine that the strong emotion choking his voice had much to do with gratitude. "*Felix* will see yet more privileges revoked."

Anazâr silently thanked Marianus for saying so. For the reassurance, perhaps, or for thinking a slave deserved to hear the inner workings of his rule at all.

As he turned, from the corner of his eye he caught the brothers glaring at each other. The masks they both wore—propriety for Marianus, comedy for Felix—slipped to reveal something savage and raw underneath. More than ever before, Anazâr was glad to be dismissed.

# CHAPTER 5

Anazâr bellowed a Latin curse in Penthesilea's ear and slapped her on the side of the head.

Her blow went wild and skidded off the side of the wooden post, striking a weakly harmonious note instead of the deep thud they both desired.

"Five more blows against the pole, undistracted," he ordered. "Venatrix, take over my position to distract her on the sixth." Penthesilea might make a good murmillo—she was the strongest and largest gladiatrix, almost Anazâr's height and thick as a siege engine—but she startled easily.

A solid week of training had allowed Anazâr to sort them into three levels: the nearly hopeless, the somewhat hopeless, and the Sarmatian. Who fought brilliantly, of course, but relied too much on techniques that were worthless against armored opponents. He understood her weakness intimately because it had been his own. He'd learned to compensate over time, but at the cost of blood. He wished to spare her the same. Sadly, she was proving as obstinate about learning new techniques as he'd once been.

Fifty-seven days until the games. A week since that night Felix had attempted to make a fool of him. Other than a couple of spats in training, especially among the antisocial Germans, it had gone uneventfully, but that didn't mean he felt even remotely prepared for the test to come. Every night he reported to Marianus on the gladiatrices's progress, and every night Marianus listened with guarded interest, showing neither praise nor disapproval for Anazâr's work. Twice, Anazâr had performed further duties, but neither time had been quite so . . . compelling as the first. Marianus had become completely unreadable, distant.

And it wasn't Anazâr's place to question that.

"Amanikhabale! I saw you resting. Another circuit with the water buckets," he called out. She groaned and staggered to her feet again. "Come, I'll carry with you." He grabbed a set of the heaviest stone hand weights and paced beside her.

"Have you . . . rethought . . . my offer?" she gasped.

"How does it go with Cassia?" he asked in return.

A banging on the door interrupted her wheezing response.

"Cyrenaicus! Ursus!" It was Quintus, the night watchman. "We've been sent to take the women to the baths."

Once the word spread, the warehouse became a very cheerful place, and a few of the Gaul women shrieked like girls. Anazâr couldn't blame them for it, really. He'd felt much the same on the occasion of his first trip to the bath with his gladiator brothers.

With Quintus were two other men, similarly ruddy-faced, thickset, and amiable. "My cousins," he explained, as they worked with Anazâr to line up the women and collar-shackle them. "We're all clients of Marianus. Where's that ass?"

That ass being Ursus, of course. "Carrying water."

"Oh, I'll bet he hates that. Being put to slave's work again."

Ursus plodded slowly into the warehouse, burdened heavily with jugs and scowling even more than usual. And he had a companion.

The white toga, the thin purple stripe, the well-groomed dark curls . . . for a moment Anazâr hoped it was Marianus, here to judge their hard-fought progress. But no. *Felix*. Gods. He carried the weight of the toga lightly—the mark of the citizen that any slave or freedman would be swiftly punished for assuming—twirling one end of it insouciantly as he stepped into the grim dimness of the warehouse.

"I'm bored," he announced. "And broke. But I have enough for the baths, so I think I'll tag along. Who speaks Cimbrian?" He broke out of Latin into a staccato monologue that spurred the Germans to respond in their native tongue. One of them began shaking as she spoke; her tribeswomen clasped her arms.

The tension of the moment disturbed Anazâr for a multitude of reasons he had no hope of even beginning to untangle.

He turned away without greeting Felix—the less contact, the better—and went to find the Sarmatian. She'd need thorough convincing before she'd let them put a collar on her neck.

Two paces later, he wheeled right back around: a loud crash had disrupted the Cimbrian chattering.

"Oh dear. I seem to have totally accidentally kicked over the water jugs." Felix let out a theatric sigh and clutched at his toga hem as if keeping it safe from a raging flood. "I suppose that means poor Ursus will have to fetch some more. Move, move, you modern-day Sisyphus."

Quintus and his cousins shrugged. Anazâr averted his glance. Many of the women smiled and gave each other sly looks, even across the tribal boundaries. It was the first time he'd seen them even close to united since—well, since the last time Ursus had found himself humiliated. It was a start, Anazâr supposed. Too bad they couldn't trot him out into the arena to bark like a dog before their fights.

*No.* He was absolutely *not* going to find amusement or worth in Felix's antics. He smothered the twitch of a smile that was tugging at the corner of his mouth.

"That's enough," he commanded gruffly, hoping his tone would convey what his language couldn't. Slowly, the laughing and whispering among the women died down into antsy, excited silence.

"Alexandros has a running tab set up at the baths," said Quintus. "There'll be an ornatrix and a masseuse reserved for them. Let's go, eh?"

Even the Sarmatian went willingly at the promise of that.

"We'll have to wait here," Quintus told his cousins.

"All of us? Right here, for as long as it takes to clean *that* filthy lot? Damn it, I want a bite to eat," complained one of them.

This section of the antechamber was right next to the women's entrance. In the other direction lay an atrium, and beyond that, an outdoor courtyard filled with food vendors, from which the alluring smell of roasting sausages and fresh-baked pastries came wafting on the spring breeze. Anazâr's mouth watered, but he had no coin to his name. The peculium he'd won in the arena was probably enough to bury them all in pastries, but its cash value was utterly dependent on the will and whim of Iunius.

He could borrow from Quintus, but no, better to play the stoic gladiator, especially with Felix around and likely looking for ways to cause trouble.

"Gladiator!" called the troublesome man himself. "Come with me. You dampen my spirits, sitting there like you're awaiting your execution." Anazâr's expression must have betrayed some hesitance or unease, because Felix added, "It's not a request. My brother says you're to bathe. Don't worry about your keeper, I'll keep an eye on you."

It didn't seem likely that Marianus would hand down such an order, especially not to his notoriously undependable brother, but even that tiny fraction of a chance that Felix was speaking true could mean terrible consequences if Anazâr refused.

Quintus shrugged. He did that often and eloquently. This particular shrug expressed an emphatic lack of opinion. No help there, then.

Anazâr, groaning within, stone-faced without, rose and stalked into the men's changing room two paces behind Felix, who didn't deign to ask again and didn't even look to confirm that Anazâr had followed. So there was something of his brother in him, after all.

The changing room was crowded with men in various states of undress, some rushing through the motions while others lingered in conversation, discussing politics or telling dirty jokes. Felix went to one of the benches along the wall, greeting an elderly man who sat there in the nude before quickly stripping down himself.

Anazâr couldn't help but note points of resemblance to Marianus. Both of them cut a lean, aristocratic figure, bodies shaped by swimming and exercise rather than hard work. In fact, there was only one major point of difference: Felix was entirely depilated. Perhaps that meant something.

*And perhaps you'd be better off not to think about it*, he reminded himself, quickly averting his gaze when Felix cast him a suspicious look over one angular shoulder. He set to undressing, hoping he'd avoided notice, but Felix's laugh said otherwise.

"I saw you looking, gladiator," he teased. "Pretending I'm my brother?"

"I have a name," Anazâr retorted before he had a chance to stop himself. He bit his tongue hard, too late.

But Felix just tilted his head, squinting his eyes. Maybe even *he* realized he didn't have the right to lecture others on their disrespect of authority. Or perhaps not. "I believe you do, but if so, I haven't heard it."

Of course he had; he'd been present for several of Anazâr's evening reports to his brother. Not that Anazâr could say so, especially not now that he'd tempted fate once today already.

"I am called Cyrenaicus," he said, thankfully keeping the incredulity out his voice.

Felix looked disappointed. He turned, neatly folded his clothes, and stuffed them into one of the high cubbies set into the wall. "Like I said. You might have a name, but I haven't heard it."

Anger flared, burning hot enough that Anazâr's hand trembled as he pushed his folded tunic into the neighboring cubby. *How fucking dare he.* He took a deep, cleansing breath. If Felix pressed, he'd lie, and speak some random name from the folktales of his people.

They walked silently through the short corridor that led to the calidarium. Felix, mercifully, did not press.

The heat enfolded him, infiltrated him, and he staggered a little at the shock. Sweat sprang up along his arms, and ahead of him, he could see that Felix's skin had already built up a sheen. Men filed back and forth with great care in the dim light, trying to avoid brushing against the heated bricks of the wall.

Felix found an empty bench attended by an elderly bath slave carrying oil and strigil. Which meant Anazâr would not be expected to clean him. *Good.* The man went straight to work on Felix's back, applying oil in neat circling motions and then scraping it off, the strigil leaving strips of lighter, cleaner skin in its wake.

Felix gestured to Anazâr to sit beside him. "I heard you fought at the Battle of Actium. I won't pretend not to be curious about it. Did you see Marcus Antonius?"

More questions about *before*. His life, separated into distinct periods, two existences and two men that could never touch but somehow did. A paradox, like a storm, raging in the heart of him. At least this question was so common that his answer felt more like a poetry recital.

"Yes. He appeared often to speak before his troops. But at the time, I knew almost no Latin." The scrape of the strigil against Felix's back lent his words measure and rhythm. A welcome relief. "He seemed a strong man and a capable general. Of course, when the fleet was lost and he ran back to Egypt, our opinion altered."

"And Cleopatra?"

"She gave speeches too, sometimes. I understood them. Whatever loyalty we had was more toward her. Our prince was from the old royal Numidian family, and her ally. He gambled us, and lost. I would curse his bad judgment, but Octavianus—I mean, the Emperor and son of the Divine Caesar—ordered him executed shortly after the surrender, so he paid his price."

"Here I was thinking you'd give me the clang and clash of battle, and instead . . . politics."

"Once encamped at Actium, our lives were not interesting. We tended our horses, and waited, and talked of home. They sent us on sorties. We would kill some men with javelins, and some of us were killed in return. And then we waited some more." He felt himself wishing he could tell the truth, that once you lived battle the poetry quickly fled. That raucous clang and clash was an observer's game.

He remembered the historical re-enactment that had brought him here. Already it felt as if it were a lifetime ago, his time as a soldier a lifetime more. His time as a husband even farther removed. He'd have enough lives to give a phoenix envy when his time on this world was finally done. But he couldn't say any of that, could he? Not even to his most-trusted brother—Gaius, did he yet live? And if he couldn't tell Gaius, he especially couldn't reveal it to a slippery Roman like Felix.

It was Anazâr's turn, now, to receive the ministrations of the strigil. He welcomed its rasping touch—the scraping away of everything old, dead—and the sensation of freshness that followed.

"I think I misjudged you," Felix admitted. "There's more to you underneath, isn't there? I can see by the look on your face that you have depths I'll never know." He tilted his head in study as Anazâr hurriedly tried to close off his expression again, but didn't comment on the change. "The women like you; they say you stood up to Ursus. You're no brute, after all."

"If you thought me a brute, you didn't know me at all," Anazâr commented, no hurt in it. "Any half-wit who follows the games would know it's cowardice and dishonor, not blood, that brought me to your brother's house." He wished immediately that he'd kept silent. Had he just called an eques a half-wit?

"You're right. I don't follow the games. I tell everyone I faint at the sight of blood. As to being a half-wit, I'll have you know I prefer to be thought of as half a man." He smiled, the expression full of sudden and surprising good-humored humility. He was actually waiting for Anazâr to speak. Not questioning: waiting without expectation. This wasn't an interrogation, it was a *conversation*.

Anazâr could say... almost anything. The words swirled around in his head like leaves caught in a river eddy. So many things. Questions. Statements. Little pointless thoughts that served no master's purpose and thus never found voice anymore, like *This bath is so much larger on the inside than it appears on the outside.*

He could even say nothing at all—not because he'd been told to stay silent, or because the circumstances demanded it, but because he didn't desire to say anything, and that was a freedom in and of itself. But the temptation to speak freely was overwhelming, here in this place where the markings of rank were set aside, so just for a moment he tricked himself into thinking they spoke as equals.

A moment was all it took. "Why do you hate your brother?"

"He promised he'd pay for my tavern bill on my birthday, then slipped out the back. I'm a grudgeful man." So Felix kept secrets, too. Well, that was fair. "I meant some of what I said at that dinner, by the way. Why does he quail *you* so?"

Gods. The astounding *ignorance* of that question. Equals? The gap between them had never yawned larger.

"Slaves have a special saying, when we curse at one other. It was one of the first Latin curses I learned: 'to the cross with you.' Have you ever seen a man crucified? A woman or child? Fainting at the sight of blood, I suppose not." *Maybe I could have been the kind of man who fainted at the sight of blood, had I the chance.* The strigiller finished the last scraping strokes against Anazâr's shins, but his muscles failed to loosen in response. "A man in my profession can't fear death, but there are worse things than death, especially for a slave. Things your brother can do. You said I treated him as a demigod. Who is *your* god? You—" He caught himself, choked off the words, begged the river to run dry.

Felix stood up and stalked away.

Anazâr sighed and rubbed at his forehead, remembering there were some marks that could never be erased.

He'd have to follow Felix into the tepidarium. Reversing the circuit would draw unwelcome attention. And if Felix was feeling as jilted as he looked—craving, like so many Romans, to bask in the martial glamor of an Actium veteran and gladiator, and receiving only an impolitic rebuff—then leaving Felix's side would give the petty Roman ass the perfect excuse to punish him. If Anazâr's outburst on its own hadn't already earned one, that was. No help for it. What was done was done. A familiar sense of resignation washed over him, carrying him to his feet and through the doorway to the next room.

The ceiling was much higher here, and the high walls held many windows of thick, colored glass. Warm, rich, syrupy light poured into the vast columned room. Anazâr forced his gaze downward from that vault of ethereal beauty into the lower realm of squalling human chaos. Vendors circled the blue-green central pool, crying their wares: depilation, massage, the ubiquitous pastries. Swimmers splashed. Knots of men stood waist-deep in water; their arguments or agreements wove into an unceasing Latin roar that was bordered, here and there, with bright threads of other languages.

Felix was obscured somewhere in the crowd.

Anazâr made a slow circuit of the pool, keeping an eye out for knots of young patrician men. Even naked, they must have a way of carrying themselves, he imagined. He did spot a likely group at the edge of the pool, but on closer approach, the extravagance of their motions and traces of makeup around their sharp-darting eyes marked them as cinaedi. Well, perhaps Felix was one of those, as well. The thought made his cock swell embarrassingly, until he remembered Felix's question and that sense of purposeless frustration took over again.

One of the cinaedi arched an eyebrow plucked razor thin in Anazâr's direction and smiled.

Anazâr walked by. He needed to find Felix.

Under other circumstances . . .

Best not to think of that. Bathhouse liaisons were held between free men, which he, of course, was not. But maybe someday, if he could just find a way to please Marianus despite Felix's perversities and capers, he could return as a freedman and fully enjoy every comfort the baths had to offer.

He found Felix at the other end of the tepidarium, leaning against a column, engaged in animated discussion with someone who did *not* look like a patrician.

An instinct to interrupt, to call Felix away and scold him, rose in Anazâr's mind. He reminded himself he wasn't here as Felix's chaperone. Quite the opposite, in fact.

The large man—he was about half a head taller than Felix, just like Anazâr—*oh. Oh.*

Subtly catching Anazâr's eyes, Felix touched the man's elbow, a casual motion that trailed off quickly, gracefully. The man's eyes narrowed and went heavy-lidded. He had the tanned complexion and heavy build of someone who carried weight for a living, but his body was unbranded.

Perhaps Felix liked that.

Or perhaps he'd chosen the man specifically because of how it would best goad Anazâr.

His fucking outburst. Not only had it been disrespectful of a citizen and dangerous to his relationship with his dominus and thus his chance for freedom, but it had revealed deep-buried resentment to a man intent on causing as much havoc as possible. Felix and the goddess of discord were obviously thick as thieves, and he called her power down on anyone who irked him. Anazâr was fucking doomed.

Felix spoke. Though Anazâr stood only a few body lengths away, the words were incomprehensible under the echoes of wavelets, the roar of voices.

Their destination obviously decided, the pair walked away from the pool, through an open doorway, and into a semi-private room lined with low, cushioned benches.

*Don't look*, he told himself. *He knows where you are. Stand stock still for as long as he takes to fuck the mule driver. Or more likely, be fucked by him. Cinaedus. Shameless. Born a master of the city at the center of the world, and he throws off his manhood and pisses on the honor of his house.* The curses he silently hurled at Felix helped distract from the shame at his own lack of control, his impolitic and wanton words.

He wished he were here with Marianus, instead.

The room was dim, probably on purpose, but the light from the tepidarium windows still stretched into it. He could see Felix bend forward over the bench and arch his back, one lean leg stretching out behind him for balance.

Felix looked back over his shoulder, a pose that should have been awkward but instead took on a taut, athletic appeal, like the form of a gymnast skillfully captured in marble.

Felix... winked at him.

*Gods.* Look away.

He didn't.

Mercifully, the mule driver blocked much of the view. As Anazâr watched, he used one column-thick leg to edge into Felix's angled form, shifting the tableau. Something beautiful became something animal.

Felix broke eye contact as his face went slack with pleasure. No lines of tension, no lifted eyebrow. He seemed so *young*, now that unguarded honesty left no room for a trickster's calculations.

The mule driver took hold of his hips and began to ride him hard.

Anazâr dared to imagine how it would feel to fuck his master's brother. To bear down into him, to use him like a whore and know that Felix would love every single moment of such use. To hold that body in his hands, knowing that, slave or no, he had the *power* to—

"Hey, you, slave. You'll poke someone's eye out with that thing. Calm down or take it into the side room."

The bath slave shook his broom at Anazâr and quickly moved on, muttering to himself as he swept.

More humiliation. He sat down carefully on the tiled floor so the evidence of his arousal was obscured, looked up at the ceiling and thought of the many unpleasant scenes he'd witnessed over the course of his eventful life. Every time he managed to conjure up a suitably withering image, though, the sound of a pleased gasp or grunt seemed to reach his ears, bringing him right back to the unique tortures of the present.

To the cross with Felix. To Hades. Anywhere but here.

He waited as long as he could to look again. This time all he saw were the soles of Felix's feet, flexed up so he stood on his toes, and the other man's feet planted between them, his stance so strong Anazâr had a strange fleeting wish the Sarmatian was here, that he might point it out to her.

Shameful, he reminded himself, for a free Roman to surrender to such a thing. Marianus would never. Marianus would take his slaves, or take other men without honor, maintaining the harmonious alignment of desire and station that the act represented. And Anazâr would submit. He hadn't yet, Marianus seemingly preferring to use his mouth, but if it did come to that, there'd be no shame. No pleasure either, really, not in the way Felix obviously found pleasure in the act, but no shame.

Or at least, no more shame than anything else Anazâr did as a slave. Like sitting on the floor waiting for his master's brother to get buggered by some ox-like freedman.

"Now *that* was refreshing. The cock, I mean," clarified Felix, not from the alcove but from the direction of the lockers. Had Anazâr been so lost in thought he hadn't noticed him leave? Another chance for punishment, but Felix didn't take it. He walked past Anazâr, heading toward the pool, then spun around for a moment, the sardonic expression fully returned to his face. "Buy us some pastries for when I get back from my laps in the pool. A man can't live on a belly full of cum alone, but I suppose you already know that."

He tossed a denarius, and Anazâr was too bewildered and taken aback to do anything but silently catch it in both hands. Which was probably for the best, considering today's record.

Buy *us*, Felix had said. Anazâr would take him at his word. A vendor at the other end of the tepidarium cried out specials piled on mixed earthenware platters, and Anazâr spent half the coin on one of those. Then he settled by the wall to wait while the smell of freshly baked bread filled his nose.

"Is that your dominus?" a man still wet from the pool asked.

A Greek, he seemed to be, so Anazâr addressed him in that tongue. "I'm contracted to his house. It's complicated."

"He's notorious in literary circles, you know. The life of the party, but never lend him money, they say. Got any good gossip?"

"I just saw a mule driver bending him over a couch."

"Everybody already knows he takes it up the ass." The Greek looked disappointed as he squeezed the water out of his shoulder-length hair. "Sextus Propertius even wrote a nasty verse about him, but they're still friends."

The name sounded vaguely familiar. "Should I know who that is?"

"Oh, you're . . . well. Propertius is a famous poet. The mentor of my dominus, who aspires to be the same. Hey, even though you look like a rough sort, I'm no snob when there's gossip to be had. Just try to keep up, eh? You must have heard of Cornelius Gallus, at least. No? This isn't some filthy gutter poet I'm talking about here. The governor of *Egypt*, man! Well, former governor of Egypt, that is. He's gotten himself into a spot of trouble involving . . ."

The Greek got halfway through the account of a brothel orgy involving two young widows of the senatorial class before he was called away. Just in time, it seemed, because right then Felix returned, wet and flushed with exertion. With no word of greeting, he snatched one of the pastries from Anazâr's tray and stuffed his face with it. When Anazâr didn't immediately follow suit, Felix rolled his eyes, grunting out, "Oh, just *eat*, gladiator. You don't need my permission. I'm not my fucking brother."

*No, that you are not*, Anazâr thought bitterly, and mutely followed him to the calidarium.

Immeasurable time passed as he shadowed Felix. The long, hot bath in the calidarium pool would have been more enjoyable if he'd known what time he was supposed to rejoin Quintus and the women. He was determined not to speak again unless spoken to; he'd let Felix take the responsibility for his tardiness.

There was a mime show at a gallery next to the calidarium that Felix had to watch. Then a long chat with a group of Egyptian grain merchants concerning musical entertainments and the latest news from Alexandria. Anazâr let his attention slip until he heard the name of Cyrenaica, and then, of course, listened with the greatest of interest. By their account, Augustus had ordered that his pet Numidian king, Juba II, be engaged to Cleopatra Selene, the daughter of Cleopatra and Marcus Antonius. The pair would rule together over a vast stretch of Roman Africa.

The news stunned him for a moment. The Divine Caesar had killed Juba and taken his throne; now Augustus had restored the throne to Juba's son. By the grace and mercy and shrewdness of the Son of the Divine Caesar, Juba II was now married to the daughter of Augustus's two greatest enemies. The Romans struck out with one hand and folded their victims close with the other.

Fortune willing, perhaps that progression would serve as model for his own life's course.

When the Egyptians left, Felix continued on to the frigidarium. Then he passed back through the calidarium and again to the tepidarium. Rooms upon rooms upon rooms upon rooms, and Anazâr helplessly tagging along through them all, silent and pensive.

By the time Felix decided to leave, and they dressed, Quintus and the women were long gone.

"I'll walk you back to the house," Felix said. His tone was unapologetic, but at least it wasn't mocking.

Out on the street, the sun had sunk behind the vast, sprawling bathhouse. A crowd of men—cleansed, marks of rank freshly resumed—poured out from the main gate on their way home to fine mansions or modest shacks or rickety insulae or slave barracks.

They set out for the Palatine Hill through the twilight streets. Thin plumes of smoke began to rise from chimneys, further darkening the skies.

"I hope my brother doesn't press about your tardiness," Felix said when Anazâr's silence had dragged on too long. Some tone of remorse, maybe, if Anazâr was being generous to Felix's character, but still not an apology. "I know you don't think so, but I was trying to reward you for your service. You've far surpassed your predecessor, and I should never have painted you with the same brush." Felix turned onto a narrow street that led up the Palatine Hill; Anazâr followed several paces behind. "The gladiatrices say you're a strict teacher, but that you haven't raped any among them."

Rather a low bar as far as standards of behavior went, but then, he hadn't exactly phrased it as a compliment, either. Anazâr remembered the meeting between Marianus and Iunius. "Don't misunderstand. I'm not a eunuch. I just don't fuck anyone without their permission." He couldn't help his slightly accusatory tone.

His hit didn't land, because Felix replied casually, "Well then, neither do I. Although back when I had elegist pretensions, I'd write poems threatening to rape my rivals *all the time*. It was expected, you see. The fashion's finally dying down now, thank the gods. Do you have any idea how unnerving it is to attend a dinner party where some snot-nosed little senator's son stands up and recites a verse about sodomizing you with a radish? Wait, don't answer that question, I just realized it's highly insulting."

Anazâr found himself smiling against his will. "So you *do* . . ."

"What, what? Finish your observation, you baffling man."

Anger had fled. If Anazâr opened his mouth again, he'd have no choice but to laugh out loud, so he clenched his teeth until his jaw hurt.

Felix whirled around to flash a rude hand gesture and a lopsided smile at Anazâr, completed his spin (which was more than a little dangerous in the darkening night, on a sloping street) and kept walking upward, homeward, without missing a pace.

Anazâr fell back a little more, just in case Felix stumbled.

The silence they shared did not feel unpleasant in the slightest.

They neared the house. Perhaps he could ask Felix one last question while this strange mood of his lasted. Felix seemed quite willing to show him a window into another world. Amusement. Laughter. Roman letters tangling together on scrolls and forming songs instead of censures on the skins of slaves.

Felix stumbled.

Because it was near dark, because Anazâr was attuned to every sound, he *heard*. As Felix fell. A hiss. He'd heard nothing like it in the arena—only when the arrows had flown at Actium.

Instead of leaning to help Felix to his feet, he jumped over his sprawled form and landed on the cobbles in a cat-crouch.

A harsh breath. The flash of a sword by lamplight. Anazâr ducked the stabbing stroke and came up inside the swordsman's reach.

There was a cold purity to this, a welcome familiarity. His body, his senses, all bent to the purpose of killing. *Ifri, my goddess, guide me.*

He hugged the man close as a lover, threw himself backward and twisted in the air.

They hit the stones hard.

Anazâr was ready for the pain. He felt the man's grip slacken and tore the sword pommel away.

If Anazâr stood to press sword to throat—to threaten into submission—the archer deeper in the alley might shoot him down. So he drew the sword closer instead and cut the man's throat awkwardly, so that pumping blood soaked his forearm and trickled warm and thick from his elbow onto the stones.

No words. Just the usual sounds a man made dying.

"Wh-what," Felix gasped, still sprawled across the paving stones. Anazâr had almost forgotten him, caught up in the fight, but there was no ignoring him now. Pale, huge-eyed, *young* again.

"Stay down," Anazâr ordered. "Quiet."

Felix nodded, gave him silence, and failed to faint. Down the alley, Anazâr heard scrabbling footsteps that quickly grew softer. An archer who only shot once—no, it was likely a crossbowman.

Anazâr tightened his grip on the dead man's sword. "We'll go. Stay between my body and the wall until we get to the house. *Now.*"

Time itself hurried and sped, a storm cloud racing over the western desert, eerie and skin-prickling in its passage. He protected Felix with his body, edging them both through the network of mazelike alleys back to the domus Marianus. Felix didn't fight his orders, didn't pull *any* of his usual frustrating pranks; and though he seemed terribly shaken, he still didn't faint.

And what of Anazâr? He had a naked sword made from killing metal and not practice wood, and a tunic soaked in the blood of a stranger: another slave, a freedman . . . or, perhaps, a citizen. Well, no matter who he'd killed, he had no choice but to hope Marianus would sanction the act. Whatever quarrel lay between the brothers, Felix was of his house.

He even dared to hope this would bring the two closer together, against a common enemy.

Felix gripped his left forearm, the one that didn't hold the sword. "We're here," he said. "I—thank you."

"Go rest." Anazâr clasped Felix by the shoulder, giving it a reassuring squeeze. "I was about to ask you to tell me some poetry. Maybe tomorrow. If I'm not crucified."

A look of fear crossed Felix's brow. "They wouldn't. My brother—"

"I was joking." Anazâr's hand drifted upward, but he pulled it back at the last moment, curling his fingers shyly into his palm.

"You're supposed to smile when you joke, you know."

 CHAPTER 6

Although they entered a silent, sleepy house, it didn't stay that way long. News of the attack spread quickly. The full staff mobilized, a doctor was summoned, and all the while Marianus stood at the threshold of his study, calm and collected and somehow directing the chaos. At the center of the storm, Anazâr silently awaited judgment or orders, head bowed. And by Anazâr's side, Felix waited too, wavering on his feet but resolute. He'd stubbornly refused multiple offers of a place to lie down, and Anazâr was secretly thankful for that.

"Call your brother-in-law, Marianus," a client advised. "Tell him to send a cohort!"

"Overkill," countered Alexandros. "By the account of Cyrenaicus, the cutthroats have fled."

"What do you know of military matters, old Greek?"

"Nothing. I've merely run politically active households during decades of civil wars."

Marianus cut the client off with a wave of his hand. "I will investigate the scene myself. We'll take ten men." He turned to Alexandros. "Should we take the gladiator?"

"I would advise not. If there are allies of the dead man on scene, it would inflame the situation. And a gladiator having wielded a steel sword outside the arena . . ." Alexandros let the silence at the end of his sentence speak for itself.

"I could say I was the one who killed the man," Felix offered, his voice uncharacteristically low and faint.

As well-schooled as Alexandros was in being the ideal inoffensive slave, even he couldn't help the quirk of an eyebrow at the offer.

Marianus ignored the suggestion and thrust himself into motion, men filing behind him as he led the way out. "Clean the sword and lock it away," he called to Alexandros over his shoulder.

Anazâr watched the thing go, wrapped in cloth and spirited away by Alexandros, feeling like it had taken some unnameable part of *himself* with it.

A short while later, the party returned, dragging a corpse.

"This is an interesting development," said Marianus, pointing toward the gaping, horrible face. "One of my own freedmen." His own face was drawn tight, eyes blazing, in stark contrast to the flopping fish-eyed corpse.

Anazâr cursed in his own language—a brutal phrase about fucking a scorpion hole—not sure if he was cursing himself or Ursus. Because the dead man *was* Ursus, no questioning it now. Perhaps he should have known before, but the mouth of the alley had been very dark and their struggle frantic and over quickly.

"Leave. Everyone. Alexandros, arrange a watch by the door, and send word to my brother-in-law. I would speak with Cyrenaicus alone."

"I'm not leaving," said Felix. Anazâr snapped his head to stare at him in surprise, but there was no trace of his usual caustic jesting.

"Felix, even you must grasp the seriousness of this situation," said Marianus.

"I do," Felix growled back, "and that's why I want to stay. It was me they were trying to kill and—"

"Are you so sure of that, brother?"

"Of course I am! What, do you think he was trying to kill Cyrenaicus?"

"Just go to your room, Felix. Go, or I'll have you taken there."

The look they shared did not radiate the same intensity of pure hatred as the night of the second report, but it was still unnerving.

"Cyrenaicus saved my life," said Felix at last, defiant in his defeat.

Marianus took Anazâr by the shoulder and led him away.

"You smell of blood," said Marianus. "Take off your tunic. Here, have some water as well."

"Thank you, Dominus." Anazâr pulled off his tunic immediately, glad to be rid of the thing. He wet part of it with water from Marianus's offered cup and rubbed at the dried bloodstains on his sword arm.

"I'll protect you if anyone brings the charge to a magistrate. You fought to save a citizen's life, above all. I doubt that anyone will bring such a charge, not for Ursus."

"He mentioned a wife," said Anazâr.

"His slave. She reverts to me now; I'll send men to bring her in the morning."

"She... won't be tortured?"

He shouldn't have asked that.

"No," said Marianus. "You're... nevermind." A faint smile curled across his face. "Alexandros will question her to see if Ursus shared the plans of his betrayal. Reward will achieve more than punishment, I imagine, if she knows anything at all. Throw that thing in the corner."

Anazâr tossed the stained tunic in the corner of the room, taking care not to get it close to the spinning wheel. This room seemed designed solely for use of women's crafts, but the walls were still richly decorated, inlaid with mosaics and hung with embroidered tapestries.

"Is there anything else of value I can tell you, Dominus? I've tried to list every detail." He'd even made a point of mentioning Felix and Ursus's conflict that morning, even though it seemed like too small a slight to drive a man to murder.

The real questions writhed underneath that politic one. *Who could have done this? What will happen to me?*

Marianus tightened his lips. "I don't know. I think it wise, at this point, to tell you some of our family history, so that you know what to look for in case of another attempt." Anazâr's heart pounded, not with the fear of danger, but with the exhilaration of trust. "When I was newly a man, my father loaned Aelia's father a substantial amount of money to further his political career. His ennoblement and my marriage to Aelia ensued, once her father Aelius's fortunes increased. But Aelius's enemies became our enemies, as well. One of them overstepped. His lands and assets were stripped by Augustus and granted to our houses at the beginning of this year. In fact, this was how the gladiatrices came into my possession."

Marianus paused to adjust a toga fold that lay crookedly across his shoulder; Anazâr felt emboldened to fill the silence. "Do you think...?"

"I wouldn't jump to conclusions just yet. My brother has his own enemies, after all. Men he's insulted, men he owes money, jilted ex-lovers. There's really no end to the scandals in his sorry excuse for a life. But I can't shake the feeling that the bolt could have been meant for me."

The alley *had* been dark. And there was no reason from an outsider's point of view to assume that Anazâr and Felix would keep one another company.

"I was once a soldier, as you know, Dominus. If you wish, I could examine your daily routines and see where you're most vulnerable to attack. You *and* your brother. If he'll follow instructions, that is."

"Felix pretends to be a fool, but he has a keen sense of self-preservation. I've learned, at great cost, not to trust his outward appearance. I promised my father I'd never turn him from the house, but still . . . well, perhaps this attack will sober him."

Admiration for Marianus—for his patience with Felix, for his ability to manage the affairs of his hectic household with dignity, for the way he held himself in a crisis—swelled in Anazâr's chest. Marianus carried a heavy burden and he carried it well.

"I hope so, Dominus," said Anazâr, because everything else he was thinking, everything he really wanted to say—it was all too intimate.

"You saved my delinquent brother's life, Cyrenaicus, and for that I thank you. The two of you together so late in the evening was unexpected, but fortuitous. In future, though, if he commands you in anything, confirm with myself or Aelia or Alexandros. Felix may be your superior, but he isn't your master."

The unspoken end to that speech: *I am.*

"Understood, Dominus. He didn't . . . He only . . ." Their passage through the baths became hard to recall in any detail now that he was standing so close to Marianus.

"It doesn't matter." Marianus's hand came to clasp the nape of Anazâr's neck, the gesture stiff, tentative, but undeniably wanting. And the smell of him . . . expensive wine and oil and day-old sweat; Anazâr *wanted* too.

Anticipating the command, he sank downward, preparing to serve.

"Not like that, Cyrenaicus. Not tonight." Marianus's eyes flashed and Anazâr froze, feeling a strange fearful lump rise in his throat. "No, you do well. Hands and knees, this time."

"Yes, Dominus." He swallowed in relief and continued down to his knees, then further. The rug was of soft, thick, clean-smelling wool; his palms sank down into the fibers, crushing them to form hand-shaped impressions.

Marianus paced around him. Anazâr heard the rustle of his toga and endured the full force of his calm regard. *This is the way things are supposed to be.*

"You're bruised," Marianus remarked. "Here." A trailing touch on his side. Anazâr tried to stay impassive, but a shiver perhaps escaped.

"I didn't know. It's nothing."

Marianus stepped away then, going somewhere deeper into the room. Anazâr waited patiently.

When he returned, it was to spread an unguent onto Anazâr's bruise. The gesture and the warm, slick touch shocked the breath out of him. The words *Thank you, Dominus* died on his lips.

"You're of great value to me, Cyrenaicus."

He had not expected this tenderness.

Marianus spread him open, his soft, delicate hands smoothing across the insides of Anazâr's thighs and up, displaying him more intimately. Anazâr's cock was hopelessly hard, but he tried to quell any other signs of shameful lust, forcing his breath to flow evenly in and out, in and out—a little raggedness when Marianus began to use his fingers, that was all.

He couldn't help wondering how much the unguent cost that Marianus was so liberally pressing into him. Whatever the cost, he was thankful for it.

"Be ready," Marianus told him.

"I'm ready, Dominus."

He'd taken the full length of his master's cock down his throat before, but *gods*, up his ass was another matter entirely. He *ached*. No, it wasn't quite pain, but it was almost unbearable nonetheless, that feeling of helpless invasion. Trying not to moan or hiss, Anazâr kept his mouth shut tight as Marianus gripped his thighs and levered him backward onto his engorged prick.

"Yes, there. Now *hold*."

Anazâr's eyes rolled back in his head in silent protest of the statuesque stillness he forced body his to assume. His body, which wished to buck and thrash, to be free and be *taken* all at once. He would do this. He would perform. He clenched his muscles, pulling Marianus deeper, and didn't even let himself smile with triumph as he heard his master's jagged, undignified moan.

Marianus took his pleasure then. The pounding rocked Anazâr forward, nearly toppling him onto his elbows. He lowered his neck, but he held.

By the time Marianus achieved his climax and pulled out, gasping, Anazâr's erection had faded. Satisfaction remained, at least, in having seen Marianus to his own gratification.

Marianus tossed him a torn scrap of fine cloth from a basket. His toga had fallen slightly askew and there was a light sheen of sweat across his forehead, but he was otherwise as stoic and disaffected now as he had been when discussing his brother's indiscretions.

"Clean up with this. I'll leave you here to take care of your own needs… unless you'd like me to send for a house slave? Man or woman, I'd be amenable to granting your choice as a reward for your actions today."

"Thank you, Dominus, but if I'm to stay here tonight, all I desire is a simple dinner and a new tunic."

It had been a long time since the bread at the baths, and now that the tension had worn off, his stomach gnawed at him.

"Very well. I'll have both sent to you right away. And as I said before, Cyrenaicus, I value you highly as my slave, but I think, perhaps, you would also serve me very well as a freedman."

Before Anazâr could respond, beg and scrape and cry *Yes, yes, yes, please Dominus, yes*, Marianus swept out the door.

Anazâr dreamed.

He woke up, in the dream, from a restful sleep on the floor of the same room. He scratched at his chest and forehead to awaken himself, and a wide swath of skin sloughed off. Translucent skin, like the inner membrane of an egg, that carried the letters of his slave tattoo. Below, his new skin shone clean and tender and blank. He peeled the old skin away from his chest, from his shoulders, peeled it like a tunic, tearing and pulling in his eagerness to have it off. As he set to work on his legs, panic surged, because what was he meant to do with his shed skin? If he left it to dirty the house of Marianus, he'd be punished. There was some ritual to perform, but he'd forgotten the words.

He was close to his new life. So very close. He began to sob in frustration, but the tears never came; by that, he understood he was still in a dream—*gods*, what an infernal dream—and let his dry eyelids shudder half-open.

A man stood silhouetted in the doorway. Even in the dim predawn light of the house, Anazâr could see the toga that swept the floor. Marianus. Here to fuck him again? Dream-fog faded; his cock throbbed with immediate interest.

*No.* He was a slave who'd been the only witness to an attempt on a noble's life. Maybe they even suspected that he'd taken part. Perhaps his master's earlier tenderness had been in apology or regret for what was about to happen now.

Not here to fuck him, then. Here to torture him for information. Here to send him to the cross.

Now his heart pounded instead, every muscle in his body preparing to fight or flee. But he wouldn't fight, and he wouldn't flee. He'd go willingly and honorably and be done with this life, dying as neither coward nor animal. He closed his eyes again, taking a deep, cleansing breath, and feigned sleep. It would be all right.

Marianus paced softly from one end of the room to the other, then back again. None of this made sense. Perhaps he was still dreaming. No, this wasn't Marianus. The nervousness, the strange half-skipping step—even with his eyes closed, he could tell.

Felix.

What in Hades would Felix want with him? He waited for something: an order, a touch, a purposeless strand of conversation. Maybe Felix was drunk.

*. . . if he commands you in anything . . .*

A rustle of cloth.

Anazâr risked a curious glance, still feigning sleep.

Felix lay on his back on the bare floor, out of arm's reach from where Anazâr lay, and let out a puffy, distracted sigh. His arms were crossed on top of his chest—an uncomfortable pose. So far from restful it veered on corpse-like.

*I should offer him my pallet. It should be me sleeping on the bare floor.* But Anazâr didn't say anything at all. Whatever Felix meant by this, Anazâr wouldn't risk embarrassing him by revealing he was awake.

The man had seen his death tonight. Perhaps for the first time, even.

Anazâr could barely remember his own first time. A night attack by bandits on a trading trip to the coast; one of his uncles had died under their scimitars. Then, after he joined the levy sent to Alexandria, there'd been times beyond counting.

He counted anyway, drifting off into the past, into sleep.

"Where's Ursus?" asked the Aethiopian.

"He won't be coming back," said Anazâr. "I have a new assistant, a Gaul slave named Rufus, who'll arrive shortly."

Amanikhabale played nonchalantly with her newly plaited hair. "What happened to him?"

Cassia, sitting next to her, looked up from her wooden bowl of porridge. Other women followed her lead, until he faced a semicircle of staring gladiatrices.

"Why would you ask—" Anazâr cut himself off in frustration.

Switching to Greek and lowering her voice, she said, "You might as well have it out. Slaves *will* gossip."

Gods damn her, she was right.

"He's dead," said Anazâr, and watched a gasp of realization run through the ranks of the gladiatrices, language barrier by language barrier. He put up a hand before they got out of control. He'd give them the whole truth, no room for scandal. "I killed him. He—" *How to best phrase it?* "He made an attempt on the house of Marianus, and I acted in its defense."

"Yes! Killing!" shouted the Sarmatian, in Latin. Good—she was learning.

"Well, well." Amanikhabale's eyes narrowed. "Quite surprising. Although now that I recollect certain experiences with our previous master, I have theories regarding such an attempt. I'd be happy to share them *directly* with our new master."

He admired the quickness of her maneuver. Her goal, obviously, was to convince Marianus she was better employed as a domestic slave. Whether her information was true or cleverly spun from air . . . now that was another matter.

"Then I'll report your offer tonight." As he shifted, a beam of light from the high window dazzled his eyes. He blinked and rose from the floor. The gladiatrices remained in shadow, hunched over their bowls, conferring like crows. "Talk, but keep eating. We have no time to waste; I want you all training in armor soon."

The three Germans looked at him dumbly.

"Eat," he said in Latin, and mimed the motion of spoon to mouth.

"Eat," repeated Cheruscia, the German with the pale green eyes. "Eat!"

"Atalanta would like to know if you took the head of Ursus," said Venatrix.

"That's not done here," he replied, and stalked off to fetch the armor. He found himself wanting to stay and teach them—*we are a civilized people, not savage headhunters.*

*We?*

He shook his head, ill at ease and wondering if traces of the dream-fog still lingered.

"Feint, shift, strike! Feint, shift, strike!"

The row of women did not move in harmony, but at least they *moved*.

Anazâr kept them at practice until arms began to tremble and the weakest could no longer raise their wooden swords above waist level.

After a short rest, he summoned one of the Gaul women forward. Enyo seemed to be the oldest among them; as he drew her hair away to fasten the murmillo helmet, he noticed a few strands of gray at the temples of her auburn hair. She spoke little Latin, and he suspected she had some slight fighting experience. Perhaps she belonged to one of the rebel tribes.

"Enyo does well," he told the resting gladiatrices. He turned to face her, lifting his sword and judging the weight, so cumbersome compared to the true steel he'd swung last night. "Attack. Feint, shift, strike, repeat!"

She came at him slowly, though with good form. He blocked every blow, retreating a calculated half-step each time.

With the helmet on, it was possible to imagine he was facing a man. Perhaps their opponents, if they were men, would perform the same mental trick to make killing them easier.

"Stop. Rhakshna! Take my sword."

The Sarmatian was at his side almost instantly. He retreated a few paces and gave the signal to begin. "She will attack in return," he warned Enyo. "Steel yourself."

A Gaul woman called out something in their language, too long to be a translation. Enyo attacked. The Sarmatian let her go through two series before she fluidly rocked forward to ring a punishing blow to the side of Enyo's helmet.

She fell. "Roll!" he shouted, and grabbed the Sarmatian's arm, knowing that she had the instinct of every good warrior—to stab a fallen enemy.

Rhakshna hissed in frustration, but lowered her sword.

Enyo raised herself to a sitting position, gasping for breath.

"Next time, *roll*. Who's next?"

"Me!" called a man's voice from across the warehouse. "But can I avoid the fighting and go straight to the rolling? That seems like the most entertaining part."

Anazâr's stomach lurched. *Felix*.

He forced a look of bland courtesy onto his face, putting up a hand to halt the practice. "Lucius Marianus Felix," he greeted. "To what do we owe the pleasure?"

Felix's head tilted, eyes crinkling. All traces of yesterday's honesty—pleasure, fear, frustration, cold-gutted horror—were gone, like that man had been a figment of Anazâr's imagination. Felix appeared the same thoroughly unpleasant trickster as always.

"Oh, you find my presence pleasurable now, do you, gladiator? Well, that's an exciting turn of events! Don't worry, I won't tell my brother . . . *if* you let me stay here, that is. I thought I could do a turn translating, you know, as thanks for saving my life."

Ugh, the mooning way he said that: *saving my life*, dripping with undeniably sexual appreciation, like one might praise a sweet overripe fruit as the juice dripped down one's chin. A quiet murmur went up among the gladiatrices—the ones who spoke Latin, at least—and Anazâr could see his carefully tended control of this situation slipping away from him again.

*—if he commands you in anything—*

"Leave to fetch scroll and ink. Write down a list of Latin words and their Cimbrian partners. You'll begin with *eat, drink, run,* and the like."

He'd hoped to unsettle Felix with the mere suggestion of actual work, or at least throw him off balance by not reacting with the scandal he was obviously hoping for, but no such luck. Felix nodded studiously to himself. "So I'll start with tits, bollocks, piss and shit, and fucking."

"You joke with these women's lives," Anazâr said, unable to keep the tone of condemnation from his voice. "As is your right, of course. Though I'd thought for a moment . . ." He shrugged his shoulders.

"He's a pretty man," said the Sarmatian, twirling her sword and smiling rakishly.

"I am indeed," replied Felix in Greek, and bowed to her, although when he rose again, his mischievous eyes had locked on Anazâr alone. "And, Cyrenaicus, I'll do as you ask. No games, I swear."

*We'll see about that*, Anazâr thought, but outwardly nodded his assent. "Thank you," he said, and despite today's many efforts in that direction, was *finally* unbalanced by Felix when his begrudging thanks was met with a surprised, pleased smile.

He called Amanikhabale aside at the midday meal. "I accept your offer," he told her.

"Very good. Should we retire to your chamber? If you're concerned about being seen taught by a woman, I could always claim we're having sexual relations."

"You think of everything. No, that won't be necessary. Tomorrow we'll have the implements."

"Oh yes, you've turned the master's brother into your personal scribe. Much respect."

"Don't praise me yet; there's no telling how horribly this arrangement might end for me." He hadn't meant to say it. Hadn't meant to confide in her—as a rule, he didn't confide in *anyone*—but there it was. Out in the open. He waited, falsely nonchalant, for her response.

"I have a favor to ask of you, in return." She lowered her voice and switched to Greek, even though the other gladiatrices were beyond earshot, clustered around the food baskets carried in by the boy Rufus. "It's not for myself. It's for Cassia."

Anazâr shook his head briefly in surprise, wondering at first if he'd heard right. Of course. He'd asked that Amanikhabale speak with her after her suicide attempt, though he hadn't expected they would get along to this degree. This was better than he could have hoped for. "I'll do my best," he replied.

"She has a daughter. When she killed her husband—and he was a man in great need of killing—his family turned out her daughter. She's with Cassia's sister now. Cassia seeks to send her daughter a letter, and hopes to receive one in return. That's all. She's too timid to ask you on her own account."

Anazâr was about to explain that this was clearly impossible. That his movement was circumscribed to a well-defined, escorted path between warehouse and domus.

Another memory: far away, in an oasis in the desert beyond Cyrenaica, his brother and his wife. Perhaps they had a daughter, too, now.

"Your own kin, in Nubia—" He broke off, knowing he'd crossed a barrier that slaves were accustomed to guard against the past.

But Amanikhabale seemingly took no offense at it. "Ha! I'm not Nubian. They gave me the name of a Nubian warrior queen, but I'm from farthest Eastern Aksum, by the Red Sea. Too far for letters to reach, but Cassia's old life lies only one hill away."

"I'll see what I can do. I might be able to find someone to deliver the letter."

"One last thing," said Amanikhabale. "Not a favor—a warning." She paused, and her eyes, usually so darkly flashing and bold, turned to the shadows. "The Sarmatian spoke rather freely about the other women at the baths. She may mean to claim a wife, perhaps by force. The customs of her people are . . . enigmatic."

Anazâr suppressed a groan of frustration. He'd assumed that this particular issue, at least, would not surface among *women*.

"There will be no fighting or forcing, and no allowances given to Rhakshna. Beyond that, I care not." That was the simplest way, and how the old ludus had worked.

"I see. Another wise decision." She blinked and smiled.

"Go."

Felix did not return that afternoon. Anazâr assumed he'd balked at the effort required of his task and been distracted by drinking or gambling or fucking.

As the light faded, his escort dragged the doors open: Quintus, pulling double duty.

He wasn't alone.

"Welcome, Domina," said Anazâr. She looked beautiful in the evening light, dressed in deep regal purple, with the red of the sunset filling her curls with strands of copper. Beautiful, and bizarrely out of place. The gladiatrices stared, cast their eyes down in fearful deference, and raised them up to stare again.

"Good evening, Cyrenaicus. I'd like to speak with you alone." She raised a fold of her stola to her cheek, then lowered it with a strange hesitance.

Without her husband hearing? Why else would she intercept Anazâr at the ludus, before his evening report? "The second level?" he asked, gesturing up the stone ramp.

She floated past him, ascending by lamplight. He followed. When she turned to face him at the top, her eyes were level with his, and the little flames of the lamps danced in them.

"Here," she said. "This is a delicate matter. I'm not deceiving my husband, nor am I asking you to deceive him. I intend to tell him of this visit, even. I love him and obey him . . . in most matters. But I can't come to him about this, not yet. Not until I'm sure. I wouldn't cause him strife over unsubstantiated suspicion."

*The murder attempt.* That was why she'd come. He nodded mutely, urging her on.

"I do wish that you keep my visit secret from Felix."

Something rotted in Anazâr's gut, like bad fucking meat.

"I will try," he said. *Slaves* will *gossip*, Amanikhabale had warned; it was an inexorable fact. All the gladiatrices had seen Aelia.

"I'll have to take that chance. I believe that the cutthroats were meant for my Lucius, and that Felix is involved somehow. No—" she raised a small hand glittering with rings, stilling Anazâr with a single sharp sideways motion "—no, it would be the height of foolishness to fall into his own trap, and Felix is no fool. But the bolt strayed wide, and there was no second shot. And Felix and I . . . we have a certain history which causes me to doubt any protestations. Again, nothing hidden from my husband. But Lucius is willfully blind when it comes to his little brother, always holding out false hope. I would have you not be blind in such a manner. To keep your eyes open very wide indeed. Ears, as well. What have you heard from other slaves?"

He felt as if he were standing at the edge of a shadowy abyss, an almost unspeakably strange feeling, because he was standing at the *real* edge of one as well. He swallowed, dry throat suddenly aching, and leaned his elbow against the wall, propping himself away from where the ramp dropped. "The Aethiopian says she has information about her former master, the enemy of your father."

"Send her to me. And *watch* yourself around Felix. He'll use your inclinations to his advantage, if you give him any chance."

Anazâr jutted his jaw in defiance of the weakness she perceived in him. "I would never sway from my loyalty to your husband." A promise, proudly given.

"I believe you," said Aelia. Her face softened. He remembered her carrying Lucullus on her hip, consoling her crying child. Then the moment of vulnerability passed; the senator's daughter put on her public face again. That stoic, beautiful mask, as perfect and removed as the face of Juno.

"I'll send her up to you now, Domina." He nodded to her, turned, and walked down the ramp, trailing his hand against the wall to keep the dizziness at bay.

Aelia spoke with Amanikhabale for a while as twilight fell. Anazâr used the time to painstakingly recall every nuance of Felix's words and actions the night of the attack, over and over again, searching for any sign that might prove Aelia's theory.

He didn't want the theory to be right. He didn't want to believe that Felix, the infuriating man who had somehow made him smile, could plot to murder a brother by blood. Felix had looked genuinely shaken and fearful that night, hadn't he?

Actium all over again. The information that could save their lives, hoarded by generals and the highest born. A rebellious voice deep inside shouted to let them all die on their own swords. *Why should I fight your battles?*

For the sake of freedom. For the sake of loyalty.

He'd be called on to make a choice very soon. He could feel the moment coming, sure as a legion marching in lockstep, sure as the flooding of the Nile.

She floated down the ramp again, Amanikhabale pacing behind, towering over Aelia's slight form.

"Quintus will see me to the shop down the street where my litter awaits," she said. "Then he will return for you. Farewell. Keep us safe. And you—" she turned to the gladiatrices "—bring honor to this house with your swords!"

The men at his old ludus would have cheered and howled like wolves at such words from a lady. His gladiatrices merely looked to each other in confusion as Aelia slipped out the door.

 CHAPTER 7

## The month of Maius.

The morning started auspiciously. Unlike all the mornings before, when breakfast was a cold, quiet affair, punctuated only by petty fighting, today the gladiatrices spoke in excitement with one another, and even the wary, tribal Gauls intermingled, inviting the Aethiopian into their midst. They'd been sharing speech more often. Beyond reminding them to practice their Latin, Anazâr didn't intervene.

It had been a week since Aelia's visit, and Felix—doing nothing to alleviate the suspicion she had laid upon him—had not returned. In his absence, and Marianus having yet to provide an alternative, they went without a translator, making do with body language and the Aethiopian's linguistic talents.

Anazâr seized the time to scratch on the stone floor with a piece of charcoal. Moving from left to right, the arc of his alphabet was smooth, though its letters were rough, unsteady, blurred. *The count of them is twenty and three, twenty and three.* He counted and began a chant, forcing his lips to stay closed so that the sounds echoed through his mind in strange, thunderous silence.

He knew the shapes of many words—shop signs, street markers, his slave name of CYRENAICVS—but they had always struck him as somber and static, not at all like the clamoring, perplexing little letters that writhed inside the words.

Felix would have grown up in full mastery of them. As of other things. And people. Anazâr, besieged by this battlefront of ill-shaped letters, would appear to Felix as a crawling baby, an idiot, an animal.

*No. Felix has flaws too numerous to count, but he never shamed me in* that *way, did he?*

Had he shamed Anazâr at all? Teased him, yes. Toyed with him, frustrated him, tested him, but always in the same way he did his brother. Never as a slave.

Damn him. It didn't matter how egalitarian he was in his mischief, and what that said about his character. It didn't prove anything, so long as he stayed away. So long as he let Aelia's accusation rest unchallenged on his face, as damning as the TMQF etched into Anazâr's. *Damn him.*

A shadow passed across his letters, looming over his shoulder like an omen.

"Scratching in the dirt is no good for a warrior," advised Rhakshna. "Those things, they'll make you sick in the mind. Maybe she wants you that way, eh? Weak, like her."

"Would you cross the steppes without knowing how to ride a horse? *This* is where we live. This city. Think about it. You're not stupid."

"You can go back."

Anazâr laughed as he rose. He felt nothing more than rueful nostalgia, echoes of old pain at the worst. He'd burned the blood from that wound. "The very name of my people means *free*. I can't go back." *Not now. Not like this.*

Even if he could go, even if he were not a marked man, even if he were free to leave this place, how could he ever look his brother in the eye, knowing Marianus had had him on his knees?

He looked directly into Rhakshna's dark, guarded eyes. "We're dead to our people, Sarmatian. I don't imagine yours look kindly on warrior women captured alive." An educated guess. He tensed in preparation for the potentially explosive reaction.

"Fuck me, you're right. I'll not be going back either. At least in this shithole I know I won't have to die old." She spat to the side and stalked away.

Once she'd gone, Anazâr heaved a heavy sigh and returned to his letters, crouching like he'd seen generals do over strategy. But the lines seemed to wash together, individual symbols curling into each other in tangled nets and chains. Any scrap of meaning he'd recently fought for, lost to him once again.

"Cyrenaicus?" More distraction. The boy Rufus approached. Anazâr rose again, not too quickly—Rufus was easily spooked. "I'm supposed to give you this." He held a scroll.

The Aethiopian hurried over, snatched it from Rufus, and began to read aloud. "Attack, defense, front, back, left, right, above, below! Excellent. Oh, and this combination of letters is to be pronounced much the same as a death rattle, according to the side note. Very good."

"Felix?" asked Anazâr, unable to hide the surprise in his voice.

"Who else?" She raised an eyebrow. "Here, I believe this is meant for you." She turned over the scroll, pointing to a crude drawing scribbled into one corner: two figures, both in equestrian togas, one with . . . yes, that was an erect cock depicted in loving detail. Felix's cock, Anazâr had to assume, judging by the obscene, egotistical size of the thing. The drawing of Felix was locked in a cage, like one used for lions, and outside it the other figure stood with a key in one hand and what looked to be writing implements in the other, tongue stuck out in an obvious taunt. Marianus?

It told Anazâr three things: one, that Felix's punishment for his various misdeeds was well underway and was the reason for his absence; two, (shamefully for Anazâr) that Felix knew Anazâr to be illiterate; and three, that knowing this, Felix still cared enough about Anazâr's estimation of him to put out the obvious effort required to communicate with Anazâr personally so as to offer an explanation for his absence.

"Very well," said Anazâr, and turned to hide the twitch of a smile. When he surveyed the women again, he made sure to banish all traces of mirth. "To your armor, gladiatrices! You'll jump like frogs in a frying pan this morning. No more lazy legs. Move!"

No hesitance. No grumbling. They did.

"I'd hate to bore our guests with talk of business," warned Aelia while she cut a piece of honeyed pastry. Her tone was light, and she spoke through a smile.

"Give me! Give me!" Lucullus's chubby hands flailed, snatching for the pastry, which Aelia tidily kept out of his reach, not even acknowledging his cries. "Nooooo!"

"But this is *gladiator* business, so it's rather exciting! Please, Marianus, let your man make his report." Aelia's matron companion turned a gleaming, somewhat horse-like smile toward the couches where the men reclined, before her roving gaze landed wide-eyed on Anazâr, who stood against the wall. Hungry, that was the expression. But for what?

He quickly looked away. *No, not at Felix.* Too late. Felix smiled, eyes threatening something unspeakably disruptive.

"If our other guest is agreeable," said Marianus. The young man by his side nodded vigorously. Gladiator-struck too. But then, what Roman wasn't? "Aelia?"

"Oh, all right. Here, Lucullus, I'll let you have a piece if you share with your father. Take it to him. Go on, but be careful!"

Lucullus rushed over to his father, the pastry flopping precariously back and forth. Marianus took a portion, ruffled his son's hair, and sent him back to his mother with a pat on his padded bottom. "Good boy. Cyrenaicus, step forward and make your report."

Anazâr tucked his hands behind his back, stepping forward and fixing his stare somewhere just above Marianus's head. He took a moment, hoping it looked outwardly like he was composing his thoughts. In reality, his throat was stuck with a knot; something about the sight of Lucullus pained him in a way he couldn't name.

"Training proceeds well. Some of the women will be able to fight in heavy armor. In the next month, I'll know enough to assign specializations. The top fighters are Rhakshna the Sarmatian, as expected, Enyo and Penthesilea, both Gaul women, and Cheruscia, of the Germanic tribes. I would match any of them against the lowest rank of gladiator and expect an excellent fight, or in the case of the Sarmatian, certain victory."

"Will they be fighting *men*?" asked the young guest. Anazâr realized he must be the wholesaler's son from Pompeii. He stifled a grin remembering Felix's antics with the scroll, but when the full import of the question sunk in, even his silent laughter died. *Up against men in the arena.* Most of the women did not have the arm strength, the weight, the killing urge. He could only pray to the gods that the fights would be held to submission.

"Probably not. I don't know," said Marianus. "That's a thorny issue at the moment, because the administration of the games isn't wholly under control of the aedile any longer. I can't rely on him for definitive match guidelines, and it's rather frustrating." He shrugged and twisted his mouth into a stoic half-smile. "We need to be prepared for all eventualities."

"Fighting naked?" asked the young man.

Aelia sighed as she adjusted Lucullus, who had gone to sleep in her lap. Her companion groaned audibly.

Felix rose from his reclining couch. "If that's the kind of fight you want to see, I know just the place! The women are well-oiled and deliver the finishing stroke with the help of a clever little harness—"

The young man punched his leg, barely wincing at his own blow. "By Hercules! That's exactly the sort of—"

"I don't think so," interrupted Marianus. "My brother will be leading no expeditions any time soon." He turned to Anazâr. "Was his lexicon of the German tongue of aid to you?"

"Yes, Dominus. Very much so." Anazâr caught Felix's gaze and held it. "Thank you."

A soft smile, performed for no one, passed as quickly as a cloud overhead.

"No expeditions," Felix quoted. "I'm a prisoner in my own home, you see. I hear my brother thinks me a *murderer*, or at least a conspirator to the same, and we all know it's impossible for men to commit such deeds when they share close quarters . . . and a staff of watchful slaves, I suppose." He turned his cruelest smile on Alexandros, who stood silent vigil by the wall and gave him no reaction. Felix wasn't disheartened, though, and strode across the floor with the confidence and grace of a seasoned orator. "But then, Marianus Lucius stands a lanista, now, so there's no supposedly impossible task that men of the house of Marianus haven't risen to, isn't that right?"

"Oh dear," said Aelia's companion. "Perhaps I should retire."

"No," said Aelia. "Felix, who is being an *ass*, will retire."

Marianus nodded and flicked his fingers dismissively in Felix's direction, not even bothering to glare at him. "Go."

"I'll go, and wish for Mercury's winged sandals. Or a grappling hook to scale the walls. I'll go mad as the women of Thebes, caged here, and you'll be a bunch of sorry bastards when I start biting off chunks of my own arm and spitting them at you . . ." His voice trailed off into an aggrieved mumble as he stalked away from the dining room.

"His imagination is fevered," said Marianus to the gaping dinner guests. His tone was calm and unperturbed; Anazâr couldn't help but admire his resistance to Felix's near-godlike powers of perturbation.

"He has always been so," said Aelia, and *tsk*ed softly. "Shall we return to the subject? Dear husband, perhaps you could order a public demonstration of the gladiatrices? That way, we could all see the progress of their fighting abilities, and, of course, the excellent training of Cyrenaicus."

"I'll have it done. Four days from now. Mark the date." Marianus turned his gaze to Cyrenaicus. "You can fight one of your pupils, and arrange another match between them. Blunted weapons for now, although in another month I'd like to see one with edged, to submission."

"Yes, Dominus." Four days until they faced the crowd for the first time. Another thirty-eight days after that, and Anazâr would send them to face their likely deaths. Another word from Marianus, and he'd kill them himself.

Marianus turned to his guest. "My man here is also ex-cavalry, and no doubt a good judge of horses. Would you like to take him with you to the race tomorrow? He can advise you on betting."

"What a wonderful proposition!"

"Dominus, I—the training is at a stage that's—every moment with . . ." The words fled. He felt himself on dangerous, shifting ground. The women deserved their greatest chance, though, and wasn't Marianus a just man? "I stand ready to fulfill your orders in any way, of course, but perhaps my time would be better invested with the gladiatrices."

"Insolence." Marianus's guest raised a hand, as if to strike.

"No," said Marianus, raising a hand of his own, this one to forestall. "Honesty. My offer was ill-planned." He smiled at Anazâr. That sign of forgiveness sent a warmth curling in Anazâr's chest, freeing him to breathe easier. "The pursuit of pleasure should not detract from the conduct of serious affairs. I'll have Alexandros find some other guide for you, Titus."

Anazâr would have liked to suggest the Sarmatian, but he didn't trust her not to kill when angered. Gods willing, she would learn.

Lucullus woke up crying, then, and the party drifted apart. Marianus left with an arm around Aelia's slim shoulders, pausing to nod at Anazâr in acknowledgement, in reinforcement of his forgiveness.

Now that the masters had left, Alexandros stared at Anazâr, studying his face, intense focus written across his own.

"What is it?" Anazâr asked, feeling unnerved.

Alexandros's gray eyebrows knitted together. "Nothing. For now. Continue to step carefully, Numidian."

Anazâr fully intended to follow Alexandros's instructions. However, it seemed the Fates conspired against him at every turn. The very next morning being the first.

"We could just continue walking," argued Amanikhabale. "After all, if walking to the end of a street and back again is good exercise, then walking down and up one of the seven hills, well, wouldn't that provide a superior result, thus increasing our value to our most beloved and financially astute master?"

Their morning rounds were tedious, true. Sometimes porters passing to another warehouse would attempt to flirt with the gladiatrices, or a granary cat would cross their path. Today, the street was empty, and therefore safe.

"No," replied Anazâr. "Orders. We stay close." He picked up the pace. Amanikhabale to his left and Enyo to his right both followed suit. He escorted them two at a time now.

"If challenged, we would have an excellent excuse. And a detour to deliver a letter—"

"Enough! I *will* have it delivered to Cassia's family by some other means." Via Rufus or another household slave entrusted for deliveries, that was his intention. "Why do you press so hard?"

Amanikhabale puffed up in indignation. "You ask me to look after the woman. I look after the woman. Now you ask me why?"

"Yes. When I set you to the task, you begrudged it. Now you attend it with single-minded purpose. Why?"

Enyo walked silently alongside them. If she was curious, she didn't show it. It emboldened them both to speak more freely than they ought to have in front of a third party. "I *always* dedicate my entire self to a task. I'm the consummate slave. Anyway, I'm concerned that whoever receives the letter may not be able to read it. If I deliver it myself, I'll know for certain its meaning is understood."

If only she'd put the same verve into her gladiatrix training.

A third voice cut in before Anazâr could say as much. "I can't mistake the sound of intrigue. Will this be a comedy of the slapstick sort, tunics torn and sausages flung and all that?"

Fuck Fortune for a whore. Of course this situation would slide further out of his control. Felix stepped around the corner of the warehouse. He'd been lurking, no doubt.

"Master Felix!" Amanikhabale greeted sweetly. Enyo stopped in her tracks, face gone tight, an expression Anazâr mirrored, if perhaps for different reasons.

Felix bowed to them all, paying no mind to the less favorable reactions. "Hello, my Nubian warrior goddess. Causing strife for our gladiator friend, are we?"

*No, that's your role,* Anazâr almost said with some bitterness. "Thank you for the scroll," he muttered instead. "Why are you here?" He stepped in front of Amanikhabale. His intent was to form a barrier between them, to keep Felix from disturbing the hard-won order he'd established, but being closer to the man was disturbing in and of itself.

Felix sighed. "I was—" he raised both eyebrows and twisted one corner of his mouth "—curious. Or bored. Oh, I don't know. This isn't about me, this is about you. And your Aethiopian, who has a fire in her eyes that I'm not going to try to piss on to put out."

"Delivering a letter to a nearby insula would be a wonderful diversion for you," said Amanikhabale, who from the sound of it was actually leaning out from behind him in order to address Felix. "Much more diverting than the construction of disgusting metaphors. In fact, I carry a letter this very moment."

Anazâr's heart lurched. "Absolutely not." *I'd never trust him with anything so important. Not for myself, and not for my gladiatrices either. Cassia would be better off going without.*

But despite his racing thoughts, he looked to Felix with an expression schooled into that of a placid, obedient slave. An expression he didn't often take on with Felix, who didn't seem to require it. No. He just hadn't earned it. That was all. "I'm sorry, Dominus. She spoke out of turn. She had no right. Excuse us. We'll be going."

He needed to get away. He needed to get away immediately, before this situation spiraled out of control. Felix wasn't worthy of trust. Unlike Marianus, he wasn't even worthy of respect—and no matter how Felix smiled and jested and lulled him into a false sense of security thanks to their strange companionship, Anazâr couldn't let himself forget it.

"Don't be ridiculous, gladiator. Of course I'll deliver a letter. How else am I to occupy my days now that I'm penniless? Perhaps if I perform the task well enough, I could make a business of it. What do you say, a letter-carrier for slaves, now there's a profession with—"

"This is serious," Anazâr growled, unable to hold his tongue. "A mother separated against her will from her daughter, trying to comfort her child in her absence. Even *you* must be able to understand the depth of feeling between a mother and her child."

*Even a childless, severed man such as myself can at least imagine it.*

"Better than you might assume," Felix acknowledged in a low, meaning-laden voice. His face had fallen, and in that moment, Anazâr heard Enyo swallow thickly. She had just enough Latin to understand, then. Families left behind: a pain all slaves shared that could never be alleviated or soothed.

The sadness that had settled around them vanished as Felix smiled again. "Give me the letter, then, and I'll see it faithfully delivered. I wouldn't keep a mother from her child any more than I'd keep myself from the breast of a beautiful woman." At the last, he looked to Amanikhabale meaningfully, but the flattery missed its mark.

She produced the letter. "The directions and descriptions are contained within."

No more games; Felix took it solemnly. Some part of Anazâr still imagined that Felix would toss it over his shoulder, or read it aloud like a comedy to passersby, but he merely touched it to his lips in a gesture that was both thoughtful and affectionate, and then tucked it away safely into the folds of his toga.

Then he turned and walked away, down to the end of the street, crossing the invisible line that separated the strange, stagnant tide pool of their lives from the greater sea. Anazâr, left standing behind, was suddenly struck by the realization that he trusted Felix far too little . . . and simultaneously, far too much.

In the scant days leading up to the exhibition match, Anazâr had introduced the practice of showman skills.

"This is alien to the battlefield of real soldiering," he'd explained to the dubious gladiatrices. "And I am sure some of you know that well." The Germans, once Amanikhabale translated his words with the aid of Felix's scroll, nodded in agreement. He knew, now, that they'd fought defensive positions in the encampments of their wandering, warlike tribe. "But in a gladiator match, dramatics can, and will, save your life. The crowd is inclined to spare those who entertain them."

Too much flashy swordwork left you open to a killing stroke; too much grim efficiency and ground-grappling lost you the love of the crowd. He'd done his best to explain the balance, even if he hadn't been able to follow his own advice during his time in the arena. The arena he'd be returning to, if he couldn't convince Marianus it was worthwhile to grant his freedom.

Now, with the match at hand, Quintus opened the warehouse doors, letting the bright noonday sun vanquish the shadows. "The crowd is gathered. Come!" he called.

Marianus had ordered this side road blocked off for the purpose of the exhibition. Anazâr motioned to the gladiatrices to wait so their eyes would become accustomed to the sun. Blinking like owls as they were, they would impress no one with their fierceness. They looked well, though, he thought with pride. All standing perfectly straight in their leather armor and metal greaves, long hair well-combed and arranged in battle-practical cords and buns.

"As you walk through the door, issue your war cry. Keep your heads held high—you too, Cassia." He walked toward the door, and as his gladiatrices fell in line behind him, an unsettling sense of *command* swept over him, swelled inside him. Even as he schooled his body into an imposing hardness, designed to impress the awaiting spectators, he reminded himself, *This is a performance, an imitation, a shadow of a battle. Never forget who you are and where you are.*

Though it was hard, sometimes, to remember in the first place.

He paced over the threshold. Time to call upon the gods. "Mars, may you be increased!" he shouted. "Minerva, too, may you be increased!" *Ifri, give strength to my charges.*

There was an answering roar from the crowd. He had not expected so many people.

Rhakshna screamed. High and quavering, unfortunately—her people fought in dead silence, and her newly learned war cry was more grudging than fearsome. The spectators blocking the street to the right of the warehouse still gasped. They were Marianus's clients and freedmen and knew of the gladiatrices by reputation. "The Sarmatian!" several called out.

The Germans yelled out the names of their rough gods in unison. The Gaul women screamed the names of their tribes. Cassia managed another call to Mars and Minerva, and Amanikhabale delivered an ululating Nubian war call, since she knew of no Aksumite ones.

Anazâr spotted Marianus at the center of his clients. Aelia's litter was there as well, raised up to give her the best view. The left side of the street began to fill with passing spectators and neighboring shopworkers, all no doubt thrilled at the prospect of a free gladiator match. He felt their eyes upon him, and was glad in that moment for his plumed thraex helmet, glad that his forehead was concealed.

"I'll keep them back," said Quintus. "And here are your swords." They were specially made exhibition swords, crafted with costly attention to detail: metal cores wrapped in hard oak heartwood, then painted silver to lightly deceive. The gladiatrices took them solemnly, except for Rhakshna, who could not hide her disdain for what was, to her, a glorified play weapon.

Alexandros—with input from Anazâr—had paired off the gladiatrices for a series of quickfire individual fights, with the winners of each moving on to face one another. The high noon sun had passed overhead, and the exhibitions could easily go on into the twilight.

Anazâr intended to fight the winner of the tournament rounds—almost certainly Rhakshna—and by then, he'd have to consider the position of the sun. She'd know enough to take advantage of that.

The women hadn't yet donned their helmets, making a show of their femininity for an audience hungry for the novelty of female gladiators. But when Anazâr called Enyo and Amanikhabale forward, he beckoned them to strap into their helmets, then checked the fit himself. "Strike hard. I want to hear ringing. Amanikhabale, you will gain *nothing* with a poor show. Focus on swordwork, not scheming."

Amanikhabale gave a sharp nod, her dark face lost in the shadows of her helmet. "I know. Believe me, I'll play the warrior queen I'm named for. Who wants the timid scribe of Adulis?" She sighed, and her head twisted oddly, as if she couldn't bear to look at Enyo's impassive, helmeted face.

Anazâr turned to face Marianus's side of the crowd, hoping he hadn't made a mistake with this choice of opening. "Enyo, a captured rebel Gaul woman, set against Amanikhabale, of the Egypt-conquering Nubians! Let the battle begin!"

He stepped back, slashing his arm down.

The pair bowed to each other, touched swords, and began. Enyo struck upward, fast and cold and without warning or sound. Amanikhabale's helmet rang a harsh note as she staggered backward. Enyo pressed in, but her second blow fell against a raised shield with a muffled thud. Amanikhabale pivoted and lunged forward against Enyo; Anazâr let out a quick sharp breath of relief.

Amanikhabale would lose. Enyo was shorter but had the speed, the strength of blow. But at least she wouldn't lose without fighting back.

A few moments, a few more flurries of blows, and Amanikhabale was driven down to one knee. A cacophony of applause filled Anazâr's ears, but there was no time to pay it mind. Anazâr stepped in, raised Amanikhabale up, led her to the side and sat her down. "See to her," he ordered Quintus. She was likely dazed. "Enyo, victorious!" he yelled to the crowd, and they echoed him back, cheering and tossing coppers.

But there was only one reaction that mattered. He looked to Marianus.

Saw him smile.

This world of artifice and confusion became a simpler, easier place, knowing that Marianus was well served.

He noticed for the first time that Felix stood close by Marianus, his complicated shadow. Felix's expression was nowhere near as easy to judge.

The next match, between Diana and Venatrix, lasted longer. They were more evenly matched, but held their blows back too much, and the crowd was not as pleased. Venatrix caught Anazâr's curt hand gesture, however, and stepped up, raining blows against Diana's shield and then down onto her unguarded leg. Diana screamed in pain, but didn't yield. Anazâr ended the match, then, and raised up Venatrix's shaky hand as more coppers fell at their feet.

Atalanta won her match against Verecunda with a feint and a kick. A dangerous move, and one a more experienced opponent could easily have turned against her, but it made for a showy victory. Through an opening in the gauzy curtain of Aelia's raised litter, he could see her clapping her hands.

Penthesilea, the only one equipped in heavy murmillo armor, easily overpowered Provocatrix, who spat blood from a lip split by a sword blow, and stayed silent otherwise.

Cimbria and Batavia, the two Germans matched together, fought hard and long. Felix called out something to them—perhaps he'd caught the spirit of the event after all—but Anazâr had no clue as to the meaning. Cimbria drove her opponent far back, almost into the crowd, winning the match and a long roar of acclaim.

Anazâr was already looking to the Sarmatian, and not liking what he saw. She shifted her weight subtly back and forth, scanning the crowd, and nothing in her carriage reminded him of an actor nervous before a performance. No, this was pure battle-wariness, and rather than glorifying it for the pleasure of the crowd, she was attempting to *conceal* it; if he had not studied her so closely for the last month, he would have passed over it. A full-lipped half-snarl, flickering eyes under heavy frozen eyelids—*damn*. She held all life, including her own, in low regard; perhaps she thought to regain her lost honor by taking Romans with her.

And Rhakshna didn't need a real sword to kill.

He couldn't call off the match on a faint suspicion. "Cheruscia, of the howling German savages, set against Rhakshna, of the legendary Sarmatian raiders!" As he checked the fitting of her helmet, he whispered in her ear, tempting her, assuming that task with a disconcerting ease. "Hold back your blows a little. Draw it out with flourishes. This is only the beginning. You can gain freedom with the years, and gold, and lovers, and another kind of honor."

Her only acknowledgement was a low hissing noise.

He stepped back and signaled for the match to begin, making sure to stay between her and Marianus. He knew that if she did lash out at the audience, Marianus would be her first target, the man into whom she could funnel all her hate and resentment. If she could take down only one Roman before being killed, she would make it count.

Because that was what Anazâr himself would do.

Cheruscia held her ground and barely staggered under the first blows. But the outcome was never in doubt. Rhakshna danced around her, feet skimming in fluid patterns while her sword licked out in unpredictable intervals. The crowd cheered her, except for the men of veteran age. *They* were struck silent.

She tossed her sword from right hand to left, feinted—

Cheruscia's shield wasn't where it needed to be. Rhakshna's stab sunk into her unarmored left shoulder. The blunt tip did its precise, anatomically calculated damage. Cheruscia's shield dropped from nerveless fingers, and her sword dropped a moment later as she clasped her shoulder, sank to her knees, and keened through clenched teeth.

Anazâr thrust himself forward and between them. His intervention was perfectly timed, but unnecessary. Rhakshna smiled sanguinely and extended a hand to Cheruscia.

*Thank the gods.*

The last fight of the first round did not eclipse the drama of Rhakshna's elegant feint, but it ended well enough. Cassia's swordwork was clumsy, but she used her shield well against her opponent, Nemesis. Victory came when Cassia lunged shield-first, bearing Nemesis down to the ground with her superior weight.

From the sidelines, Amanikhabale shouted, "Well done, indeed!"

Anazâr approached Marianus. From the corner of his eye, he kept watch on Rhakshna. "Dominus, shall we begin the second round?"

Marianus didn't reply, just gestured a regal "continue" with one hand. At his shoulder, Felix imitated the motion with an added lurid bulging of his eyes.

"Gather the coppers, boy, and keep a few for yourself," Anazâr told Rufus, who set himself to the task immediately, skipping and picking like an unusually happy crow. Raising his voice to address the crowd, Anazâr called forward the victors. "Enyo to fight Venatrix!" His small store of crowd-pleasing flourishes and epithets was quite exhausted by now, and he couldn't think fast enough to replenish them, occupied as he was with keeping track of every single gladiatrix, but most of all, Rhakshna. Guards had been hired to oversee the proceedings, watching the crowd, the gladiatrices, and likely Anazâr himself, but there was no saying what amount of force they would resort to if called upon. Better for Anazâr to employ foresight.

Enyo and Venatrix fought in a hybrid style—straight swords, small rectangular thraex shields—and for a while, the swordwork proved exciting. But Venatrix tired quickly. For every one of her blows, Enyo gave two, hitting increasingly below the shield, or above, each ring against the helmet sounding out pain and defeat, until Venatrix staggered backward and Anazâr stepped in to steady her.

Penthesilea again overpowered her opponent, Atalanta. She was unstoppable in her armor and, what was more important, untiring. Her resilience surprised and pleased Anazâr, who hadn't expected much of anything from her.

When Rhakshna lunged through Cimbria's defenses, she was positioned nowhere near Marianus. Anazâr swallowed his sigh of relief. He spoke with her sharply, though, before ending the second round. "Too fast," he whispered curtly. "Fall back next time. Make it look like you're in trouble."

He planned on beginning the third round with Penthesilea and Cassia, who by necessity of numbers had skipped the second round. Something was wrong with Cassia, though: her skin had gone pale and clammy, a condition strongly visible under such a bright sun, and her eyes were unfocused. "She took a blow to the head," said Amanikhabale, pressing a rag against Cassia's forehead and gathering her protectively under one arm. "These are unpredictable. She'll recover."

Anazâr didn't recall seeing Cassia take a notable hit to the head. *Something is wrong.* No time to query the cause, though. "Enyo and Rhakshna!" he shouted. The crowd's favorites, and they showed it, screaming and chanting their names, already dividing into opposing parties.

As he fitted their helmets, he noticed the crowd in front of Marianus thickening; some of the passers-by from the left side had migrated to the right for a better view. Jostling and cursing were the order of things. "Make way for the house of Marianus, you street rats!" bellowed someone, maybe Quintus. Marianus and Felix stood at the front now, assured a view, protected on either side by clients with jabbing elbows.

Felix was looking as unwell as Cassia. The sun? But no, it wasn't even full summer yet and the day wasn't all that hot, especially standing in the shade as they were.

Anazâr gave the signal to begin, and stepped back so that he stood in front of Marianus—no, gods damn it, he couldn't do that. He was here as a showmaster, not a bodyguard; remembering that, he stepped aside to give Marianus a clear view.

After the first engagement, Rhakshna fell back, as he'd wanted, before pressing forward again. She didn't once look at Marianus or the crowd in a threatening way—she performed completely admirably, herding Enyo around the square with efficient but acceptably showy grace. Perhaps she could make a name for herself as a gladiatrix, after all.

In fact, both of them would. He knew Enyo would ultimately be defeated, but she fought well; her slightly greater age gave her an advantage in experience, in dedication to training. He knew from practice the strength of her arms, the force of her strike. She changed her direction mid-step, pivoted, executed a feint—

—No. Not a feint. The arc of her arm ended in a knife drawn from a greave.

Three steps to Marianus. And she'd already taken one, the blade brandished and glinting in the sun. Sharp. Two steps until slave killed master and woke the dark beast at the heart of Rome, dormant but *waiting* since the fall of Spartacus. *To the cross.*

He hurled himself into her path.

Too late. The knife—

Enyo stumbled. Behind her, Rhakshna stood with an arm extended in perfect javelin form—had she thrown her damn sword?—and then leaped forward like a panther, *exactly* like a panther, he'd seen one leap on a condemned man in the games last year and *keep the master safe oh gods keep him safe.*

Rhakshna fell on Enyo a heartbeat before Anazâr. The pair struggled, rolled, rolled again, and Enyo was screaming, but Rhakshna was deadly silent, jaw set in grim determination as she straddled Enyo's chest. The knife jerked. As Anazâr rolled, he caught sight of Marianus's clients grabbing fistfuls of his toga, pulling him backward, swallowing him up into the safety of the crowd.

The rest of the crowd, sensing the threat of real violence in the atmosphere as surely as an oncoming thunderstorm, roared in delight. Coppers fell around them like rain.

Rhakshna had blood on her hands. Blood, pumping up from Enyo's throat. Anazâr drove a fist into Rhakshna's face. He knocked her backward onto the ground and she rolled away, came up shouting on her knees, waving empty hands.

*We're all going to die here. If I kill her now, will I save anyone?*

No. *Think.* He unwound the chain of events as best he could in the moment it took to turn back to the crowd. Rhakshna—she'd thrown her sword to trip her target. "A murderess was executed here!" he shouted, raising both arms victorious and feeling the stickiness of blood run down one cheek. *Enyo's blood.* "All free men are safe! Justice has been done!"

His pronouncement was met with shouting and applause, the likes of which he'd never heard after a victory of his own.

"Thanks to *me*," said Rhakshna, looking up at him from where she still knelt over Enyo's body. "And I want some of what you promised earlier. Damn your fist, my tooth is loose."

He strode over to her, impervious to the infectiousness of her bloodied grin. "You knew the attempt was coming," he accused in a low hiss. "We'll talk later. In private." *Amanikhabale, too*. More events were coming together in his mind, and a net began to weave together, still full of gaping holes but promising the most troubling entanglement once complete.

Quintus grabbed his arm. "Marianus wants them all chained back at the warehouse. He'll spare you the same treatment . . . for *now*. I'd suggest you get to the fucking bottom of this *quick* if you don't want the whole lot of you sent to the fucking cross."

Two slaves dragged Enyo's body by the legs out of the square, leaving a wide swerving trail of blood to paint the stones.

# CHAPTER 8

"Some of you were born into slavery," said Anazâr to the chained women. "You must know the law."

"Yes," said Atalanta. Her voice slid up and down, quavering from girlish to croaking as she spoke. "The entire household is sent to—put to death. I know. I want to live. We all want to live. We have no reason—"

"Enyo had a reason. So *that* is my question to you: what reason does a Gaul ever have to seek their own death and doom their companions as well?" He counted off from five stiff fingers held angrily high. "One, tribal honor. Which means almost nothing, absent free tribe. Two, religion. I know little of yours, save that you're known to sacrifice by burning. A remote possibility. Look me in the face, all of you! This is your life at stake. Three, madness—hard to determine. Four, witchcraft, even worse. Five, threat to family." He held up a closed fist now.

Venatrix flinched.

He sat cross-legged at her level, letting no veil of mercy fall between them as he stared into her eyes. "Speak of this."

"She had a daughter sold to the port of Ostia. That's all I know."

*Oh, Enyo.*

Rhakshna stopped rubbing the salve onto her bruised lip and met his gaze easily. "The Aethiopian bitch warned me. I didn't believe her at first. I thought it was a plot to make me look bad. But I kept my eyes open and it paid off."

"You should have come to me."

"Like I said, I didn't want to play the fool. Instead, I come out the heroine, the savior, and you keep me in chains. Roman justice is shit."

"*I* don't keep you in anything. Our master does, and for good reason after one of his own slaves made an attempt on his life. We're all lucky we're not on the cross right now. No. Luck has nothing to do with it. Marianus's generosity."

"Oh, you are soft on *him*. You're as bad as Cassia, mooning after—"

"You make it extraordinarily hard to be grateful to you, Sarmatian."

"You told Rhakshna you heard Enyo talking in her sleep. Plotting to kill her master *in her sleep*. No wonder she only halfway believed you. I don't believe you at all. In what fucking language did she happen to disclose?"

Amanikhabale adjusted her cuffs and shrugged, meeting his stare without fully meeting it, giving away absolutely nothing. "It's true. She mumbled in a dialect of Lepontic that I recently learned."

"I think you had some part in this, but didn't trust that you'd survive the attempt, and covered yourself. If I find out this death is on your shoulders—"

"*Someone* got her that knife." Amanikhabale's counteroffer.

"Come to me with a better story. One that makes the outside influence obvious. I will expect that your memory becomes clearer by morning."

Amanikhabale nodded.

Gods willing, he'd find out the truth eventually. Until then, a half-truth would serve best to keep them all alive. He was a loyal man, but not to the point of suicide.

In the privacy of his spacious storeroom quarters, he finally stripped his armor. Though he wanted to throw it aside in frustration, years of instinct took over, and he arranged it carefully over a chair instead. He poured himself water from a tapped amphora, and kept the tap running after he'd drunk his fill, enough to splash his face and chest and wash away any last traces of blood.

The water darkened the stone floor, then ran into cracks and disappeared. Beyond the beam of sunlight from the one high window, the whole storeroom was darkening with the twilight, and the bolts of cloth muffled sound.

They didn't muffle quite enough.

"Step forward," said Anazâr quietly. His mind was already turning to tactics. He could rip off the chair's crossbar, use the jagged point as a weapon...

"You don't miss much, do you?"

*That voice.*

Felix stepped out of the shadows, his face strangely blotchy and his gray eyes wide and blinking.

"Why are you here?"

*He's behind it. He's behind the attack. He could have visited the warehouse months ago, before my time, and offered to retrieve Enyo's daughter in return for his brother's murder. Maybe he'd met the daughter himself on one of his trips to the whorehouses. Seen his opportunity. Orchestrated it all.*

It was as if Felix sensed his accusation, or maybe he saw it written across Anazâr's face, because he immediately leapt to his own defense. "My brother made sure I stood beside him today. I'm a fool and I've been playing a fool's game, but I never thought it would come to this."

Not a defense. Not a denial. Only a maddening riddle. Anazâr kept his fists lowered. He wouldn't strike, not yet. Felix was a fit young man, but he could easily be taken down. Anazâr had the size and the strength and the skill. Marianus would reward him. All his problems, solved. But he needed a confession first.

"You tried to kill him. To free yourself from his punishments."

Felix's brow crumpled, the tension in his mouth snapping apart a heartbeat later. "Do you truly believe that? I'm damned beyond all hope, then." He strode to a nearby column of cloth and leaned against it, slumping almost drunkenly. "Fortune's rags. If not for you, I'd be dead twice over, and now I find that even *you* have turned against me. Well, if that's the case, you may as well kill me yourself now. Spare me the indignity of dying at the hands of the next cutthroat."

"More acting. More drama." And why did he even *care*? The melodrama of his petty Roman masters . . . he should only be as involved as his prescribed loyalty to Marianus demanded. No more. Yet he couldn't help the hurt in his voice.

"This is the first in a very long time that I speak with no artifice. The fucking words fail me, the ungrateful bastards. I need your help, gl— Cyrenaicus." He turned the name over in his mouth, like it was too large to fit. "*Cyrenaicus.* No tricks. No games."

"Tell me then," said Anazâr, crossing his arms. "No tricks. Before, you said you fainted at the sight of blood, but at the first so-called attempt on your life, you did not."

"It's a lie, it's a lie, lie, lie. I find gladiator games . . . repugnant. The fact that my feigned weakness embarrassed my brother was simply an added benefit."

*Repugnant.*

"You think I'm a barbarian," Anazâr accused. The Romans called his people that. *Bar bar bar bar.* Of course Felix was no different.

"It's just a word. We're all the same, bags of bones and guts and brilliance. Me, you, and every other slave, and I can't stand to watch you die like dogs. That's all."

*He asked me my real name. To know me as a man and not as a slave.*

*No. To have compromising information he can humiliate and control me with, like he controls everyone else around him. A spider at the center of a web, and when he couldn't seize my name, he seized my body—my desire—in its place.*

"Why did you come to me that night? Did you hope to taunt me, the way you did in the baths?" *Is this all a manipulation?*

Felix covered half his face with one hand and laughed, a broken, rueful sound. "I was afraid. I knew I'd cheated death once, but it could come again. *Would* come again. Whoever wanted me dead wouldn't give up so easily." More blinking, wetter now. He barked out another laugh. "And coming to that conclusion, I realized . . . I realized that after all my fucking *games* . . . there was no one—*no one* I could trust. No one I could turn to."

*No one but me. He'd faced his death, and then he came to shelter by my side.*

"I'm a slave. I'm not even *your* slave, I bear no sword, and you come to me—"

Felix pushed off his leaning post and lunged for Anazâr, who flinched but didn't shy back. Felix's white-knuckled hands gripped the rough fabric of Anazâr's tunic and wrenched at it in useless protest. "This isn't about your skills with a sword. How do I— You—" He thumped the heel of his curled hand against Anazâr's chest. Once, twice, three times, each blow more ineffectual and flailing than the last. His disheveled toga slipped farther off his shoulder. "You think a man like me can't find some fucking brute to follow me around, kill anyone who crosses me? You don't strike me as an egotistical man, Cyrenaicus. You must know your skills aren't exactly unique."

Another strike against his chest, but this time Anazâr grabbed Felix around both wrists, clutching hard enough that Felix hissed in pain and twisted on his heels, trapped. "Then what. What do you want me for?" Anazâr pressed their foreheads together, boring his glare into Felix's wide, startled gaze, those eyes that shone gray like his brother's. "Why are you *here*?"

"I shouldn't have come. I don't mean to endanger you." More ridiculous hysteria. Now Felix's knees gave out from under him, his entire body sinking downward, held upright only by Anazâr's punishing grip on his slim wrists. *He's right. I could be killed for this.*

"Stand up. Please, Felix." *I have to see your eyes again.* Anazâr ran his hands down, nearly to Felix's elbows now, softening his grip until it was enough to anchor Felix but not enough to hurt.

Felix staggered, and his clammy hands clasped Anazâr's elbows in turn, linking them both together. Then he took a deep breath and raised his eyes, and oh gods, he looked nothing like his brother— everything he was, every tortuous contradiction, was right there on the surface of his face. No barriers, no masks. "Love's a crazy whore," he said. "That's all there is, really."

Anazâr couldn't reply. He couldn't even *breathe*.

Felix gathered his composure, setting his shoulders and lifting his chin. A hastily drawn curtain fell lopsided over his features. "But I'll go. Maybe it's better that way. A rope out the window and I—"

Anazâr pulled him roughly closer. *I'll have the truth from you yet.* But the truth had undergone a metamorphosis into something embodied, held warm in his arms. Felix, already here for him. Stripped of everything. Everything except...

A quick pull was enough to send the toga sliding to the floor. A few more sufficed for his loincloth and tunic. Felix's body was fine and smooth, even in places where Anazâr usually hungered for musk and hair, but somehow it only increased Felix's appeal. Noticing Anazâr's hungry interest, Felix smiled softly, canting his hips to draw Anazâr's attention to his flushed, slowly rising erection. But he didn't act. This Roman master of men, waiting on Anazâr's will.

Anazâr would take this offering, take Felix, seize this moment even if he died on the cross for it later. He was tired of worrying about *later*. He'd live like he did in the arena, one passionate horrible glorious moment at a time.

"My name is Anazâr," he said, so close that his mouth brushed Felix's ear. It was the first time he'd heard his own name aloud in years, and it was like a spell, transforming Felix again. Earlier he'd gone from the trickster to a fearful, lonely boy seeking solace and now, again, he changed, this time into a minor god. The only man in this universe who knew—would *ever* know—Anazâr as his complete self. Now he had that man pressed against him, shivering, but not with fear.

Gasping. "Thank you. Gods, *yes*, yes—"

A spell, yes. More powerful than anything you could buy at a temple, more powerful than anything you could conjure up even with baths of blood. It transformed them both.

And it was terrifying.

"Quiet." Anazâr pushed, edging Felix's legs open with his thigh. Rocked him backward and up against the bolt of cloth. A low laugh sounded, and then a soft growl in the back of Felix's alluringly tipped-back throat. "I said *quiet*." Anazâr silenced him with a hand over his mouth. Felix's freed hand went straight to Anazâr's cock, and his eyes were wicked as they peered out over Anazâr's fingers.

Anazâr wanted to groan out, to praise Felix's skillful hand, but long years taking pleasure quickly and silently, in crowded barracks or cells, had given him a discipline that Felix no doubt lacked.

He bit off the words and pinned Felix harder against the bolt of cloth. *Rough use, but he'll like it.* He let go of Felix's other arm and rubbed his palm down Felix's hipbone, down into the whorishly smooth area around his cock and sac, exploring the fascinating contrast between feminine-soft skin and jutting hard shaft. Felix moaned, a strangled sound that Anazâr felt against his fingers more than heard.

"I'm going to kiss you now," he warned in a whisper, transfixed by Felix's smothered, glassy expression. "Make a sound, and I'll stuff my cock down your throat to silence you, and then your pretty hole won't get fucked at all." He'd never used words this way with a lover, but Felix inspired him—Felix was his *muse*, better than any of the nine the poets called on.

Felix nodded, the motion quick and eager, and, satisfied, Anazâr slowly released his grip. Felix's lips were swollen and red, halfway to bruised by Anazâr's crushing hold on his face. *Mine*. All he had to do was complete his claim. He covered Felix's mouth with his own. Opened him and tasted him. Those same poets always spoke of kisses sweeter than wine—untrue, but the taste sent him halfway to madness anyway, so perhaps they were right after all.

He wanted to growl when Felix's hand left off his cock, but feeling them entangle in his short-cropped hair, combing and tugging lightly, almost made up for it.

And then Felix leapt up, wrapping his legs tight around Anazâr's hips and settling Anazâr's shaft against the cleft of his ass with one of his trickster's smiles. So athletic, and as light as he was, they could fuck just like this, standing, Anazâr spearing into that tight heat every time Felix inevitably fell toward earth. The thought nearly unmanned him, so he bit Felix's lips as punishment for being so fucking tempting.

When his gasping became less ragged and he could trust himself again, he finally pulled away from the dizzying kiss to spit on his hand.

He didn't ask permission. Didn't worry that what they were doing—gods, what they were *doing*—was the exact opposite of everything good and proper. That he was overstepping every conceivable bound that ought to govern him. Just for now it didn't matter.

Felix's lips twisted into a snarl. Having to silence his own clever mouth must have been sheer torture. What quips waited on his tongue, what praises and outcries and filthy fucking lines? Anazâr took mercy on him and kissed him again, swallowing his moan. And then he slid his fingers between Felix's legs, pushed two spit-wet fingers up into his tight hole. Felix's entire body convulsed and Anazâr had to press him harder against the bolt of cloth to keep him still. But he yielded. Just ready enough for Anazâr's cock.

Taking the base of his cock in hand, Anazâr worked into Felix methodically, probing the limits of his so-called better's body at the pace of his own desire. Inch by excruciating inch, Felix opened around Anazâr's shaft. The power he felt, stretching that willing body, *taking it*, made Anazâr feel more animal—or god—than man, enough that he had to press his mouth to Felix's pulsing throat to smother the growls that rose unbidden from deep in his chest. As he sank down, Felix threw his head back hard a few times, thudding against the cloth, but Anazâr was too close to determine whether the look on his face was pleasure or pain or some chimeric state in between.

Seated at last. For a moment, each kept perfectly still, and Anazâr let himself savor the tight clench and the warmth of being buried so deeply and completely in another man in a way he'd never known before. Felix's hands swept down from Anazâr's hair until he'd wrapped both arms around the back of Anazâr's neck, pulling his face close enough that their cheeks brushed. Gods, the sounds they made together... the sawing rasp of Anazâr's evening stubble against Felix's smooth skin, the pounding of their hearts. "Such a marvelous prick," Felix whispered, his voice broken but still somehow teasing. "Ever since I saw it rise in service of my brother, I said I'd have it for my own. It's wasted on him. *You're* wasted on him."

Some furious, territorial emotion boiled in Anazâr. He shoved Felix harder against the sturdy bolt of cloth. "Don't speak of him here."

Felix rolled his hips, shifting the angle and pressure of Anazâr inside him. "Make me shut up, then."

Anazâr ground his heels into the floor and set himself to the task. No more limits, nothing held in reserve. Thrusting, attacking, achieving an effortless brutal perfection of form as he slammed Felix's smaller body up and down on his cock and fucked up into him at the same time. So hard it even hurt *him*, but Felix took his punishment nobly, clinging to Anazâr for his life and letting out harsh high whining breaths through clenched teeth.

To fuck his master's brother like a whore... Anazâr had fantasized about it before, but now that it was happening, he realized no whore could ever love this treatment the way Felix did. The pleasure itself was his only payment. Felix *abandoned* himself to it.

Anazâr let himself do the same.

The friction against the drum-tight skin of his cock was... it was ecstasy. Outrageous and fucking unbearable. He fell against Felix, crushed him, drove up into him, held him tight.

And safe.

The pulsing of his cock and balls echoed through every single muscle as he clasped Felix to him over and over again. The delight of spending into such a willing lover ever increasing until at last his arms grew weak, his whole body convulsed, and his softening cock slipped away. *To submission, to satisfaction. Mine to give, mine to take. Yes, oh yes.*

Felix touched feet to the floor at the exact moment Anazâr's legs gave out. Anazâr sank, panting, to his knees, and it was so much like kneeling at a shrine except suddenly it *meant* something—a warm glow of serene happiness. He nuzzled against Felix's hip in gratitude.

Felix cupped his cheek, tilting his chin and guiding his gaze upward again. His gray wolf's eyes were shadowed by heavy, satiated lids, his cheeks were flushed, his mouth as tender-looking as if he'd been struck. "Forget something?" he asked, and gestured to his untouched erection, heavy and sweetly tipped with a drop of precum.

*I'll suck him. I'll take that cock and make him forget his own name. Swallow his seed.*

"Mmm, never mind," Felix said flippantly. "You've done enough today, I think." In illustration, he reached behind himself, probing at what must have been his incredibly abused hole, and proved Anazâr's suspicions correct when that touch elicited a hissing wince.

But he didn't stop. He fingered himself, circling and rubbing. Anazâr caught his breath admiring Felix's shameless grace, especially when his slow motions caused a hypnotizing trail of cum to trickle down his inner thigh. Anazâr's cum. He couldn't help but groan.

That seemed to please Felix. "Oh yes," he said, pulling his questing hand free and spreading his fingers, examining the thin strands that webbed between them. "Shall I eat it for you? A Roman eating a slave's spunk like honey, that would certainly give my br—"

He cut himself off with a strangely catlike coughing sob and a jagged smile, wrapped his cum-drenched hand around his own shaft, and jerked it hard and fast and in that familiar way that marked him as unselfconsciously devoted to his pleasure. The thing Anazâr had most hated about the man became the thing he most loved, the act inspiring in him a mix of fragile tenderness and fervent lust.

Felix came without warning, his hips bucking wildly and his head thrown back, but oddly enough, he didn't make use of Anazâr's mouth or even obscenely paint his face, as Anazâr would have expected. He covered his cockhead with his palm, filling that instead, mingling their seed. A passing wonder—would he lick it neat and clean with his clever tongue, as catlike as before?

Yes, yes he did, and grinned at Anazâr all the while.

When he was done, he slumped down, seating himself on the hard floor with his legs sprawled and Anazâr still kneeling between them.

They rested.

After he'd caught his breath, Anazâr stiffly rose again, finding some scrap of cloth to clean them both, tending to the mess on Felix's inner thighs with a studiousness that would shame the best body slave. When he looked up from his work, Felix's eyes were closed, his head tilted back to rest against the bolt of fabric. Anazâr laid a gentle, chaste kiss on the point of his chin and then his mouth.

"Come lie with me," he invited softly. "My pallet isn't comfortable, but it's better than the floor of your brother's house, and this time I'll keep you warm."

"I'd like that."

The sound of Felix's voice pleased Anazâr immoderately. It was a musical voice, a skilled voice, a voice that contained a multitude of intonations, most of them deep and rolling rich.

As they eased onto the pallet, everything he'd studied of Felix, every detail of body language, assumed new meaning, new grace. The way Felix traced Anazâr's collarbone with the edge of his hand spoke of confidence in expressing affection. There was honesty in the wideness of his eyes, lazy happiness in the angle of his hips. Anazâr couldn't stop taking it all in, *reading* Felix, even though a part of his mind held back and warned *your judgment is not to be relied upon in this of all moments.*

He was beautiful. Handsome. All the names, all the appellations, all the words in all the tongues.

*But he is not your master.* The only thing that made this allowable under Roman custom was the interplay between power and duty. And since both were so confounding as concerned Felix, Anazâr had every reason not to let this happen again.

He tried to recover his senses. "Where will you go tonight, if the house of Marianus is no longer safe for you?"

The dazed satiety vanished from Felix's features. "I can't stay here? No, of course I can't. You're right." He shook his head, sitting up abruptly. "I have a friend, well, an acquaintance really. He drunkenly promised me use of his—well, I don't think he really promised it, not genuinely, but if I show up, he won't turn me away. And my brother doesn't know him. They never met, not even that time at the temple, the day the hailstones fell." The words kept tumbling and tumbling, all fragmented and insect-like flittings to and fro that spoke of overwhelming anxiety.

Anazâr couldn't align Felix's rambling paranoia with the man he called master. "How can you be sure? For brother to kill brother . . ."

"Don't you know how this city was founded?" Felix darted to where the white folds of his toga lay pooled across the floor. As he hauled it over his shoulders, it let out angry rustling noises like a living thing. "Romulus and Remus, brothers by birth and wolf-fostered, fell into a squabble over survey lines. Since we live in Rome, not Reme, you can guess which one ended up dead."

Felix twisted, ducked, and threw a fold in the air. Anazâr had always supposed a toga could only be donned with the aid of a very skilled slave, but Felix was doing the best he could, cursing as his furious jerking motions only entangled him more. Anazâr rose, overcome with the urge to help, even if it all seemed incomprehensible.

"No," said Felix, nearly in tears. "I— Just help me tie a rope somewhere, all right, and I'll lower myself out the window. I won't come again. I won't. Wait, I can't climb down a wall in a fucking *toga*, what was I thinking?" He twisted again and loosened a fold.

Anazâr grasped Felix by his shoulders and held him still with the lightest of touches. Felix froze, swaying neither away nor toward him. "You're not thinking at all. You've even forgotten your under-tunic. Wait. We'll make a plan. We'll talk."

"I'm a danger to—"

"Lie with me, just for a while, and we'll talk. Please."

Felix's twitching face stilled, but didn't calm. "I'm a fool. A fool and an ass. You risk your life for me and I can't even give you . . ." He sighed, spreading his hands.

Anazâr pulled him closer, using so little force against Felix's shoulders that the motion was more like a guidance, a teaching. "Come then, fool," he murmured.

Felix, shuffling, followed him back to the pallet.

The window's beam of sunlight had long gone, leaving them lying in deep shadow. Anazâr nestled down face to face with Felix and stroked his brow with the back of his hand until the deep creases there smoothed away. Felix settled a fold of the toga over both their legs, and Anazâr quietly marveled at his turn of fate to be wearing, in some fashion, such a noble thing.

*Talk*, Anazâr reminded himself.

"I believe you," said Anazâr. "Someone is trying to kill you. But why would it be your brother? What does he have to gain? He could cast you out if he wanted, couldn't he?"

"Perhaps it's over Aelia. No—" Felix shook his head, forestalling the question on Anazâr's lips "—it's nothing like that. Well, it was, I suppose, but it was never about love. She'd been married to him for three years with no issue. She came to me."

Anazâr felt as if the stone surface beneath the pallet had turned as treacherous and dizzying as the ocean, rocking him to and fro. He quelled the ridiculous urge to steady himself with an anchor, somehow. *These are complicated people indeed.*

"She's not barren. She had a son with her first husband, after all. But that one fell from favor with Augustus. Her father decreed a divorce, and her ex-husband kept the son, as usual. So she needed another. A child of my seed . . . well, everyone remarks on the brotherly resemblance. I was a safe choice."

"Did you do it out of regard for the family?"

"Gods, no. My hatred for Lucius is pure, refined, unambiguous. But I have no quarrel with Aelia. Fulfilling her request was quite pleasant, in fact. She has breasts like—well, pick a fruit, any fruit. Except for grapes and cherries, of course. Those are too small."

"Your language is improper, to say the least, but I've grown to expect that." Anazâr could barely see Felix's face in the darkness, but white teeth flashed, the signal of an impish grin.

"I'm awful. I know. But I've kept it a secret, I swear, until this very moment. And I can't fathom why Aelia wouldn't keep her peace also."

"Would he have to kill you all, if he knew?"

"It's complicated nowadays. The paterfamilias can't go about killing family members willy-nilly. At best, he'd be tied up in lawsuits for the rest of his cursed life. Perhaps she told him. Perhaps he found out through some other means, and she's unaware. I don't know. But I'll tell you what I do know. I'm sure he means me dead."

"I can— I'm not sure what I can do. Keep my eyes and ears open. Your brother... well, I suppose I'm practically furniture, now."

"Furniture, and a hole for him to—"

Anazâr cut him off, refusing to explain himself, explain the complicated bonds that tied him to Felix's brother. "Where does your hate come from? You've never said."

"I don't want your help, *Anazâr*. I don't want you in danger. I don't want you as anything except a lover."

How could he press matters after such an admission? He could barely comprehend such a thing. *Thank you*, he wanted to say. *Thank you, thank you, thank you.* Joy seized the words before his tongue could speak them. Joy even more fervent than he'd felt when Marianus had dangled a morsel of freedom in front of him.

And then the fear hit like a whiplash. Could he really trust that Felix's words were true? And even if they were, what power did those words have in the real world, on the streets of Rome, beyond this tenuous sanctuary where they embraced in shadow?

He stared through the darkness to see his fear mirrored in Felix's eyes, and awe there, too, because the fear was not sufficient to drive away the hope, and Felix understood. What this meant. What was between them.

Felix could see him as both slave *and* man, and with that sight, finally free him. Maybe not in the eyes of Roman law, but what did the law matter, really, compared to everything else that made him a slave?

 CHAPTER 9

The next morning, Anazâr was escorted through the city under the light guard of Quintus and the cousins whom Anazâr hadn't seen since the baths. A quiet indignity, quickly overshadowed by the fact that when they arrived at the domus, Quintus had him shackled, offering no explanation or apology. The weighted metal of the cuffs dragged on his wrists, heavier than their size would suggest. It pulled the rigidness out of his shoulders and neck and left him slumped and hunched like a beaten animal.

The night before seemed a distant dream, though one he was desperate to recall in every detail, haunted as he was by the fragile image of Felix's last strange, tentative smile as he slipped out the window on his makeshift rope.

Anazâr followed Quintus through the silent, strangely empty house, back to the garden where Marianus sat half-dressed on a stool at the head of a dainty man-made pond, attended by a young male body slave who massaged glistening oil into his chest and shoulders. Despite the tranquil setting and the slave's ministrations, he didn't look remotely relaxed.

And he didn't even deign to look up when Quintus cleared his throat to announce their arrival. Just said, "Have him kneel."

Quintus's foot jabbed at the back of Anazâr's knee, but Anazâr knelt of his own accord before he could be knocked into position. He lowered his head, awaiting his master's judgment.

"Leave us."

The moments it took the footsteps to recede stretched like whole days, but finally they were alone. Anazâr still didn't look up.

*He knows. He knows about Amanikhabale's lies. About Aelia's infidelity. He knows about Felix. About our—*

"My brother-in-law thinks I should have you all killed. Sent to the cross before anyone else in your pit of snakes can be convinced to rise against me." Marianus sighed. "But I'm too damn softhearted and I . . . I'm fond of you, Cyrenaicus. Against my better judgment, it seems. And no matter how often my advisors tell me I should just have you killed, I can't shake the feeling that sparing your life and trusting your loyalty will increase both our fortunes in the long run. That we rise or fall together, and as a freedman, you will honor me with the kind of loyalty a slave can never offer. But I need you to get to the bottom of this and prove yourself worthy of the gifts I so desperately want to give you. Do you understand?"

Cold fear settled into hot shame. How could he ever think this generous, overtaxed man a murderer? "Yes, Dominus," Anazâr murmured.

"Now is the time to prove it, then. Tell me what you've learned."

Anazâr's heart pounded, pulse throbbing in his forehead. That morning, before Quintus had come to collect him, he'd spoken with Amanikhabale. She'd given up on the "talking in her sleep" story for what she promised was the truth but was likely just a more convincing lie.

The truth—he was kneeling alone in the vastness of the desert, taunted by mirages. Would he really become complicit in her deception? Betray his master that way? No choice. If her lies came to light, he would say he'd relayed the information in good faith. *Lie again. Lies, lies, lies.* Marianus didn't deserve it, Anazâr *knew* he didn't, and yet he didn't see a way out. Or at least not one that didn't endanger Amanikhabale without just cause.

"The Aethiopian saw a man stumble into Enyo on her daily escorted walk. They didn't speak, but their collision seemed . . . rehearsed. She pressed Enyo later, received evasions, and relayed her suspicions to the Sarmatian. That could have been when the knife was passed to Enyo."

Marianus's voice revealed nothing when he spoke. "Is that so?"

"I believe she tells the truth, although I am not an expert in such matters." *I am not a torturer.* "But her actions aren't those of a liar."

"Maybe not." Marianus sat back, rolling his head on his neck, eyes closed. "Did you learn why the woman would make an attempt on my life, knowing hers would be forfeit?"

"She had a very young daughter sold to Ostia, surely into a whorehouse. Someone must have promised her daughter's freedom.

Or perhaps threatened her life. To investigate if her owner was involved, you could buy the girl through an intermediary, make her part of your household." He remembered himself. "I beg forgiveness, Dominus, if my advice is—"

"No. I hear you. Perhaps I'll follow that course."

Anazâr fervently hoped so. At least Enyo's daughter's fortune would be aided that way, even as hope for his own diminished. "I'll offer more advice, then. The Sarmatian—she proved her loyalty, and she's feared. If you set her as your bodyguard, it would give your enemy pause. And of course, I stand ready to fight in your defense, down to the last breath."

Marianus's gaze darkened, those luminous silver irises half-shaded by his eyelids. Finally, some expression—a glimpse of an inner garden behind high, austere walls—and what Anazâr saw there was *lust*. He found himself unable to hold his master's stare. He ducked his head.

"Come here," said Marianus.

Anazâr . . . didn't want to.

"Yes, Dominus."

He rose to his feet, even that motion hunched and shameful. Maybe it was an effect of the shackles, which Quintus had not removed.

*You lie to yourself. You know the true reason.*

*Felix.*

"Cyrenaicus, I would hope that you need no reminding about how it looks to me, on this of all days, to see you hesitate in carrying out an order." Still sitting on that stool like a king or an emperor, but now Marianus stroked an imposing erection, shiny with oil, the motion erratic. Impatient. Annoyed.

Anazâr forced himself to step forward, and then lurched, unsure of what Marianus was asking of him, specifically. Should he return to his knees again? He half lowered himself, but froze when Marianus shook his head.

"Give me your back," he directed, twirling a finger in illustration. "I'll have you sit on it this time."

Anazâr swallowed hard, but turned, praying his actions appeared quick and eager and obedient to Marianus, even though they were anything but. No preparation this time. No touching or promises or cooling ointment. Just Marianus's firm hand on Anazâr's hip, guiding him down. Marianus's cock, slick with the oil but *burning*, piercing and splitting his body.

The position was an unexpected mercy: all Marianus's scrutiny focused on the complacency of Anazâr's well-trained gladiator's body, the body with which he was forced to kill and die and starve and suffer and scrape. But none on his face, where he could escape behind his closed eyes.

And find refuge in the tiny, flickering memory of Felix's sex-pained smile.

A long stretch of solitude passed after Marianus's departure. Anazâr remained kneeling, trying to clear his mind.

A yellow-throated lark dipped down from the sky and rested on the empty stool, cocked its head, sang four brilliant notes, then hopped away into a corner of the garden obscured by flowering reeds. Heralded by the bird's passage, strange, unwelcome thoughts began to enter Anazâr's mind. He shook his head.

Footsteps approached.

"Hold out your hands," Alexandros said. Was that pity in the weathered old man's eyes? Anazâr realized he was shaking slightly as he raised his arms. It was the weight of the metal around his wrists, he told himself, and he hoped Alexandros assumed the same.

No clue as to whether he did, though. Alexandros remained as inscrutable as ever as he crouched in front of Anazâr and produced a key from the folds of his cloak.

"Is everything as it was?" asked Anazâr, and sighed when the key turned in its lock.

"More or less. Reward the Sarmatian according to your discretion, and inform her that a sum of a hundred denarii has been advanced toward her peculium."

Anazâr thought to ask for his own. But no, he should have discovered the plot much earlier. Marianus was fair. "What's her value?"

"Very high. Higher than mine, perhaps."

"Do you see the day when you'll reach your own value?" He wasn't sure why he dared to ask Alexandros such an intimate question, but something in the moment seemed to call for it. The tension of waiting for the bird to tire of the garden and rise back into the sky, perhaps.

Alexandros took the empty shackles and stood in stoic pose, unoffended. "I've paid for the freedom of my son. I had a daughter, now gone to the afterlife, and I would have paid for her as well. But as for myself? Freedom is wasted on the old. I'd rather die sleeping on fine linens than starving in the street."

"Understandable." Anazâr rubbed his wrists. The pressure marks were fading already.

"Come with me."

Alexandros led him not to the vestibule but to the women's craft room Anazâr and Felix had once spent the night in, when Felix had so strangely slept by the threshold. It was occupied now by Aelia, sitting by the spinning wheel, toying with a skein of crimson yarn.

The Aethiopian stood against the wall, faded into the mural as successfully as a born house slave.

"Cyrenaicus," Aelia greeted, smiling serenely at him. Two symmetric curls framed her heart-shaped face; otherwise, her hair was gathered and pinned into artful seafoam curves. As always, the perfect picture of a Roman wife, calm and collected in the face of chaos.

"Domina."

"You saved my husband's life," she said. "You and your Sarmatian. I would thank you."

Two voices spoke in his mind at once. *She is generous but there is only one thing a slave wants, only one thing and oh my desire I will die before I ever reach my freedom but she is generous, she is a noble lady and she is generous.*

"I'm honored, Domina. But no thanks are necessary. I merely fulfilled my duty. I would lay down my life for your husband."

"I wanted him to advance your peculium as well, you know. That won't happen. But I wonder if perhaps there are ways to reward you that are available to me as a wife."

*She fucked Felix. And now she wants the same from me, oh gods.*

He didn't speak. He wasn't sure he could.

She continued. "The life of a slave . . . it's an impermanent, lonely thing, is it not?"

Aelia blazed brightly in the center of his field of vision. Too brightly. Still, he managed to notice that over Aelia's shoulder, Amanikhabale's left eyelid twitched. He would have given anything to read her mind in that instant, to draw her counsel.

"I try to live day-to-day, Domina. If you do not attempt to sew anything lasting, the lack pains less."

"Your metaphor is confused, but I appreciate your effort to speak within my feminine domain. I'll speak soldier-plain in return. Perhaps I could have a message conveyed for you. A message of simple regard and concern to one you hold dear."

*Fortune, you are merciful.* An uncomplicated kindness was truly all she offered. And he knew just the way to avail himself of that kindness.

"There is one, Domina. His name is Gaius. He belongs, as I still do, to the lanista Iunius." Gaius, whom he hadn't dared to linger on in his thoughts because it was too heartbreaking, just as it was too heartbreaking to think of his other gladiator brothers he'd lost, or his friends, or his wife, or the child he'd never had the chance to give her.

There just wasn't room for sentimentality in a slave's life, but now, thanks to Aelia's generosity, he was able to indulge in it. Just this once. His heart swelled with a bittersweet sadness that wiped away everything else. *Please be alive.*

"Very well. I will send a house slave and ensure confidential delivery to this Gaius. Along with a few denarii of peculium."

"Thank you, Domina."

"As for this one—" Aelia gestured behind her with the tip of the skein "—she should have come forward earlier with her suspicions. The decision has been made to leave her discipline in your hands. If she's lashed, though, give her no more than five strokes. All these women are valuable to our house."

The thought of whipping one of the women, even one as untrustworthy as Amanikhabale, turned Anazâr's stomach. He could have Quintus do it, or one of the other women . . . no, that would be even worse. If the order came down, he'd harden himself to the task.

But not today. Not while there was any choice.

Amanikhabale spoke. "I regret my error, Domina, gladly receive correction, and thank the gods that the house of Marianus remains unscathed."

"Study your swordwork, Aethiopian, and win a higher place in our esteem. Cyrenaicus, you may go now."

Alexandros beckoned.

As they passed through the atrium on the way to the vestibule, they skirted a milling group of clients. Here to complete their morning ritual of deference and financial sustenance, no doubt. Waiting for Marianus to appear before them, as stately and resplendent as the sun.

Anazâr caught a glimpse of toga fold, and flinched.

When the red doors closed behind him, he felt as if some titan's fist, some brutal ethereal force squeezing his ribcage, loosened its grip, and he could breathe once again.

Returning to the warehouse and their daily practice brought him further relief, and Anazâr could tell the gladiatrices felt so, too. Well, maybe for them it had more to do with being unchained and allowed into the sunlight than about the rigors of the exercise or the renewal of purpose, but Anazâr enjoyed their apparent enthusiasm regardless.

But it wasn't just relief. Something had changed in the way they looked at him. The habitual shadows of distrust that came upon them—only rarely, of late, but still enough to be of notice—had apparently vanished the moment he'd walked in to unshackle them, Amanikhabale unharmed at his side.

None of them could stand to look at the Sarmatian. Torn between gratitude and fear, perhaps. He kept her aside from the others, away from the sparring.

"You're to be rewarded," he told her later, after the exercises had ended. Rufus and an older slave woman were dragging in the heavy clay vessels filled with mashed beans and barley, their usual dinner staple. "In my old ludus, that would mean provision of wine and a woman for a night. In your case, well . . ."

"What, I can't have a woman?" Rhakshna smiled at him, baring teeth, and Anazâr couldn't tell for the life of him whether she meant it. "That fucking Aethiopian has one, why can't I?"

It seemed a casual insult, at first, or maybe a strange diversion tactic, as patently false and absurd as pointing to the sky and shouting, "Look, there's Jupiter!" But then, when he thought about it, he did recall Cassia, freshly unshackled, immediately moving to clasp Amanikhabale on the arm, like long-parted sisters. Well, maybe not sisters. And Amanikhabale, that day after the baths, circuitously asking about taking a wife. Not sisters at all. He wondered if he and Gaius had ever played roles in a similar revelation.

He shrugged. "I'll have a woman hired. From *outside*. You can't expect the women you fight with to serve your desire at command."

"Ha! You and your incomprehensible morals. I was jesting anyway. I don't want a whore. I don't even want wine. That's how I was captured, you know. I was piss-drunk at an ambushed wedding party. Too drunk to get on my fucking horse." She curled her bruised mouth into an expression of naked self-disgust. "I haven't let a drop touch my lips since then. For reward, just bring me meat carved off something with four legs." She stabbed a finger at the clay vessels. "I'm sick to death of that fodder."

A fair request. He sympathized. It would not be difficult to arrange, either. He beckoned Rufus over.

Their communal meal proved a somber affair. If the Gaul women mourned Enyo, they did so very quietly.

Later, alone in his quarters, watching the shadows draw closer to the window, winning their battle with the fading sunlight, he finally let himself think of Felix.

Marianus, Aelia, Alexandros. No one in the domus had even mentioned Felix's name. Where had he gone? Had he reached his destination safely? Anazâr felt compelled to check behind the bolts of cloth, as if he could discover Felix hidden there, a crooked smile drawn across his face.

Gods, that smile. The absence of it left a hole in the world.

There was still some light. He sat up on his pallet and turned to a less pensive pursuit: the tracing of letters on a wax tablet. He would improve his rude hand.

He remained hunched over his tablet, working single-mindedly until darkness fell and he was forced to set the tablet aside. A few faint stars shone in the window's black rectangle.

And then a *rock* soared through it.

He jumped to his feet, heart pounding. Dropped back down to his knees, fumbled for the tinderbox, struck a spark and managed, after a time spent softly cursing, to coax a flame and transfer it to a candle.

He scanned the floor with the meager light until he found the rock—tied, of course, to a folded scrap of papyrus. Letters only, letters tiny as ants, and he had no hope of understanding them unaided.

Did Felix wait outside, cloaked in the deep darkness? Anazâr went to the window and held up his candle, once, twice, three times. Perhaps this would be the last time they would . . . well, if not *talk*, at least acknowledge each other's presence.

If Felix couldn't reconcile with his brother, there were other cities where a quick-witted man could make a good living. He imagined Felix in Alexandria, strolling along the marble colonnades of the Greek Quarter while arguing some obscure poetic convention with a handsome man or a pretty, disreputable lady. He could be happy, if only he would just *leave*.

And he would leave. Of course he would.

Anazâr pinched out the candle flame and joined Felix in darkness, wherever he was, wherever he was going.

# CHAPTER 10

In the morning, he summoned Amanikhabale. No choice, really. He'd thought maybe if he looked at the letter by light of day ... but no, it was as indecipherable as before. He just had to hope Felix had the sense to realize a translator would be necessary and thus not write anything incriminating.

"Another lesson?" she asked as they walked into his quarters.

"No. *This*. And I'll trust you to decipher it truly. After what happened yesterday, our fates are closely tied."

"So true." She took the scrap, unrolled it, and peered at the little crawling lines. "I suppose I should thank you for not whipping me, as well. That would have put me off my dinner, and it's difficult enough to choke down as it is. I wouldn't mind some meat either."

"The additives are for strong bones; gladiators get used to the taste. The message, now." Looking down at her hands, he noticed, not for the first time, that several of her fingernails were misshapen, discolored, ridged where they should be smooth. Given that their fates were—as he'd remarked—so entangled, perhaps he should finally ask why. "What happened to your fingers?"

"Torture. Following a setback in Nicaea, I ended up slave to a slippery Bithynian. He wasn't a bad master, but he *was* outrageously dishonest, and made a fantastic living out of it. Our household moved to Rome, where I once lived in a domus much like that of Marianus. Then my master was accused of forgery. All his slaves were tortured for evidence, according to Roman law. Most of us left behind a few fingernails and teeth, but lived through it."

She'd rather talk of anything but the message. Even torture. "You've read it already."

"Yes. It's just . . ." She wouldn't meet his eyes. "The first part is a reply to Cassia. The family wouldn't let Felix see her daughter. They said they've told her Cassia is dead. That it's more merciful that way. I did not expect to be charged with telling . . . with carrying . . ."

"Tell her. Honesty leaves a cleaner wound. I'll let you be the one, since you and she . . ."

Amanikhabale narrowed her eyes. "Since we *what*."

Surely she didn't think their relationship a secret? He shrugged. "I was led to believe you were intimate. Well, whether or not you are doesn't matter to me. As long as it doesn't affect your training, you can do as you please. I was much the same, before."

"Maybe we are, maybe we aren't. But I'd prefer if you didn't mention it again. To anyone." She gave a huffy sigh and combed her fingers through her braids, deep in thought a moment before her expression relaxed into its usual polite opacity. "There's a note here for you, as well. From the master's brother. It begins, 'To my big man.'" A grin, showing teeth.

"Me? I'm only middling size, for a gladiator." Half a joke, and he soon had half a smile on his lips, too. Of course she knew Anazâr was the target.

"To my... middling-size-for-a-gladiator man. I have not been able to get you or your huge—" Now she snorted into her hand, gripping the letter so tightly it crumpled in her fingers.

So Felix *had* realized Anazâr would need someone to read for him, except the knowledge had done the exact opposite of what Anazâr had hoped: instead of encouraging him to use discretion, it had spurred him into his usual sadistic compulsion toward scandal. But then, perhaps a bawdy letter would at least keep the true depth of their feelings for one another—all the tenderness they'd shared—a secret.

Which didn't stop him from being embarrassed, of course, but he didn't let it show. "It's his way. Continue."

"—sword," she finished, "by which I mean cock, out of my fevered imagination. Meet me at the Archius insula by the Tiber at the edge of Tanner's Row, second floor, eastern room, in the first watch of the night. Have the Aethiopian, who's no doubt reading this to you, write you a master's pass. Aside: I know a rich poet who's looking to buy a scribe, and I've already put in a word for her. Let the dice be cast, and eat this dangerous message, perhaps with some fish sauce. No, burn it. *Vale*, my Hephaistion!"

Anazâr looked away, toward the window where dust motes danced in the clarified morning sunlight. He could let down a rope ladder, he supposed. "You know the danger. If I'm caught, lashing will be the least of it."

She sighed. "I'll write the note. I've no choice but to play this game, even though the masters have weighted the dice. Including your Felix. Your *Alexander*. Don't lose your head with him. Not the big one, at least."

*I trust him more than—*

No. He would hear Felix out and discover anything that would provide advantage. Quiet, subtle advantage. Neither loyalty nor love would save Anazâr, not standing where he was under the specter of the cross.

*You should have left.*

The day that followed was their rest day, and their bath day, but the escorts never came. Instead, the gladiatrices made do with buckets of sun-warmed water, squatting and glowering as they splashed their filth-striped skin. Anazâr could see the fragile remains of their morale withering in the sun right before his eyes, and there hadn't been much left of it after Enyo's death. At least there was more than a month until the games, because if they fought tomorrow, they'd be slaughtered.

However, if their spirits remained this low, a month to prepare wouldn't be enough. A *hundred years* wouldn't be enough.

So he drew on the floor again—not letters this time but lines for a game of tables—gathered wood chips for counters, and ordered them to play. At least they could practice their Latin this way, and pass the time with less danger of falling into fearful imaginings.

Cassia shivered and wept every once in a while, letting her long dark hair fall over her cheeks to hide the tears. Amanikhabale brought her water and stayed silent.

Their grim tournament lasted until nightfall.

Quintus accompanied the delivery of their usual dinner. "And next week?" asked Anazâr.

"I don't have the slightest idea. I just lock up, guard the door, and do as I'm told. Ask Marianus tomorrow about the bath trips." Quintus had a curt manner about him tonight—not hostile, no, but any prior amiability had entirely vanished. Distancing himself from potential trouble, Anazâr had to assume.

When true night fell, Anazâr unshackled Amanikhabale. The women sleeping next to her awoke, stared, and closed their eyes again, pretending not to see. He took her hand and guided her up the ramp to his quarters, wondering what story to tell them all the next day.

He recalled his earlier platitude about the value of honesty with some ruefulness as he set to work on the rope ladder and a disguise. Amanikhabale lit a few more candles and began her own work.

A gibbous moon shone over Rome's dark streets. He'd weave his way down to the Tiber by its light.

"It's not a good disguise," said Amanikhabale, adjusting the drape of the hood that hung low and shadowed over the incriminating half of Anazâr's brow. "I can't promise that you won't be stopped, or that no one will recognize you." *Or that the forged letter will prove convincing, or that either of us will survive this.* "But maybe . . ." She waved a hand through the air in a vaguely circular motion.

"Maybe you'll change your sword for a quill, and I'll fly back to Libya on a winged stallion."

She anchored the end of the rope to a sturdy post. "Association with Felix brings out an odd sense of humor in you, I believe."

"It certainly brings out *something* absurd in me. Let's hope Fortune will be amused, and spare us."

A whisper of a farewell followed after him as he climbed out of the window and down. Down into the black chasm of the unlit streets that stretched out before him as bewilderingly complex and dangerous as the Minotaur's labyrinth.

The main streets flickered with the irregular light of lamps, which were tied to the carts prohibited from the city during the day. They rolled on their delivery rounds, wheels creaking and bullocks lowing, guarded by watchful men with clubs and whips.

Anazâr kept to darker, smaller, parallel streets, straining his vision for any clue to the shape of the world, trailing his hand along walls when the lack of lines grew too dizzying.

The street leveled. He continued until the sound of rushing and a noisome stench indicated he'd neared the bank of the Tiber.

Two cloaked men drifted toward him from an alley mouth, one bearing a lamp on a staff. Thieves, by their ragged tunics. Anazâr looked directly into the black oval pools of their hooded faces, and bared his teeth.

"Closer," he said to them. "Closer, please." He reached, quite conspicuously, into his own tunic. Nothing belted there but a practice sword, but it was likely all he'd need for men such as these.

Just the threat of retaliation was enough. They drew back. He walked on.

He wondered if the people he passed by could sense he was a slave, the same way he'd sensed the cloaked men were thieves. Even with the tattoo covered, did he hold himself a certain way? Walk too quickly? Seem too determined to hide his face from passersby?

The signs on the walls begged light to read, which he couldn't do anyway. He stopped by a group of carters unloading amphorae and asked directions to the Archius insula while keeping his voice casual, his posture guarded yet unaggressive.

"Down that way. Tavern with a red awning, Tiber-side." The man barely glanced at him.

Down a few building lengths, the sound of music—drum and ill-played flute—drew him toward the tavern and its awning, stained and bruise-purple in the gloom. He wondered if the fabric had come from a Marianus warehouse. From a bolt much like the one where he and Felix had— No. He needed his wits about him. With the patrons of the tavern, who could still report him, but with Felix, too. This suspicion, this paranoia, this uncertainty . . . it all had to end. He had to decide his loyalty *tonight*.

A man leaned against the wall to the left of the tavern. Anazâr knew Felix at once by his eyes, even in the guttering torchlight. He'd foregone his striped toga for one that didn't mark his class. They were both, in their way, in disguise.

"Felix." Just that. He had no idea what else to say. Felix was the one with all the words.

"Anazâr." He flinched. Hearing it aloud still felt strange and strangely threatening, even though the circumstances of their meeting actually made the Roman name *more* dangerous to speak aloud. "I'm glad you're here. Come with me, inside. There's someone..."

Felix drew closer, placed his hand around Anazâr's wrist, pulled lightly. Anazâr remained statue-still, muscles locked into place. "You *involved* me. And others, as well." *I want to go with you. What I truly need is another matter.* "In your stupid family quarrel. A woman is *dead*. The Aethiopian and I risk our lives even now."

No response. No look of apology. Only an ineffectual, impatient twist. "I know, but—"

"No. You *don't* know, Felix. You don't know anything. That's the fucking issue here." Anazâr fought back the urge to lash out and strike. Hit him. Fuck him. *Like an animal.* Felix unmanned him. "Spoiled impetuous little fucking child of a man."

Felix's breath came faster, faster still, and then stopped entirely as he held tight and turned his face away. But his hand never left Anazâr's wrist. A drunken chorus roared into life inside the tavern, spilling out into the street, over the shrill flute. Felix finally breathed again, and spoke. "I'd hoped that our bond would include some measure of trust, but at least it includes honesty. I thank you for that. Speak from your heart and know that I hear you."

"The *point*, Felix."

"For once, I'm not acting the fool. I have information for you. I'll tell you everything. And then, once you've heard, you can decide... you can decide whether I'm worth risking your life for." His expression at that was so unguarded, so heartbroken, that Anazâr almost relented on his strict stance.

Almost. He shook off Felix's hand. "I'll follow and hear you out. Don't touch me again."

The shape of Felix's eyes changed then, although the darkness masked just how. Whether they'd widened or narrowed, the effect was disconcerting, nearing predatory.

*I take too much liberty with my own body for one like Felix, born a master. Damn him to Hades, anyway.*

"This way," said Felix, his expressive voice stripped of all emotion and character. He turned, leading Anazâr up a narrow, rickety staircase that scaled one side of the building and disappeared into darkness. What awaited him there?

*Someone to kill me.*

A wooden door. A low-ceilinged, lamplit room lined with pallets. Bags and pots and cloaks hung from pegs on the soot-streaked walls. This must be how the poor lived, hunching in little cells of the massive insula like larvae in the beehive. He'd never imagined such a life before. All he knew in Rome was abject slavery or obscene wealth, and nothing in between.

Curled on a pallet at the edge of the room was a young girl, no older than ten, with matted blonde hair. An elderly woman sat watch at her side, withered mouth set in a tight seam as she worked a needle and thread in some menial task.

The woman nodded at Felix and returned to her work. The girl drew her shoulders tighter at their entrance, but even at this angle, there was a familiar cast to her face.

"You said I didn't understand," said Felix. "Well, neither do you. Not as much as *her*."

The girl on the pallet.

"Enyo's daughter." It came out reverent and hushed.

"Her name is Litis. I found the whorehouse she'd been sold to. There was no way I could have afforded her, so I pulled rank and invented some insanely complicated court case and swore in my name of Lucius Marianus that I'd send her full price tomorrow, plus bonus."

"So this will come to light soon."

"Yes," Felix said. "But she's safer here."

"Why?" The thought of such a young child set to whoring made him want to vomit, but still, any life was better than none. He had to believe that. He moved a step closer to her, opened his mouth to speak some word of comfort—

Felix barred him, laying a hand against Anazâr's shoulder. And then he snatched it away a heartbeat later. "Sorry. But Dara—that's Dara watching her—says to leave her space. She's frightened and mourning her mother. I had to tell her."

"You—"

"Listen to me, Anazâr. A woman had Litis brought from the whorehouse into a richly curtained litter. This noblewoman spoke of her mother, made sympathetic promises, extracted certain information. It was *Aelia*. And Aelia told Litis she would be sent for again, soon, so that Litis could join her mother, as soon as a task was done."

"The lady lied to me," said Litis, in a high, dull voice. "Maybe you're lying too. I want—" her Latin tumbled into Gallic and then trailed off into weak, hoarse crying.

Anazâr knew the rest, anyway. *I want my mother.*

Felix, standing next to his brother at the match . . . he'd been the target all along.

Dara glowered briefly at them both before turning to hush Litis and pet her flaxen hair. "There, Master Felix," she said in a high, artificial sing-song. "Your man's seen her with his own eyes. So now I'd say it's time for you both to leave." Sweet as it was for Litis's benefit, her tone brooked no argument.

Whatever Felix's motivation, he'd found the girl an able, fierce protector. And still, it would never, *ever* be enough to replace what she'd lost.

What Aelia had *taken* from her.

"Your mother was brave, and loved you very much," said Anazâr, and turned to leave before the crying cut into him any more deeply. He'd made it as far as the foot of the stairs before he rounded on Felix, gripping the smaller man's shoulders fiercely. "Why!" he demanded. "Tell me why you showed me this. Why you *did* this. Don't stall, don't fucking mince words, just tell me plain."

"I . . ."

"Now, Felix!" Anazâr shoved him against the wall and pinned him.

"I did it because it wasn't right to leave her, not after her mother died as a result of my feud. And I showed you because . . . I showed you because . . ."

*Because you want my loyalty and this is the easiest way to procure it.*

"At first, I thought it would prove a comfort for you. To know the affairs of your charge were properly taken care of. I wanted to help you. But I didn't expect Aelia to be involved. I'm still reeling from that myself. I thought the girl was confused, perhaps, but now that I've gotten her free of that pit, she tells the story even clearer. I had to draw you here and show you the proof. It was Aelia. I've never had anyone I slept with try to kill me. Their husbands, wives, certainly, though I shouldn't jest at this of all times, it's a habit I—"

Anazâr covered his mouth, the gesture less forceful than before, but charged with no less meaning. "You can stop talking now."

Felix. What a fool. Using all those words to say such a simple thing. *You showed me this because you . . . Because you . . .* But no, he couldn't say it, not even in his own mind, not even on Felix's behalf.

Anazâr collected his thoughts enough to speak. "You could leave this city. Leave all this danger and intrigue behind you. You're not one of those Romans who would rather commit suicide than face exile; you love what's foreign." He let his hand drop from Felix's mouth, memorizing the intimate sensation of warm breath against his palm. "Why?"

Felix smiled and answered with no hesitation at all. "'Love knows not the meaning of the question *why*? Why do some gash their arms with sacred knives, and cut their limbs to the sound of the Phrygian pipe? To each at birth nature allotted a vice; to me Fortune allotted the doom that I should ever be in love.'"

"Your own lines?"

"No, Sextus Propertius. I 'love what's foreign,' was it? Well, I love *you*. And I'd tell you, and better yet *show* you, so many more reasons 'why.' Come with me tonight to my hiding place. It's rather luxurious. We can still get you back safe and sound long before cockcrow, if— I shouldn't beg."

"I won't make you," said Anazâr, and kissed him. His whole body seemed to melt, tension and fear running from him like sweat, and it felt as purifying and clean and right.

One kiss turned into another, and another again, hungry starving relief and thankfulness, and best of all he knew Felix felt it too, that perfect clarity and harmony between them that reached beyond everything, *everything*, even the words of the poets. Beyond joy and sadness, or perhaps encompassing both, allowing Anazâr to consider the most brutal of facts in the light of compassion. Because now that he knew Felix was not the blood traitor, he had to persuade Felix to leave. And wherever Felix fled, Anazâr could never know and never follow. Not with the possibility of torture—of revealing Felix's whereabouts—a constant threat.

Tonight, at least, he'd follow where Felix led. That was the small mercy, that this night would be theirs. The greater mercy would come when Felix left.

And lived.

# CHAPTER 11

The majordomo, a lanky Aethiopian with a short beard the color of wet steel, kept the door halfway shut. "You're really pushing it, Felix."

"Come now, he's a bodyguard. How can I walk the streets at night without a bodyguard, with liver-stabbing thieves thick as flies? If your master were here—"

"But he's not, you infernal house-pest."

"He'll be gone before first light, I swear. And I'll make it up to you. I've got an advance on a Greek translation coming in tomorrow."

Anazâr hung back, made himself as small as he could, and trusted to the hood of his cloak.

Felix eventually wrangled their entry into the domus. The disdainful majordomo led them through a vast atrium, then through a study lined from floor to ceiling with scroll shelves. Then further inward, skirting the edge of a dramatic peristyle garden where statues of nymphs rose from star-shaped fishponds clustered around a weeping poplar strung with glass windchimes. It was a tableau that could have sprung full-formed from the strange mind of a god. *No*, Anazâr reminded himself: wealth and craft alone, quite human, could make such spaces.

The majordomo left them at last in a private room.

There was no doubt as to who was staying here at present. The floor of the room was strewn with clothing and half-rolled scrolls and even a few gnawed pits of fruit. Anazâr surveyed the unmade bed with some concern, suddenly unsure of what he was getting himself into. As soon as they were alone, though, Felix wrapped both arms around his waist, tugged him close as a lover—gods, they *were* lovers, only an idiot could deny it—and reached up for the edge of his makeshift hood.

"Let's get rid of this," Felix said quietly, and Anazâr forced himself not to flinch away. It was ridiculous, his protectiveness of his face. It wasn't as if Felix hadn't seen the tattoo before.

"I can't help but see them through your eyes. The letters."

Felix's expression was soft as he unwound the hood, letting the fabric slump lightly to the floor. "They tried to disfigure you," he said, matter-of-fact. "But it didn't work. You're still devastatingly handsome, you know. I'd even wager the tattoo adds to your appeal. Marks you as a man with a dangerous past." He brushed knuckles across Anazâr's forehead.

"You're pushing." Anazâr smiled and put on a playful approximation of the majordomo's disdain.

"To be totally honest, they give me a moment's pause. Before I see past them, that is. Do you want me to show you?" Felix didn't wait for an answer before he darted away to rummage in an open chest. He tossed toiletry items to the tiles in blithe disregard for their fragility and no doubt outrageous cost. "Ha! He keeps his actress mistress in this room when he's in town. Makeup, makeup . . . here you are." He waved toward a low seat. "Sit, sit. I can't do this if you're standing, you great brute."

Anazâr did as commanded, not out of fear but from a languid, dreamlike compulsion. To paint his face, like a cinaedus, an actor, a whore . . . it was a proposition so alien from everything he knew to be true of himself that he could find no offense in it, no reason to refuse.

Felix stood facing him. Tipped Anazâr's chin up. Looked down on him with a gaze both distracted and piercing, so utterly focused on his task that he seemed a different man.

"If one of my actor friends were here, he'd do this properly," said Felix, and trailed a finger sticky with some ointment across Anazâr's brow. A moment of panicked vulnerability hit Anazâr, but he forced himself still until it passed. A fighting reflex, that was all, because his throat was bared to another man. Anazâr realized he was panting when Felix cupped his jaw and pressed a gentle kiss on one side of his mouth. "Easy, now. Just a little more, and then I'll bring the mirror."

He closed his eyes and let himself believe that Felix's sweeping touches were a sort of massage.

"Well, it's not quite your shade." Perhaps Felix meant to sound put out or critical of his handiwork, but there was an edge of quiet pride in his tone. "Although I suppose it would blend better if you'd let me do up your entire face."

"No." Anazâr opened his eyes. Reached out and caught Felix's hand in his own. "Show me, now."

He just wanted to get this over with.

And he was afraid of what he'd see. It wasn't anything Felix had done, either. Since the tattoo, he'd never *stopped* fearing his own face. He was about to beg Felix to stop this whole mad farce when the mirror loomed in his field of vision as suddenly as a striking snake.

He looked into his own dark eyes and saw a man of the Free People who'd gone far from his land.

*This is who I am.*

"You see?" Felix said. Anazâr barely heard him, too transfixed by his shifting reflection in the mercury glass. "What they did to you, it's only skin deep. Easy enough to disguise. Even easier still to ignore, if only . . ." He paused, and fear seized Anazâr again. Fear of what truths Felix would reveal. His barbed tongue could be turned to truly incisive ends, if the mood hit.

The moment stretched out between them, and over the mirror's rim, Felix caught Anazâr's gaze in his own, piercing and as silver as the mirror. "If only you realize its worthlessness for *yourself*. That this doesn't mean anything. Well, to status-obsessed fools like my brother, maybe, but not to anyone who matters. It's all as artificial as if we were actors in a play. You can't let your role consume you."

Anazâr's roles as husband and provider, as warrior, as slave, as freedman-hopeful . . . They'd all eaten him alive. Saturn devouring his son.

All the while Felix shrugged off the weight of his own role. Anazâr had hated him so passionately for that. The hero who slipped his mask and laughed at the audience, as if *they* were the fools for not knowing they were watching a comedy.

Not even a real man. Shameless. Cinaedus.

He lived for no one's expectation of him but his own.

"I don't know if I could do this, in daylight," said Anazâr. "It would be too visible."

"Well, at least I've got you thinking of a future now. And will you believe that I find you handsome? Tell me yes, or I'll be forced to get out the rouge and kohl."

Anazâr wrinkled his nose. "Fine, fine. I believe you. Don't turn me into *you*."

"Excuse me! I do *not* wear kohl. These eyelashes are the ones I was born with, I'll have you know." Which was probably true, since his brother was blessed with the same. Although they seemed less apparent on his more severe, masculine countenance.

*No. This night is not for Lucius Marianus to intrude upon.*

"But you do wear rouge?" Anazâr teased. And then was overtaken by a sudden thoughtfulness and curiosity. "How do you do that? Or rather, allow yourself to do that? Go between woman and man the way you do. Don't you ever feel . . ." He struggled for words. *Duty to perform? Guilt? Fear?*

"If I wanted to be a woman, I'd take a scissor to my balls and run off with the Galli. All respect to the Great Mother, but that's not my path. I don't have an answer. I do what brings me pleasure. Manhood isn't such a strict thing as you believe." Felix laid the mirror aside, conjuring away the glass-imprisoned stranger who wore Anazâr's skin.

"You let that man fuck you that day. In the baths. People talk."

"Let them!" And then he laughed, as if being the object of gossip gave him great joy. Well, it probably did. "The shame in some quarters is well justified by the pleasure. Or even makes the pleasure sweeter."

Anazâr didn't understand this talk of pleasure. It had never been thus for him, not the way taking a man or using his mouth or even rubbing against another could be. At best, it lacked pain. Well, perhaps for all his talk of being a man, Felix was built differently.

"You don't believe me," Felix accused, no hurt in it. He paced away, reclined on the edge of the bed, and kicked off his sandals.

"I don't think you a liar. But you have a choice. Not to subject yourself to such use. You were born a master of men, and yet you perform duties meant for your lessers." *Like me.*

"Do my brother and his ilk have you so bewitched you actually conflate pleasure and duty? You'd be the ideal slave, if it weren't for fucking me." He slid out of his toga as he spoke, the working of his lean arm muscles distinctively masculine. The gladiatrices had arms as strong by now, but there was an indefinable difference to Felix's proportions—indefinable and maddeningly alluring. The toga slipped to the floor, and inspiration dawned on Felix's features. "Do you trust me?"

"Must I?" Anazâr smiled to show he was jesting. He went to Felix and touched his arm, running his fingers up delicious smooth skin, up under the fine linen of Felix's tunic where it covered his shoulders. Their position was reversed now, Anazâr looking down into Felix's upturned face, drinking in the pools of his eyes—long lashes, indeed—and the curve of lips half-parted in candid desire. Anazâr's cock crooked helplessly upward in response.

"I'd . . . I'd like to show you the difference between the two. If you'll let me," said Felix. Anazâr's expression must have turned to apprehension, because Felix was quick to add, "It won't be like with my brother. If you don't like it, we'll stop at once and I'll ride you like a pony."

"Can't we skip directly to the pony bit?" Before Felix could answer, Anazâr regained his courage. "No, wait, I'm curious. I'll submit to you. You can take me as I did you."

"I'm not that athletic. Gods, but that was a lovely fuck. I have something else in mind. Quite as interesting, if perhaps less physically taxing. There's a chest under the bed."

"More makeup?" Anazâr's forehead had started to itch. He was anxious to fuck and sweat the paint off.

"Oh, no. Get undressed and I'll show you."

Soon they were naked and sliding over smooth sheets, touching each other. That delightful shivering sense of rightness returned as he welcomed Felix's warmth into his arms.

He let Felix take the lead, not knowing what else to do, feeling a little lost. His ever-mounting arousal drove him to crave direction, orders, but Felix never gave any.

Instead, he traced Anazâr's body. Ran fingers down the lines of one collarbone, then the other. Leaned in, pressing his thigh against Anazâr's erect flesh, then slid away, offering no release, leaving him in ardent torment. Kissed and tongued Anazâr's heaving throat.

"Do you want me to touch you in a like manner?" asked Anazâr in a voice as steady as he could make it. "So light?"

Felix's eyes had subtly changed. They were darker, warmer—less of that cold gray. They absorbed Anazâr's gaze, holding pure promise with no hint of threat. "Only if you want. I know this leisure, this freedom, must feel rare. Or you can lie there and attend on *feeling*. No duties, no expectations, I swear."

"I'll try that." He put his hands behind his head and settled down into the bed's luxurious softness. And speaking of luxury . . . Felix's hands parted his thighs, petting the sensitive skin. And then Felix pressed a wet, breathy kiss into the juncture of groin and thigh, setting Anazâr's skin alight with pleasure.

There were grapevines painted across the vaulted ceiling, barely visible by the warm candlelight, and Anazâr imagined that they sheltered the bed, concealing their lovemaking from the punishment of an angry god. *We're safe here. I can allow him anything.*

A melodious clink sounded, almost like the ringing of a bell.

Felix rose, grinning. "Look at these beauties. Should we try one?"

He made an expansive merchant's gesture, encouraging Anazâr to take in the sight: an assortment of false phalli of different sizes and shapes and materials, even one attached to some kind of complex harness.

Felix's grin widened considerably. "Like that one, do you? Me too. It's a rare fine woman who'll use that on me. Not much use for us though. And maybe not this one, either." He tossed an imposingly thick cock sewn from stuffed leather to the floor. "Don't remember where that one's been. This one, on the other hand, looks fucking *pristine*." He held up a white marble dildo shot with glittering mineral veins that mimicked the other kind of vein. "But still too big."

*Thank the gods he thinks so too.* Anazâr gulped, his remote, peaceful sense of acceptance quickly fading. "Why would you use . . ."

"Oh, I still want to end with my hot prick inside you, but we have plenty of time to play first. The problem with fucking a man is the angle. You can't quite see the *stretch*, and even if you can, you're too distracted chasing your own pleasure to really appreciate it. This way, I get to enjoy every moment, and you get the benefit of my absolute attention. Trust me."

"I'll try."

"This one?"

Translucent, blue-tinted glass, shaped by some masterfully perverted craft into a cylinder curved like a bow. One end was smoothly rounded, the other flared into a wider, bulbous base. And it wasn't much longer than Felix's palm. Certainly the least imposing of the collection, but for Anazâr it was rather like trying to choose the safest beast out of a pride of lions.

Not so for Felix, apparently. Thus decided, he rolled back from the edge of the bed and pressed his body to Anazâr's again, sweeping his hand over Anazâr's stomach in soothing circles. But despite the gentling touch, and even though Felix's lips had returned to his throat again, wet and fluttering and insistent, Anazâr could focus on nothing but the cool glass resting against his thigh. Waiting.

Felix huffed out a sigh. "Is it that much of a distraction for you? Look, it's not an instrument of torture. What if I let you hold it? Will you be able to focus on the present, then?"

It hadn't looked large in Felix's hand, but it weighed heavy in Anazâr's palm, and caught the candlelight like a jewel. Which he supposed it was, really, being not much less precious than the sapphire it resembled. And it was warm, having already leeched heat from Felix's body.

"Just think how beautiful it'll look inside you." Felix had propped himself up on one elbow and was now observing Anazâr intently, all the while smiling with the refined hunger of a connoisseur of flesh. His fingernails scratched leisurely down Anazâr's chest and up again, seeking out one nipple to pinch and roll between finger and thumb.

Seeking, finding—evoking surprising twinges of pleasure. Anazâr had to remind himself to breathe again.

"I'm not sure I want to," he still said, although perhaps not so passionately this time.

A light touch, trailing down Anazâr's arm until Felix had wrapped his hand around Anazâr's and both of them held the dildo together. Together, they raised it to Felix's chin. Felix's mouth. Holding Anazâr's gaze, Felix swirled a clever tongue across the glass. Sucked the narrow tip into his mouth, his soft lips molding around its hard surface, *yielding* so perfectly Anazâr could barely breathe.

"You've decided me, you satyr," said Anazâr. His rock-hard prick had softened during the moment of uncertainty, but that was no longer a concern; the blood and heat and desire came rushing back.

"Oh, have I?" Even if Anazâr hadn't already fully changed his mind, seeing the unmasked pleasure on Felix's face now would have convinced him. "Well, then. I'll have to take advantage of this change of heart before you lose your nerve. Or maybe I'll make you beg for it?"

He slunk backward off the bed, down to his knees on the floor, where he insinuated himself between Anazâr's spread legs. He leaned in, nosing at Anazâr's balls. Inhaled. Exhaled. Just the damp air of his breath made Anazâr's sac tighten and alter in texture—he'd never been so achingly aware of how his body changed under desire's rule. And then the wet flat of Felix's tongue lapped the sensitive hardness behind his groin.

Anazâr bucked and groaned, Felix's strong-boned hands wrapping around his thighs to hold him firmly—nearly painfully—in place. Beads of saliva trailed down the crevice between his legs, down to tickle at his hole, which twitched in a response he could neither anticipate nor control. *Control.* He didn't need it anymore. Had lost it. Lost that need. All he needed was to fuck and feel something inside him.

What followed was an absolutely debauched assault, tongue and lips and so much wet spit, and all the while Felix moaned and hummed and murmured wonderful nonsense.

*Let me please you. Let me take care of you. Let me show you every last thing you've missed or denied yourself.*

He was helpless to his own pleasure.

The glass was still clenched in his hand, slick with sweat now.

*The glass was still clenched in his hand.*

He looked down at it, vision hazy, trying to understand it, remember why it was there, what it *meant*, and it was as impossible and magical as letters, but with none of their attendant shame or frustration.

Only one thing to do. He lifted it, glinting, to his mouth and sucked it in greedily, imagining it was Felix's cock, except it was so ruthlessly hard, so impenetrably beautiful. He sucked and sucked and sucked, fucking his own mouth with it, relishing the feel of it dragging across his teeth and crushing his tongue.

"Magnificent."

Felix's ministrations had stopped. He was draped over Anazâr's thigh, watching him in quiet awe.

*I please him.* And the knowledge of that sank into him sweet and rich, touching a strange depth that being a satisfactory soldier or slave had never breached. "Do it," gasped Anazâr. He reached down, holding out the glass in offering. Felix kissed each of his fingers in turn as he opened Anazâr's grip around the toy's curved shaft and took it into his own hands.

*Oh.* There'd been oil in the cache, too—Felix glazed his fingers, rubbed them over the glass and, deft as a conjurer, nudged it into Anazâr. Just the tip, shallow and painless, and then it was out again, so quickly that Anazâr felt the lack more than the presence. Anazâr's hips rose and fell back in swift response, shifting the weight of his erection against his drum-taut stomach. He gasped again. "Yes, more. I'm ready. Yes."

Felix laughed against his inner thigh, pressing kisses there as he toyed the tip back and forth across Anazâr's entrance, never pushing it inside.

Anazâr, torn between irritation, admiration, and raw teeth-clenching need, begged at last. "Please."

Felix slid it into him so smoothly, opened him so effortlessly, that Anazâr shuddered with relief. That rigid thickness inside him, inexorable and alien, became *part* of him. Flesh of his flesh.

Usually the invasion of penetration made his cock shrivel with the effort and the pain, but now it only further inflamed his straining shaft. *Throbbing.* It was throbbing like a bruise. *Touch me. Touch me please.* He couldn't say anything, too focused on the way his channel shifted around the solid intrusion, clenching and yielding in a rhythm he could only vaguely control. He lifted his hips in entreaty—

—his nerves ran with liquid fire, the pressure, *fucking gods the pressure*—"No!"—*it's too much, it's too good*—"No, don't stop. Yes. Felix. I'll spend . . ."

The pressure shifted, the pleasure faded. "Shhh, it's all right." Felix smoothed his hand up and down Anazâr's twitching thigh. It gave

Anazâr something to focus on, something to ground him amid the wash of intense sensations. "Would you like to come with it inside you? It's an exquisite experience, I must say. I could suck you. That big thick cock . . ." He licked his lips, enthralled. "You'll tighten around the glass. I can't promise that will be entirely pleasant. *I* like it, but then again, my tastes can be—"

"Suck me."

"*Mmm.* As you command."

*As you command.* It echoed in Anazâr's head, crowding out every other thought. Lucius Marianus Felix, master of men, saying to him, *As you command.* The most dizzying height he'd ever reached. That was, until Felix's hot, slippery mouth enveloped the head of his cock and then swallowed the whole length down in one practiced dip of his head.

Anazâr seized up, his hole clenching hard around the glass. It *shook*. Or perhaps his body shook around it. He didn't know anymore. Cause and effect, flesh and glass, all merged, all distinctions erased by the surge of molten ecstasy. His prick was a heated bar of iron plunged into water at the forge. He howled because it hurt, too, howled even as he spilled his seed down Felix's tight throat and was swallowed, swallowed, swallowed.

Once Felix drew him to glorious satisfaction—Felix's mouth was fucking irresistible, no matter what use he put it to—Anazâr let his mind drift as his body relaxed, muscle by aching muscle. He'd been renewed.

Cleaned. Emptied . . .

No, that was Felix delicately sliding the glass out. Though his vision wavered in the bliss that followed release, he watched. It was amazing. He'd never forget this as long as he lived.

Which would probably not be long, but what did that matter? Death made the act of love all the more urgent. He didn't know many poems, but the ones he did, well, they all agreed.

"I'd like to fuck you," said Felix. "Once you're ready again."

"Yes," he murmured. Not just a polite acquiescence, not this time. He wanted it too. Wanted to feel Felix inside him, stretching him until they fit together perfectly.

"You don't have to move much. Shift on to your side. There, that's it."

Felix gently guided him, then lay cradling him from behind. Unlike any master, Felix was in no rush to take his pleasure, not forcing his way into Anazâr, not just yet. Instead he rocked his hips, his body swaying against Anazâr's, and they could have been dancing except for his hard smooth cock gliding up and down, parting the slick cleft of Anazâr's ass. Held close like this, it was so . . . so . . . He didn't have any name for it, any bar to measure it by.

Gentle, undemanding kisses marked the dreamlike passage of time. Anazâr lay on his left side; Felix kissed his right shoulder, his cheek, the curve of his throat, the side of his lips. Resting together in this position, Anazâr couldn't really see him, couldn't look into his perturbing eyes, but he could feel Felix watching *him*. And that was good, too.

Felix stroked his thigh. Crooned in his ear. Guided Anazâr's right knee forward, straightened the left, pushed inside him, first with fingers, then with his prick.

Anazâr moaned, because Felix's heat was better than the dildo, better than any of the cocks he'd taken before. Slow and courteous, but *insistent*, and gods, Anazâr was more than happy to accept it.

"I love the voice you speak with when—when you abandon yourself," said Felix. "Let it speak. Speak through you. I've been so eager for this. You're perfect. A strong man, a *good* man . . . oh gods, I don't want to lose you—"

Something trembled and broke in Felix's voice, and Anazâr was unable to reply, unable to give voice to the filthy words he'd been in the midst of summoning up for Felix's pleasure.

"Felix," he said instead. "Felix, Felix." Over and over again, a chanting invocation, urging his lover onward, willing him the strength to continue. Clutched tight in Felix's embrace, Anazâr's body heaved and his eyes burned.

He didn't cry.

He *wouldn't* cry.

Although he thought, judging by the slight erraticness in his thrusts, that Felix might be.

Well, let him. Let at least one of them be free enough to mourn this for the tragedy it was.

After what seemed like half a night of fitful half-sleep, Anazâr rolled Felix onto his back and took him. They petted and kissed their way through the slow, deep strokes of his cock, neither making much sound except for the occasional soft whine from Felix when Anazâr plunged into him just right.

When they'd both spent for the second time that night, Anazâr lay back among wrecked sheets with Felix cradled to his chest, pretending not to notice the sound of ragged breathing and the small tremor in his lover's shoulders.

He thought, when Felix finally stilled, that he'd fallen asleep. But then Felix's tentative voice broke the silence of the night. "There was another before you. Another slave I proclaimed to love—who I *did* love."

"Your own?" Anazâr's sexual desire was quite sated, but the prospect of comprehending the truth of Felix, why he hated and loved—well, that woke another kind of fierce desire.

"She belonged to my father's household." *A rare fine woman*, Anazâr's memory supplied. "Her work was to serve food and entertain, at times, with music. And she was . . . she was perfect. Beautiful. Poised. Talented. Funny. That was the thing I loved most, her sense of humor. She'd even laugh at my wretched attempts at poetry, and fix my stumbling lines."

"She could read."

"Very well. And when I got to know her more, and she learned to trust me, she brought out a wicked edge to her wit that stung and aroused as much as being spanked. Of course, nobody pays any mind when a young Roman boy dallies with a slave or two for practice, but she wasn't just a *hole* to me, and . . . well. My father forbade me to spend so much time in her company. It was unseemly. But he wasn't cruel. He'd manumit her in his will, he promised, and I could set her up as a freedwoman and keep her as a mistress, quietly, until I married a woman of good family. He was ailing, by then. I couldn't imagine any life without Alexandra, but I promised him my most dignified conduct."

*Alexandra.* Her name. "The daughter of Alexandros, then?"

"They had something as close to family as slaves are allowed, his position and education being so high. Alexandra and I passed love notes in code and played at Pyramus and Thisbe, though we believed our affair would have a happier end. It did not. When my father died and my brother assumed his position as paterfamilias, Lucius had all our father's small mercies burned to ashes with his body. When I didn't immediately fall into line, he ... he ..."

Alexandros's words filled the space Felix's couldn't. *I had a daughter, now gone to the afterlife.* Horrible recognition, so cold it turned his skin to ice. "By his own hand, he took—?"

"Oh gods, no. He's too practical. We're a mercantile family with plebeian origins, after all. He simply sold her. I scrambled to find her price—there's a kind of refined whoring available to boys of the right set—but after a few weeks under a new, harsh master she decided not to wait. They saw her going down to the Tiber."

"They captured her? Tortured her for running away?" The tattoo on Anazâr's forehead seemed to tingle in sympathy.

Felix shook his head. He let out a broken laugh through gritted teeth, took a long pause to gather breath, and then spoke again, in a much smaller voice. "No, she outwitted the whole world in the end. Drowned herself before they could seize her. Her owner threw out her body like garbage."

"And it's all your brother's fault." No wonder so much venom seethed between them.

"No. It's mine. My brother's a horrid man, but he only does what's correct by Roman custom. That's all he *ever* does, and I hate him for it. But blaming him for her death would be like blaming the fucking tide for washing in. It's my fault. I knew my attentions endangered her, but I plowed forward anyway. Make no mistake, I hate my brother, but I hate myself even more."

There was no arguing with that. Anazâr was a slave and a gladiator, and he carried a slave's and a gladiator's weight of responsibility.

Felix had been born a master, and now he carried a master's weight. Fortune's wheel—it was what it was.

After a time, Felix sniffed. "What, no platitudes?"

"Would they change anything?" He remembered the quiet acceptance among his gladiator brothers when they'd had to kill one of their own, or watch one of their own be killed. Each carried his guilt willingly, as much a part of him as the hands that performed the act.

"Damn you," said Felix, but already his voice sounded brighter, the knife's edge of memory dulled again by the distance of time. "After her death, I swore not to endanger another in the same way. I kept my affairs brief, and never within my brother's house. And then you arrived."

"I charmed your heart out of its slumber?" Anazâr joked. "So you humiliated me in an attempt to push me away?" He may have forgiven Felix many things, but he acutely remembered the sting of that first meeting, when Felix had taunted him for performing a slave's duty to his master. For the first time, he felt he was owed an explanation.

"No, actually. That initial cruelty was completely genuine. After the dismissal of your predecessor, I'd been lobbying my brother to send the gladiatrices to some different fate, anything but the cruelties of the arena. I tried to tell him that what had happened under the first trainer was an ill omen. That he'd be a fool to ignore it. And then you arrived and all I could see was history repeating itself. More suffering, more death, punctuated by an eventual slaughter to the roar of the crowd." He drummed his fingers almost painfully on Anazâr's chest in his distraction. "There were three more among their number before you came. Did you know that?"

"No, I did not." They'd been so ill and demoralized when he'd first taken them under his care. Disease? Hunger? Suicide? Exposure? They all seemed equally likely.

"I suppose they keep their tragedies as close to their hearts as you do yours. Well, you must suspect. After all, my brother wasn't secretive about why he requested your service, in particular." *No taste for women. The last trainer couldn't keep his prick out of the stock.* "A few of them ended up pregnant. Two Gauls, and one particularly lovely

Parthian who had the kind of singing voice that could make a drought end. When the trainer realized what he'd done, he panicked and went to a cut-price pharmacopola. The abortifacient he gave them was probably no better than rat poison. Those poor women didn't even stand a chance."

No reply for that, either. Anazâr closed his eyes against visions of blood and wailing. He couldn't help but picture his wife. To die so far from home, so far from family and clan and even your gods. And all for one man's cowardice and cruelty.

A few moments were enough to comprehend why they hadn't told him. Such sufferings among slaves were only shared when relevant to future survival. He himself would never think to tell the women—or anyone, really—of the atrocities he'd witnessed after Actium.

"I knew what they said about you, but I didn't believe it," said Felix. "I assumed you were of the same ilk as him. To be honest, I . . . I thought you something of an insatiable satyr, that day I first saw you. I couldn't imagine that a man who so visibly enjoyed slobbering all over his master's cock wouldn't also take his pleasure from his fellow slaves. But other than my brother, you were as remote and unmovable as stone, weren't you?"

*Except for you*, Anazâr thought. *You drove me half to madness wanting you, and I couldn't fight it.*

"The gladiatrices didn't like you, but when I pressed, they said you hadn't raped any of them, although they'd seen the Aethiopian go willingly with you to your quarters. Even that day at the baths, I couldn't tempt you."

"Although you gave it your best," Anazâr put in, feeling a heat and a stirring at the memory. Felix's true face, so young and open.

"And then the more I tried to humiliate and push you away, the more it became a test, to see if you could stand me, all of me, the very worst parts of me, and still open your heart to me. And I wanted—no, *needed*—you to pass that test."

"Don't expect me to thank you. I'm not accustomed to that kind of bloodless examination."

"You misunderstand. It wasn't you I was testing, not really. It was myself. If you couldn't love me, then maybe . . ."

"Then maybe you'd have to give up on all your trickster foolishness? Treat the world with the seriousness it demands, even though it hurts you to do so?" Anazâr's heart pounded in his temples, and he fought off the urge to grab Felix by the shoulders, although whether to shake him or pin him to the bed and fuck him, Anazâr wasn't sure. But he resisted, because he wasn't an animal. Not like the previous trainer. *Nothing* like him. He settled for grabbing Felix by the chin, jerking it upward so he could see Felix's eyes in the dim light. "And since I do . . . love you? Now you give yourself permission to resume your casual spite toward everyone and everything around you? Just so long as you've earned my love, you think you can refuse the responsibilities you were born to?"

"I'm *ready*, Anazâr. During this exile, I've been searching, thinking, trying to work through it all. I could seek an audience with Marcellus, the old enemy of Senator Aelius. He wasn't involved in any of this plotting, but he *could* be, if I lay it all out for him."

"You have no idea. You're grasping at straws." Anazâr sighed, kissed Felix on the forehead and softened his grip. "This is beyond intervention. Exile yourself from the city. Wait for me to gain my freedom, and I'll join you, if I live." He traced Felix's jawline with the edge of his forefinger, hoping to engrave the outline in his memory.

"You won't live! You won't live and you know it. Why else would you fail to name a place for us to meet? You expect me to leave and wait out my life, and it doesn't matter what city I choose, because I'll be able to take comfort in picturing you alive and searching for me. A fool's dream."

"You're torturing meaning into my words. But fine." The name of a city came to him, and it was a perfect name and perfect city: within the Empire, but beyond the reach of Marianus. And it was *large*. Even if they wrenched the name from Anazâr, it would likely do them no good. "Alexandria, then. Meet me there. I'm sure once I arrive, even if it takes me ten years, tales of your debauchery will quickly lead me to where you make your bed."

Felix laughed, and the sound came rich and deep from his chest—a true laugh hiding hardly any pain. "And you call *me* an impractical fool! I suppose I'll have to switch roles and be the level-headed one, if we're ever to meet again in this world. The details come to me even now. I'll wait every Kalends and Ides, midday, by some landmark. What do you say?"

"The southwest corner of the Library at the Serapeum. I remember pleasant shade there, and vendors selling cool date wine." Even if they tortured him, even if they knew Felix's exact location down to the building, Anazâr had to believe they wouldn't send a killer so far. And the promise, hopefully, would prevent Felix from ever returning.

"The Library, then. Seal it with a kiss."

They did.

 CHAPTER 12

Anazâr guarded against sleep, his naked body tangled warm and lazy with Felix's. He waited until his lover seemed at peace: breathing slowly, eyelids heavy and still. *Rest. Be safe. Please be safe.*

He slid from the bed as silently as he could. He cleaned himself with a cloth dipped in the crystal bowl of rosewater that stood by the bed—gods, the absurd luxury of this night—and made sure no traces of makeup remained. Tunic, sandals, belt, mock sword, and most important of all, the hood—

A rustle of sheets behind him.

He stepped for the door with excruciating care, willing the leather of his sandals to *glide* across the tiles. He'd rather fall on his sword than trade parting words with Felix. Words that Anazâr knew would be their last.

Let Felix have his illusions, his phantom in Alexandria. He would take Anazâr's best self there with him. And in some measure, Anazâr would at last be free.

He wanted to thank Felix for that. So he did it silently, in his soul. *You've done more for me than you'll ever understand.*

His hand touched the curtain at the door, and he had to turn back one more time, even though he knew the story of the downfall of Orpheus.

Pale gray eyes, burning inhumanly bright, a mark of the life force that animated Felix and charged his every gesture with improbable grace—those eyes were half-opened, and his face drawn tight with a grief that failed to mar his beauty.

Felix didn't speak a word.

And Anazâr passed through the curtain, bearing the guilt for that wound of silence.

He was strong enough to bear it. He had to believe it.

A slave woman bearing a lamp stood waiting at the portico. She gestured toward the exit. Her face was delicate and blank, revealing not the slightest trace of emotion.

*Let her composure be a model for your own*, he told himself with every step.

She fell in beside him. Sent, no doubt, to make sure he left properly without stealing the silver. She was Aethiopian, like the majordomo, like Amanikhabale. Willowy, though—nowhere near Amanikhabale's unusual size.

Amanikhabale's height, her thick shoulders, had doomed her to the gladiatrices' troupe, had barred her from an easier life as a scribe or tutor slave. Fortune's wheel again. He remembered how large she had loomed behind Aelia as they'd spoken together that night at the warehouse . . .

"Is there a problem?" asked the slim woman holding open the door. "You can take the lamp with you, if you need light."

"Yes, to the lamp. But there's no problem, none at all. I'm leaving now."

His heart froze as he stepped over the threshold into the night. He'd left Felix, and what was he returning to?

Amanikhabale, holding watch for him. Amanikhabale, who hadn't had any good explanation for why she'd known Enyo's plans. Amanikhabale, the only one of the gladiatrices who'd spoken to Aelia in private.

He wanted to *run*. Run, while merciful darkness still cloaked the city. *Find a horse. No, the roads are watched too closely. The fields. The Tiber. Every man and woman will turn against me when they see my face.* The folded paper square of his forged pass burned in his palm. Had she purposefully given him a poor forgery? Was he carrying in his hand a set trap about to spring?

A jagged cobblestone tripped his sandal. He staggered, clung to the wall for balance, and tried to *think*. Gods, he wanted to turn back. He was so utterly alone, and there was his lover waiting for him. They could go together. To Alexandria. Disappear in the night. Surely Felix could talk his way out of any run-in with someone trying to stop them.

Except that wasn't who Anazâr was. He may have been a runaway once, but never with the lives of so many—women who had trusted him against all odds—in the balance.

There had to be another way. A way to face this problem head-on. Prove to his gladiatrices and Felix that their trust and faith in him were not misplaced.

He reasoned that Amanikhabale must be playing for higher stakes than his death, or Felix's death. After all, she'd known where Felix was waiting, and not passed it on, or else they'd both be dead by now. She had no reason to wish Anazâr gone from the table—none that he knew of, at least. So he'd return to the warehouse. She'd let down the ladder for him, and they'd come to a new, more honest arrangement.

Damn her. *She'd* killed Enyo, not the Sarmatian.

But as he pushed away from the wall and set out again, he couldn't hold on to the hatred. The fear and the loneliness left no room for it, perhaps.

"I had no choice," said Amanikhabale. "I'd be dead if I'd refused to arrange the attempt on Felix's life. Enyo or anyone else, just so long as I found *someone* with something to lose . . . or gain, I suppose. Someone they could manipulate and dispose of. And I'm sure they plan on killing me as well, no matter what honeyed promises that wolf-bitch pours in my ear. Dead sooner or dead later, and I keep picking later; it's really very simple. Aren't you the same? Isn't that why you're here?"

He wasn't going to answer that.

"Why are you still alive?" he demanded. "Marianus and his wife know it was you who warned Rhakshna and foiled their plans." *I delivered the news to Marianus myself. That day in the garden, not knowing you'd been as much a part of orchestrating the attempt on Felix's life as you were in foiling it.* He tossed down the last coil of rope and stalked toward her. She flinched. He moved inside her reach; she didn't step back.

"I told them a good enough story," she said, the words rushing against each other but still held perfectly clear. "That Enyo, at the last, didn't believe her daughter would be saved, and was planning on killing Lucius instead. So I had to intervene to ensure failure. It was an easy enough lie to tell, since they'd purposefully arranged the attempt in such a way as to disguise which brother it was meant for. And then I immediately offered them another plot. Oh, you'll love this one. They certainly did. It's absolutely mad." She raised up her hands, palms to the sky, and grimaced like a tragic actor. "We shall use his love to destroy him!"

Anazâr glared until she left off. "Stop praising your own brilliance and tell me, then."

She responded in the same crisp, manic rush. "I told them Felix is desperately in love with Cassia. I showed them a love letter to prove it, written in blood, in his own hand. Remove her from the troupe, I said. Sell her for cheap to some freedman. Send me along, so I can write on her behalf—her family wasn't rich enough to have their women taught. She'll use my knowledge of letters to send Felix a message asking him to meet her. He'll come, and there'll be someone waiting to kill him. Probably you. And then, after the deed's done, they place all the blame for his death on *her* shoulders. She killed her husband, after all, so why not her lover? The plan appeals to their purse strings, as well—no expensive slaves to be wastefully put to death."

"By the fucking cross! How can you— What— But how— Repeat that!"

She did. It *was* mad. Her thin fabric of forgery and lies would tear apart under any real examination.

But for now, it held.

"So where's our advantage?" asked Anazâr. "It buys us only a limited amount of time. Cassia is removed from the arena, and so are you, only to be placed in even greater danger. I'm working under the assumption her life actually holds value for you. Perhaps I'm wrong."

"Love is a throat left unprotected. A knife turned against the one who wields it. I can't let them know my true—" she paused there, her glib stream of words faltering into a telling stutter "—my true loyalties. I have to believe that Cassia has a greater chance, this way, than in the arena. She cannot fight. She'll choke up. You saw her at the practice. What she did to her husband, she'll never repeat."

"So I've been enlisted to kill Felix. We're all at this location. And then what?"

"We cut down any bastard who gets in our way, and make a run for it. Your Felix, too."

"Appealingly direct. Do you think your fighting skills are up to the task? Cassia's? Escaping Rome is . . ." He gestured vaguely to his tattoo, then swept his hand away. Strange, how the gesture felt just slightly less shameful after last night.

"I'll have forged manumission papers by then. And I'm no Amazon, but if *you* knock a man down, I can make damn sure he never gets up again. I'll be most highly motivated, after all."

Her words broke some barrier inside him that he'd never even known was there. He froze with his mouth half-open, not trusting the words just yet.

Freedom—not just yearning for it, but chasing it, seizing it, taking it like a lover.

Felix wouldn't be there, though. Felix would be gone by then. But perhaps they could carry out this plan in his absence. And then . . .

*Alexandria.*

"By my tally, there's thirty-six days until the games," she said. "If they go for this plan, they'll want to avoid a scandal so close to Marianus's first exhibition, lest it interfere with his reputation. I imagine it will be afterward. But nothing is sure. Pray to your gods. I'll be doing the same." She smiled crookedly and shrugged. "You never know if it helps, but it can't hurt."

"My goddess feels very far away," he murmured. "But perhaps . . ."

"You should put me back in my shackles."

They stared eye to eye in complicated silence, each the mirror of the other's faint, fierce hope of freedom.

A miserable morning spent scraping at the old dinner dishes with no explanation for the lack of their usual breakfast and no promise of a later meal. The whole time, Anazâr wondered if Marianus had left them all to waste away and die, as if he could not even spare them the regard to have them properly crucified for their treachery.

That afternoon, though, Quintus did come. The welcome sight of slaves bearing food and fresh water weighed against the concern that Quintus was also accompanied by leather-armored guards who carried their clubs like retired legionaries.

"We'll have a couple of these fellows keeping an eye on the warehouse," said Quintus. "The baths are back, but they'll be split up and taken in shifts. Marianus still wants a daily report from you, but you'll be delivering it to me instead."

Equal parts relief and fear swelled in Anazâr's chest. He'd been dreading seeing Marianus again, dreading another incident like the one in the garden. But the decision also spoke to a fundamental and troubling change in what was between them.

Mutual respect for each other had given way to fear and distrust.

"Some of the swords are too splintered. They need replacing." Anazâr knew they could make do with the battered ones, but this could serve as a test of Marianus's willingness to further invest in their prospects. *I'm finally beginning to understand him.*

*Understand him, in order to outthink him.*

"I'll pass that on."

The baths were a businesslike affair. Anazâr paid for scraping and simple barbering and kept his eyes to himself. When he did look to other men, he tried to see them as they really were, and not solely imagine his low station and attendant disfigurement through their eyes.

"Hey, you. Got some news for me this time, I'll wager." That Greek gossip, from the first day. At least the familiar face was *him*, rather than the alternative. No sign of Felix's mule driver, or the man himself. Anazâr wasn't sure if he'd be able to maintain this constant mask of indifference if it came to that. "What in Aphrodite's magic twat is going on at the domus Marianus?"

Here to finally finish the exchange they'd started, Anazâr supposed, since last time he'd had nothing to offer other than Felix's sexual indiscretions. He should feel more torn about his willingness to pay his debt.

*Slaves will gossip.* And Anazâr was a slave. One tired of playing at loyalty, no less. If Marianus was so intent on treating him like a snake . . . well then.

"Don't say this came from me." *What lies should I spread? No, worse to tell a half-truth.* "But I've heard that Aelia has been having an affair—with Marianus's full knowledge. They attempted to blackmail her patrician lover so he now seeks permanent removal of Marianus through hired killers. I heard it from a friend of a slave of her friend."

The Greek gaped, moved to slap his palm against the wall... and comically arrested himself at first contact with the scalding stone of the calidarium. He blew on his fingers and made a hissing noise. "Fuck me with a galley oar! It's almost too sordid for belief, but oh yes, I can very well believe it. Whose side is Felix on? Or is he taking it up the ass from Aelia's lover as well?" He looked *terribly* pleased at that prospect.

Anazâr shook his head with feigned regret. "I heard he's decided to flee the city until this all calms down."

"You've heard wrong, then. He's kicking around all over Rome. Marcellus, Pomponius, the widow Metella, they've all hosted him. Never stays in one place long, looks mopey, keeps scribbling notes and tearing them up, and papyrus isn't cheap these days, I should know—"

"Cyrenaicus!"

The name, unwelcome to his ears, had been called by one of the guards. Time for Anazâr to leave.

Damn Felix for a stubborn fool.

## The month of Junius.

The new swords did come.

Starting that day, he worked with each woman on her greatest weakness.

For most of the Gaul women, that weakness was *pain*. Not the kind of pain that wracked the body—he had the vague intuition that women were, indeed, accustomed to such suffering, perhaps more so than men—but the short sharp pain that signaled your opponent had forced past the barrier of your skin. Had inflicted their rough will upon you, and would do so again.

*Submit. Surrender. Panic.*

They had to learn to ignore that signal.

He ordered them through interminable drills, sometimes striking them himself against padded heads or arms with a wooden staff, sometimes directing them to inflict pain upon each other. Blood rarely ran after these sessions, but bruises flowered plentifully.

With Rhakshna, he worked on flourishing skills and safe submissions.

"A gladiator is a valuable investment," he explained. "At the highest level, they fight only a few times a year. If you bring a man down and kill him without express direction, especially a man who's worth much more than you, the punishment could be severe."

"But he may not have the same concern for me, if I'm worth less, eh? Fucking Romans. We don't bother with this financial shit where I'm from. We just kill them all and take their things." She grinned, baring teeth, and resumed her stance without being ordered.

The Germans fought without flinching, but they were only now beginning to understand his directions for attack and defense techniques. Newly entered into common language, he began to differentiate them and understand their close bond. Their old master had named them in an arbitrary fashion after different German tribes, but they were all Cimbrians, all kinswomen. Cheruscia was a daughter of a headman and was adored by the others, either for heritage or for some other reason.

Batavia, the most expressive, came to him one day. "Man," she said, and pantomimed, thrusting her jaw out to give her face a masculine cast. "Man of us fight. Attack, defend. Fight?"

He wondered at first if she was making a statement about the nature of their tribe. But after more sessions of awkward pantomine, he began to comprehend the true, pragmatic intent.

Would they ever have to face a man of their tribe in the arena? A husband, perhaps, or a brother? The thought sickened him.

He had no answer.

Anazâr hadn't seen the domus Marianus—or the man himself—for half a month. Not since he'd been taken in chains to the garden.

So when Quintus arrived that evening and announced Anazâr would be making his report there, it took him completely off guard.

Quintus must have been feeling generous, because he caught Anazâr's perplexed expression and grunted in acknowledgment of it. "The aedile in charge of next month's games will be there. He wants to take a look. I've been told to bring along the Aethiopian and the Roman, too."

Amanikhabale's plan had been set into motion.

On the street, Cassia let her hair fall down to cover the brand on her cheek, keeping her head down as well. The hubbub of the darkening streets appeared to confuse her, and she staggered on several occasions. Every gain she'd made in the last month steadily disappeared as they were escorted into the shaming light of the master's world.

Amanikhabale kept her eyes straight ahead, betraying no sympathy, no love.

No rebellion.

*No rebellion.*

Anazâr crafted his gaze with all the care of an architect. Neck bent forward, chin tilted slightly downward, eyelids half-lowered. *I fear you are displeased with me*, the look said, or at least he hoped it did.

He had never taken on such a pose with Marianus, not even on the day he'd been brought before him in chains. He'd always held himself with slightly more pride than that, as much pride as a slave could have, and it took this day and this pose to realize that.

The aedile was a cricket of a man whose senatorial toga, with its broad purple stripe, gave him the only weight of presence he possessed. In contrast, Marianus, seated next to the aedile in the study, blazed all too vividly, centering the world around himself.

*He'll see through me. Pry away this mask. Rip me open.*

"Ask Cyrenaicus," said Marianus. His tone toward the aedile was neither rude nor particularly deferential.

The aedile coughed. "I originally had some concern the gladiatrices would give a weak show. But after the unfortunate incident at the demonstration, I now find myself faced with quite the opposite concern. Women thirsting after blood instead of bleeding it—heh, heh." By the time Anazâr realized it might be wise to force himself to chuckle, the aedile had thankfully moved on. "Well, bitches such as those might not be suitable for the entertainment I had in mind. Dwarves, gladiator. Dwarves! I shall have women fighting dwarves. And dwarves, of course, are dreadfully expensive."

*Far more expensive than women*, he didn't say.

Marianus nodded at Cyrenaicus, giving him permission to speak.

"I've trained the women in proper submission technique, Dominus. I believe they would give a good show. For best results, I would suggest a rehearsal. Perhaps even a choreography." *Cautious good news*, he told himself. A comic performance, held after the serious bloodshed, and no one need die. No casualties except their dignity. "As for the question of weapon—gilt swords or dulled steel—I believe that would depend on armor."

"I suppose nudity would be a bit over the line, a bit *excessive*," grumbled the aedile, putting a particularly displeased emphasis on the last word. It made Anazâr's skin crawl. Since Felix's revelations, Anazâr had become more protective of the gladiatrices.

"I can offer a substantial discount," said Marianus. "But given the farcical nature of the event, I'd rather not have my name bruited about as lanista."

"Yes, yes, quite understandable. But the praetor and I will be sure to mark this as a favor. We have a terrifically violent main spectacle planned: a threeway battle between Greeks, Parthians . . . and lions! Don't speak a word of this, by the way, or I'll have you crucified, gladiator. Because it's a surprise. But we were sorely lacking in the comic slot, and your women will be *perfect*."

Anazâr gave a curt nod.

*Crucified*. Damn the man for saying it with so little care. No, not just saying it. *Meaning* it as a threat with so little care. If the power of a master was a mantle to be worn about the shoulders as a constant weight, then the aedile's must be made from the diaphanous silk of distant Serica.

He prayed this trial would be over soon. That he'd be sent away from these watchful eyes, away to deliver his merciful news and breathe the anxiety out of his body. If any gods heard, however, they didn't act on his behalf. Instead, he remained in excruciatingly statuesque stillness, eyes lowered, as Marianus and his guest conversed further, paying Anazâr as much mind as the mosaic on the wall.

When at last the aedile took his leave, Marianus's gaze fell on Anazâr seemingly for the first time. Anazâr knew that look, knew that tense, anticipatory posture.

"Cyrenaicus." Marianus's voice was as gritty as sand.

Nothing had changed.

Everything had changed.

Anazâr's heart pounded against a ribcage that felt crushed smaller than it should be. The whole world seemed to tilt to one side.

"Dominus," he heard himself saying. A strange wind picked up the word, carrying it away, taking some part of Anazâr with it.

"You're dismissed," said Marianus.

Cassia sat on the low stone step of the atrium's colonnade, hugging her knees, a far-off look in her eyes. He wondered if she'd seen a songbird.

He stood beside her. They waited in silence.

"I feel like I'm my own ghost, haunting myself," she said at last.

She had a raw, strong-boned beauty, but suffered the blows of life as badly as glass. He'd seen so many people break over the years. *Not again, oh gods.*

"Wait," he told her. "There are other lives depending on yours now. You have to wait."

Amanikhabale walked into the atrium. She sat next to Cassia, their shoulders not quite touching. Their hands, however, did. The knuckles of Amanikhabale's hand were clenched shockingly pale against brown skin.

"I'm to go back to the warehouse," she said. "But they'll be moving you on. Everything will be well."

"Yes," whispered Cassia. "Everything will be well."

He moved a few columns away to give them a moment of peace.

A tarpaulin covered with a layer of sand served as practice ground for their falls.

The dull thud of Penthesilea's head raised a puff of fine sand and a corresponding growl from Anazâr. "Your chin was not tucked in!" he shouted. "Do it again. *Correctly.*"

She staggered to her feet and dutifully plodded back to the corner where the sequence—jumping, tripping, falling, rolling—was marked to begin. Hunching down, she rolled her neck in a circle, and narrowed her eyes. Evidencing such laudable determination, he judged that she'd master the sequence by the end of the day.

The mood among the women had improved with the news that their first combat would be a relatively bloodless affair. Yes, Cassia's disappearance had at first unnerved them, but like all slaves, the gladiatrices were accustomed to sudden departures and the lack of farewells.

Anazâr told them she must have been requested for other duties. They didn't speak of her anymore.

"You'll have to lash me, you balls-cut maggot, before I set myself to this *choreography*." Rhakshna had reacted to the news in a quite opposite manner to the rest of the women. As a consequence, she remained shackled. Shackled and glaring. "You tell those Roman cunts I'm a fucking warrior! A warrior! If they set me to fight a fucking dwarf with a toy sword, I'll stab the little bastard in the eye and use his warm body as a springboard to launch into the fucking stands! I want Roman blood!"

"I'll just leave you shackled until the games, then, and tell Marianus his fierce Sarmatian has a powerful terror of dwarves and isn't fit to fight."

Her stream of shrieking curses echoed off the walls, the vicious barrage causing Penthesilea to stumble.

It was an easy way out, leaving her shackled like this, hoping she'd come to her senses and perform dutifully on the day. And although she was a competent fighter, it was stupid of him to cut her practice short. But ever since the news of the dwarf fight, his mind had moved onto seemingly more important battles, ones with actual life-or-death stakes. For him. For Felix. For Amanikhabale and Cassia. What if they weren't strong enough to fight their way out of the city?

All pressing concerns that weighed heavily on his mind, far heavier than Rhakshna's unpredictable mood. But one weighed even heavier still: what if Marianus had another killer in mind for Felix? The Aethiopian's plan was mad, but held the glimmer of a hope of success. Though if Anazâr wasn't there to intervene...

He couldn't afford to dwell on it. He left Rhakshna behind, and in the line of those awaiting their turn, he tapped Amanikhabale on the shoulder. "You. Come with me over there. We'll work on swordplay."

She nodded.

Anazâr pushed her harder than ever, but no word of complaint crossed her lips, not anymore.

That night, he stared at the blank wax tablet until his lamp guttered out.

His will to learn was as strong as always, but grief and dread weighed too heavily on his shoulders for him to even lift the stylus. The letters...

He imagined Felix slashing lines across precious paper, a look of otherworldly concentration in his eyes. The letters, writhing together like coiling snakes, like outstretched limbs in an erotic tableau.

He lay back and imagined Felix's concentration again, this time shifted to a different context. Felix, kneeling studiously between his legs, serving him with single-minded intensity. His stunning eyes. His wet tongue, darting and thrusting.

In the part of his mind not ruled by desire, the plea of *leave this city* still resounded. Even as he stroked himself to completion. Even as he drifted into sleep. *Leave this city. Leave this city. Leave this city.*

*By my love for you, leave.*

# CHAPTER 13

Rain pounded down from the black sky. Two house slaves stood in the peristyle garden, holding a protective covering over what Anazâr assumed were the most delicate of the flowering vines. The slaves looked miserably wet, but at least the summer night was warm enough to save them from fever.

If Jupiter did not relent, they might be standing in the garden all night.

"Come," said Alexandros. "The Dominus and Domina are ready to see you now."

He led Anazâr into the room farthest from the street, the richest room of all . . . and the only room in the house that had a door.

"Close the door behind you," said Marianus. He was seated next to Aelia on an ebony couch slung with leopard fur.

Alexandros left. The door closed. The sound of the rain abruptly ceased, then drifted back into his ears as a chorus of murmurs, eerily human-like. He fell to his knees and stared at the ground, melting himself into a mold of submission and desperation, the one feigned and the other true.

"Rise," said Marianus. "You've pleased me. You made errors, but you've done much to redeem yourself. I bought your contract from Iunius today. You belong to me fully."

*You belong to me.*

He'd thought he was used to being owned, to being another man's property, but hearing it now filled him with cold dread, as if he were standing at the edge of the world and looking down into the abyss. Aelia had taken him to this place before, at the warehouse. It would mean something like relief to finally fall.

He stood. "Thank you," he said.

"After the games tomorrow, you'll have another chance to prove yourself in my service. I've concluded, with heavy heart, that my brother is trying to have me killed."

*And now it begins.*

"The first attempt was a ruse, to shift future blame," added Aelia. "We're sure of it. For the sake of this house, for all our safety, we cannot allow him to succeed. Marianus has long overlooked Felix's evil intent out of loyalty to their father. But my husband is most certainly *not* the soft-hearted fool that Felix believes him."

"No," said Marianus, and stretched a protective arm over Aelia's shoulders. Months ago, the sight would have pulled Anazâr's heart into his throat. Now, he . . . noted it, and drew a look of discomfort and vague anger onto his features, simply because that was what Marianus *desired* him to feel. "A fool I am not. I'll give Felix one last chance. One last test. I've sent a message from a supposed friend that I'll be asleep in the house of one of my freedmen on the outskirts of the city, where I keep a mistress. If he comes there to kill me, his own life must be forfeit."

*This is my time.*

"Dominus," said Anazâr, and fell to one knee like the soldier he'd once been. "I will not hesitate. I will not falter. This house is my life and your word is my law."

"And I promise to protect you, of course," said Marianus. "No one will know. And you would be freed."

*A freedman.* How many times had Marianus said that word to Anazâr? Made that promise? Anazâr would have done *anything* to see it fulfilled, to see himself bound in service to Marianus that way. And now it seemed such a pale and impermanent thing in comparison to Alexandria.

"My fortune is in your hands," said Anazâr. "It will always be so."

"I take great joy in your loyalty," said Aelia, smiling. "I was full of natural fear. Fear for my dear husband's life, fear for the future of my son. They have an able protector now."

"The time is set for the day after the games," said Marianus. "If this hateful rain continues—"

There was a knock at the door.

Marianus's voice rose greatly and took on a hint of anger. "Alexandros, I am not to be disturbed."

"I apologize, Dominus," came the muffled voice. "But it's a courier from the aedile. He seeks urgent audience."

Marianus was striding to the door the next instant. The touch of his hand against Anazâr's shoulder was fleeting, but shocking to the core. Hopefully his shiver would be taken for gratitude or desire. And then Marianus was gone.

"Come a bit closer," said Aelia. Her smile had vanished. "I'd have words with you. Very *honest* words. And I'm quite relieved I don't have to go to that fetid warehouse to have them."

"Yes, Domina." It was hard to keep Aelia in his vision. Not that hatred consumed him—hatred was an emotion he could not afford to suffer—but now that the role of benevolent mistress no longer framed his perception, he had nothing to replace it with. She was a wraith, a crossroads, a new moon.

"I know you a little better than my husband knows you, I think." He dared a look into her eyes. They gave nothing away. "He thinks playing to your physical desires and dangling the promise of freedom is enough to secure your loyalty, but I'm not so sure. I think you're a much more complicated thing than you like to pretend."

*Reveal nothing.* Anazâr swallowed hard and didn't speak, didn't acknowledge or refute her accusation. Wished for Amanikhabale's talent with words. That woman could talk a lion out of eating her; surely she could handle a battle of wits with Aelia.

"Anything I tell you will stay in this room. If it does not, I'll have you killed slowly—no, never mind. I'll have some of your gladiatrices killed slowly. Oh, now *that* gets a reaction." She smiled serenely. "You and I are alike, I think, in that both of us play very well the part we are given, regardless of our true desires. You, the loyal slave. Me, the loving wife. The kernel of it? My desired outcome in this world diverges greatly from that of my husband."

A strange sense of relief swelled through Anazâr as he realized this was no trick to test his loyalty. *No. It still could be. Reveal nothing.*

But whatever her goal, Aelia at least seemed unperturbed by Anazâr's lack of reply. Perhaps she was enjoying the freedom to speak at length, without interruption from Felix's barbed wit or her husband's patriarchal proclamations. She swept across the floor, circling Anazâr in a certain predatory—no, carrion-seeking—gesture. Her small, soft hand traced delicate patterns over Anazâr's shoulders. "Don't mistake me for your pet murderess, however. I don't hate Lucius. He's not a bad man. But he *is* beneath me, a fact brought into sharp relief by this new venture as lanista to this freakish troupe, and the fact that his damnable brother seems so determined to sully their name. Unlike my husband, I don't have blind faith that Felix's . . . dispatch . . . will solve all our problems. A higher, better marriage and a return to senatorial circles lies within reach, if my father decides. He's gotten the money he needs from Marianus, after all. But I'd prefer this marriage ended with Marianus dead or in disgrace. Otherwise, I'd have to leave Lucullus behind."

At last, a desire he could understand. She'd left one child behind in her first marriage, he remembered Felix saying. But the first real swell of rage washed into him. What of Enyo's child? Aelia may have a mother's gentle compassion, but it was a selfish thing of limited influence, and Anazâr would do well to remember that.

"Kill my husband. I'll have you freed just the same. Or kill Felix, and I'll have my husband blamed. Deny me, and I'll have my husband buy your Gaius up and sell him to the mines to die. A colossal waste of money, but he'd do it for me. *He'd do anything for me.*" She smiled and spread her hands. "But do it my way, and no one else needs to die. Cassia won't be blamed and crucified. You and I will be free. Felix is irrelevant. Kill him, keep him alive as a lover—" her eyes flashed in triumph as if to say, *Oh yes, I know you better than you realize* "—as you wish. He's of no consequence to me."

He opened his mouth, but it was the reflex of drowning man seeking air. He had no words to speak.

"I think your path will become clear once you understand more of my husband's plan, and who will suffer for it. So I'll let you go now without an answer. If you think to curry favor with my husband by revealing me, know that he loves me beyond all measure. He would never believe you."

"I believe you," he managed to whisper. At last, he understood why Marianus had set out to kill Felix, when disinheriting him would have been so much easier. It was all Aelia. Marianus was a hollow man.

"Good. We understand each other very well, then." She lifted her hand from his crawling skin, relinquishing her claim.

For now.

"I hope the sun comes out tomorrow," she said, as bright and gracious as ever. "In the meantime, you can sleep in the basement, and join your gladiatrices at the Circus in the morning for rehearsals. Go now."

"Yes, Domina."

He wondered if his final answer could be anything other than *yes*. And if she'd have him killed anyway, afterward. Everything was possible. Nothing was forbidden.

"Apollo, may you be increased," prayed the Circus Maximus custodian. He was a man of middling age named Egnatius; Anazâr had known him for many years. "By your merciful light, the games may begin this day."

The dwarf, who stood by the custodian's side, scowled and crossed his arms. It was hard to tell his ancestry, but Anazâr imagined he must not hold to Roman gods. "It's still too fucking wet. Where will we rehearse?"

"We'll figure something out," said Egnatius. "I'll clear out a few shops on the upper level, if I have to. You're not scheduled until twilight, anyway. I'll clear a space after the mid-day show. Yes, that's it." He scratched at his head, gaze darting all over the vast archways of the Circus entrance complex, obviously distracted. "The flooding last night was— I've got to go again. Go buy your people some breakfast. It's on me." He set off for the entrance to the underground staging area, the infernal land of death below the clean yellow sand.

"There's a decent pastry shop over that way," said the dwarf as he turned to Anazâr. "I think it's open already." And then the dwarf squinted upward at the turbulent sky, at the ranks of towering clouds whipping away from Rome toward the far horizon.

Nearly mid-day. A high white sun glowered down on them, casting the vaulting form of the imperial shrine in silhouette. It stretched above the stands like a white eagle, Jupiter's avatar, raising a space to the heavens for his chosen representative on earth. Soon, the sun would pass overhead and the shrine's shadow would stretch down across the stands, onto the ground of the Circus Maximus and beyond, darkening the streets of the city itself. A constant reminder of Rome's power and dominance, as if the gladiators in the arena who fought and died under its shadow needed such a thing.

They'd stationed the gladiatrices on the second level of the entrance complex, all gathered in an impromptu, wooden-walled pen against the side of a rich little temple whose bricks were painted an eye-popping scarlet. Barbershops and food stalls and vendors selling cheap jewelry made from stained leather lined the rest of the walkway to the stands. The crowd swarmed restlessly, waiting for intermission to end, while guards in the employ of the Circus Maximus kept watch for cutpurses.

"I have some good news for you," said Anazâr. "I've been back and forth, talking to some of my former brothers-in-arms. Your old trainer will fight in the midday event."

As he'd hoped, every single head raised.

"I thought only condemned criminals would be fighting then," said Amanikhabale. "Won't the number of fatalities be too high for someone associated with an elite ludus—someone like that walking excrescence we all know and love so well?"

"Apparently he's fallen from favor," replied Anazâr. "A combination of Marianus's displeasure at the failed contract and skills diminishing with age. He'd already won his freedom and sold himself back, not knowing what to do with it. It's likely he won't survive this bout."

"So I'll never get to kill him myself," snarled Rhakshna. "Shit! That's the *opposite* of good news."

"Hard to please as ever, Sarmatian. No matter. Play nicely tonight, like you promised, and I'll make sure you get a real fight the next game."

A lie, of course, but perhaps he could beg a favor on her behalf.

Amanikhabale opened her mouth as if to speak, half of Cassia's name shaped—and then she tightened her lips and looked away.

Venatrix left off translating into Gallic and turned to Anazâr. "Can you go and see? And tell us if he dies?"

"I don't know what he looks like, but I'll ask around and do my best."

He smiled as he left their pen and fell in with the crowd that surged toward the stands at the call of the horns. Whatever happened after the fight, at least *they* would be safe, and perhaps, in some measure, avenged. And then later . . . well, at all costs he'd have to avoid the appearance of having killed a master. Roman law. He wouldn't be protecting his gladiatrices anymore. He'd be putting them to death. But then, did he really have to kill Marianus?

"I've heard it's going to be Parthians besieging a Greek castle. Plus *lions*," the man to his right shouted to his friend.

The friend shook his head in disgust. "Terrible idea! I'm fine with damnati fighting each other to death, or being eaten, but not both at the same time. Too muddled to provide any real spectacle or lesson of moral value."

"Men to the right, women to the left," cried the guard at the archway that led to the stands.

A hand fell on Anazâr's arm.

"Cyrenaicus. We need to talk. There's been a change of plan," said Egnatius.

*Kill.*

The passages of the underground were ankle-deep awash in foul water, worse than galley bilge, reeking of death-fluids. A line of slaves mopped and bailed furiously, paying Anazâr no mind as he stalked onward. He had no need of a guide; he knew this place well.

*Kill him. Make him pay with his life.*

But that would never happen. In Rome, the masters never paid.

He'd seen people he cared about die in the arena before, watched helplessly as they risked their lives. *Gaius.* But it had never hurt like this, never terrified him and made him so impotently furious. He didn't know where to throw the rage. Not yet. So he walked.

*We had the Parthians in one of the stone cells on the lowest level. Mistakes were made. The floodline went up to the ceiling. And the lions are either drowned, too, or vomiting up their guts. The aedile got on his knees and begged your master—*

Lies. He wouldn't have had to beg. Maybe once, Anazâr could have believed that, but no longer.

*How much did it cost, you bastard? How much did that sniveling fool have to pay you for their lives?*

Their lives. Anazâr pressed the heel of his palm to one eye, smothering the urge to punch the closest wall. A stupid, adolescent compulsion.

*—passed the new script to the announcers. It's to be the Amazonomachy. The Amazons attack the Athenians to recover the sister of their queen, but are repulsed and annihilated, symbolizing the triumph of Greek civilization over barbarism. They already have blunted weapons laid out anyway, so it won't be too hard to ensure the outcome.*

Anazâr had reassured Egnatius that he was, above all, a professional. Disappointed at the waste of his training, certainly, but life was uncertain, and one had to be prepared for losses. Anazâr would skip the spectacle and drown his disappointment in a wine flagon at one of the taverns on the third level that served well-off slaves. After all, he was no stranger to wasteful death. That was what he told Egnatius.

Egnatius believed him.

And once he had gone, Anazâr went straight down to the underground.

A group of guards with long spears came at him from the other end of the hallway. He moved aside for them, flattened his back against the slimy stone, made eye contact with them and nodded as if he had every right in the world to be here. They moved on.

He made a sharp right and climbed a short stairway. These stones were dry. The smell receded. The sound of the roaring crowd increased, pulling at him like a tide.

A man stood silhouetted in the passageway: one of the usual guards who was posted at the sally port to repel cowards with a spear thrust through the gate's iron grill. He and Anazâr had never come to blows during Anazâr's time in the arena. Now, Anazâr approached him with the same confidence that had allowed him to win through this far.

"Cyrenaicus! What are *you* doing here? No one told me you were on the program."

Anazâr walked up to him, smiled crookedly, spread open-palmed hands—*orders, you know, there's nothing to be done*—and headbutted him.

They both stumbled back, the guard clutching his head with a low groan, Anazâr shaking stars out of his.

As it often did during such violence, time slowed. The roar of the crowd diminished. Anazâr grasped the guard by the head and pounded him into the stone wall. Crushed his fragile face with a barely perceptible crunch of his nose and a sad little gush of blood.

The guard groaned weakly as Anazâr crouched and methodically stripped him of his armor. A leather over-tunic and greaves—weak protection. The sally port offered nothing better.

A bundle of javelins left by the gate, though, he'd take those. And the guard's spear. And—there was a dead woman propped by the gate, her throat a mass of twisted flesh. *Atalanta*.

*No more.*

He unbarred the gate and burst out onto the sand and sunlight, running. Running for *their* lives. Not his own, not anymore.

 CHAPTER 14

There was a castle. And there was an Amazon army. Not the fierce women of legend, but a ragged gang with blunted weapons who milled in confusion. Soldiers who clung to each other and wept.

There was a story and it wasn't being followed. The crowd shrieked, the chorus rising into the painful upper registers of rage.

Anazâr noted the displeasure as he pounded over the sand. *Rally, move, fight back. Don't let the crowd turn against you.*

A detachment of crest-helmeted Greeks—or the rebels, brigands, or criminals who played at the role—came at the women with long spears. One, two—five of them.

Fifty paces away. Close enough to see Rhakshna screaming and pushing at the Germans, ordering them into position in a language they didn't understand.

"Cyrenaicus! Cyrenaicus is with us!"

No time to turn, no time to tell who'd called. He rounded the gladiatrices. On his left now was the castle, a squat square of wood painted to look like brick. If there were archers inside, he was exposed and as good as dead. *I've fought through a hail of arrows before.* To his right, the gladiatrices.

He had a clear shot at the Greek detachment.

"Shields up! *Attack!*" he shouted, and threw his spear.

The guard's spear was ill-balanced for throwing, and clanged off the shield of a Greek. But the missile shocked them into faltering their march, gave him time to ready a javelin—

And then Rhakshna was upon them. Rebellious as ever, she'd cast her shield aside to throw herself tumbling *under* the wall of spears. She rose up under the chin of a Greek and swung her scimitar into his face. Even blunted, it slashed across the unprotected softness of an eye socket—the man howled like a dog. She took his short sword, cut his throat, and rolled away as another Greek dropped his spear to stab at her.

Anazâr sent a javelin high into that one's chest, where the armor left him bare. He fell. Rolled through the sand. Didn't get up again.

The Germans followed after Rhakshna, shields held at the same height, as good as locked. The other gladiatrices rallied in their wake, a Gallic war chant sounding high and steady over the roar of the crowd. Fickle as ever, the crowd's anger had turned to delight at the Sarmatian's antics.

Three men left now, their longspear angles thrown into chaos by the advancing Germans. Rhakshna came at them from the back. Anazâr sent a javelin over Cheruscia's shoulder and into the throat of another.

Red crests on the sand—the sand, stained dark red.

"They're all dead!" shouted Rhakshna. She faced the teeming stands to the southwest, both fists raised, but basked in the glory of applause for only a moment before turning to her sisters. "Now tell these sluggish bitches to get to work. We've got to take their weapons and cut out these javelins."

Amanikhabale—she was here too, they all were, thank the gods, except for poor Atalanta—was already translating into Latin along with Anazâr. The women rushed forward and pulled at swords, wrested spears from loose hands.

"What were the instructions?" Anazâr asked Venatrix, who seemed stolid as ever, and he thanked his goddess Ifri for that. "What did they tell you at the sally port?"

"That we must fight as we were. We didn't go easily. We thought it was a mistake. Then they killed Atalanta. If we capture the standard in the castle, we can live, that's what they said. I didn't know you'd fight with us. We had no hope before, now I have—"

"How many do we face inside the castle? What weapons?"

"I know nothing."

Of course. Why give them the tools for tactics, when they were meant only to be gruesomely and gloriously slaughtered? The thought didn't dishearten him, it made him *furious*.

Just then, Diana tossed Venatrix a sword, and as she weighed it in her hand, the sun struck a savage light from its mirror-polished surface.

"We hold real steel," shouted Anazâr in the booming voice he'd used every day in the warehouse. Not a performer's voice, meant to whip up the passions of the crowd. This conviction, this expression of genuine feeling, was for his gladiatrices alone. "We fight damnati without training." A damnatus sentenced to die in the arena was what he'd once been himself—another life, another time. But he knew their weaknesses well. "We'll march into the heart of the castle and take their fucking standard! We'll live! As victors!"

"Would this be a bad time to inquire about strategy?" asked Amanikhabale.

"Tactics, I think you mean," said Anazâr, grinning madly, to his surprise—a strange soaring mood had come upon him. He switched to Greek. "We have to keep the crowd on our side, and they love bravery above all else. An all-out frontal assault through the entrance, our strongest fighters in the lead. We'll need to position everyone carefully, but we can't take too much time. Even now, the crowd's cheers are dying."

"I'll take care of that," said Rhakshna. She pulled up her breast band to her armpits, exposing her chevron-etched chest, stalked to where the vast rows of spectators could best look down upon her, and raised her hands to the heavens and howled. The cheers rose again.

"Right," said Anazâr, and switched back to Latin. "I've seen these stage-forts in use before. The walls are low enough for the crowd to see all—but too high to vault. There'll be a corridor about thirty paces long before it opens up. It's done so that the defenders can beset the first attackers from three sides. They want to see attackers pressing forward over a mound of their own dead." *Stepping on the faces of your comrades and brothers and fellow soldiers.* "But if we go through fast enough, break through their line . . . I have the javelins." He tried to think of some role for the women behind him and could not. He was no brilliant general, no Agrippa, and gods forbid he take Marcus Antonius as his model. "We have to stake everything on moving faster, striking harder than they expect."

"Very well," said Amanikhabale. "Shall we start lining up?" She lowered her voice and spoke to him alone. "You know, I halfway thought Marianus and Aelia would let me live, even though I suppose I really knew better. Felix and Cassia may have a chance, at least. I've already cast my dice and it's a damn poor throw."

"I'll hit you worse than in training if you keep talking like that," said Anazâr, soldier-rough, although he, too, had to hope that Felix was long gone to Alexandria and safe. Even if he did survive this battle, he doubted he would live through the night. But maybe the gladiatrices...

Anazâr in the front, Cheruscia to his left, Rhakshna to his right, knowing she'd be crouching much of the time so he could throw over her head. Batavia, Cimbria, Penthesilea in the next row—the next-best fighters, ready to step forward, lock shields, and burst to the right. He ordered them all, giving spears to the ones in the rear, even doing a quick drill for positioning.

There was no movement from the castle. The top of a crested helmet showed over the edge of the wall; judging by the height, they were holding someone up to watch. But they had no javelins, no arrows. He wondered how many were inside, whether they were armed or armored, and how well.

A little beyond where Rhakshna had capered, there *was* an archer's balcony. The man held his bow at the ready in the service of the Circus Maximus, but would not interfere in the fighting in the arena unless called to. He was undoubtedly excellent. Anazâr had seen one of these archers shoot a wall-climbing panther in the eye, first try. No escape, then, though there never was. Win or die. Or perhaps win *and* die.

"If your sister falls, you cannot stop for her," said Anazâr. "Avenge her. Fight on. *Go.*"

They surged forward.

The world narrowed. Darkened.

At the end of the corridor, a wall of bright shields, red-crested helmets, shadowed eyes. Men who wanted to live as badly as Anazâr. No, *more*.

He cast his first javelin. This was what the men of his tribe were born for. The reason they'd ridden halfway across the world, called into the service of pharaohs and imperators. *The Numidians have come with their javelins.* The Greek in the middle fell back, an iron shaft sticking out of his face, flipping upward to point at the sky like a sundial.

In the turmoil that followed, a throat left bared. Another javelin, another life. And then he gripped the last, too close to cast, and sank it into the mouth of a man.

A shield crashed against the side of his head. He jerked away, saw himself about to stumble into Rhakshna, who was hamstringing a Greek.

He had no sword.

Penthesilea pressed a hilt into his hand. "Cheruscia has fallen," she gasped.

He turned around, ripped away the shield of a Greek and hacked at the closest bare skin until the man's arm hung by a tendon and he stumbled back, whining.

Blood. Bodies. His gladiatrices fought bravely, but it was as if they were thrusting into deep raging tidewater. No space opened. No ground taken.

*There were too many.*

"Fall back!" he shouted. "Retreat to the mouth! Hold fast there!"

The press of bodies washed him back and drew him into its fold.

They stopped the line of shields at the mouth of the corridor. The foremost Greek, skewered by a spear through his shoulder, struggled briefly until Provocatrix hacked his neck open.

Over his body, a line of shields stood still. A curse sounded in Latin. "Pull back to where we have the ground! Wait for the bitches to come to us!"

A javelin came flying out of the corridor, but it was ill-cast and slow. Anazâr knocked it aside with his greaved arm. The shields pulled away, the men rushing backward, obeying the command.

"What's our count?" he asked of the women.

"Cheruscia, dead. Rhakshna—there were many men on her..."

"I've got a hole in my fucking leg the size of my thumb!"

He turned to the right. Rhakshna—alive somehow—leaned against the fort's wall, right at the corner, gone pale as milk under the smears of blood, her mouth a rictus of pain.

"Keep your thumb pressed in it, then," ordered Amanikhabale as she tore up strips of Rhakshna's tunic. "I need leather. Leather I can tie—"

Anazâr gripped the spear shaft and hauled the Greek's carcass around the corner. *A fisherman of the dead.* "His armor has leather ties." He turned to the rest of the women. "Hand me that javelin. We'll mount another attack. Their numbers have lessened. We'll win through." *And two of our best warriors are out of the battle.*

The crowd's roar took on that discordant edge of irritation, of impatience.

Batavia's ragged sobs—less cries of grief than sounds of raw pain, as if her lungs were turning inside out—sawed apart all his thoughts of tactics. There was nothing left to do. Attack, attack, and attack again. They'd die one by one. The Greeks would clamber over their bodies on their way to the open sands and the glories of the crowd.

The crowd. The coughing sobs. The taunting voice from the end of the corridor. "I know you all! I know the names of your living and dead! I've fucked half of you whores and now I'll kill the rest, and then I think I'll fuck your whore daughters!"

Diana hefted her sword and lunged for the corridor, howling in Gallic, and gods help him, Anazâr was too far gone in frozen despair to stop her.

"Cyrenaicus!" someone called behind him. Too many voices, too many sounds.

Venatrix and Cimbria hauled Diana back again, gathering her thrashing body between them, patiently weathering the blows from her flailing fists. But Anazâr could see it, the desire that burned in them to follow her on her suicidal charge.

"*Bastard,*" hissed Amanikhabale. "I'd hoped to see our old trainer this day, but with his head on a fucking pike. Not like this." She tied a strip of leather around Rhakshna's thigh with a vicious, desperate tug to staunch the bleeding. It wouldn't hold for long.

"Cyrenaicus! You must look!" Nemesis stood on the other side of the corridor mouth. She'd walked away from the wall and was pointing up to the stands.

He looked.

He saw nothing.

And then he knew. The archer's balcony was empty. *The archer was gone.*

Did they have an ally?

*Felix.*

Anazâr was a master of the javelin and only a decent shot with the bow, but Sarmatians were the deadliest archers alive, raiding a bloody path through the East, whittling down proud armies with their relentless arrows. If they could get a bow to Rhakshna...

"Amanikhabale. Penthesilea." The largest and tallest. "Take Rhakshna and go! If the weapons are on the sand, lift her up on your shoulders and have her shoot over the side—from behind the fort. Go! And Rhakshna—your wound had better stay closed."

"I can't walk, but I'm not dead yet."

That same taunting voice: "Come for your standard, whores, before the crowd turns against you! The games' masters will unleash the fucking lions on you if you delay!"

*No lions left to unleash*, Anazâr thought grimly, but that didn't mean they were safe from the crowd's displeasure. "Let him rage," he hissed. "We wait."

He dared to step back from the mouth, taking enough paces to see past the edge of the fort.

The protective pit that lined the wall—the rains had made it a moat, half-filled with brown floodwater. Two figures clung to its side. Almost too far away to tell...

Amanikhabale stood out against the yellow sand. She'd dropped to the edge of the moat, leaving Penthesilea supporting Rhakshna.

She was pulling someone out. Long dark hair lashing wet down her back—*Cassia.* It was Cassia. Not Felix.

They fell into each other's arms.

A pang of jealousy plucked at Anazâr's heart at the sight of their embrace. Disappointment that it couldn't have been Felix coming to their aid. That it wasn't Felix and himself now, in each other's arms, touching one another's faces in disbelief and wonderment.

It didn't matter.

Cassia had a bow across her back, arrows clasped in one hand. Already, Rhakshna was reaching for them.

They had a chance.

He had told Cassia, before they'd parted, that other lives were depending on hers. He hadn't really known what he'd meant by it at the time, only that she needed to hear it, but it seemed the gods had heard, because now she was playing savior to all of them.

New harsh notes sounded in the cacophony: the creak and scrape of metal. The gates of the sally port.

A full squadron of guards, and Molossian mastiffs on leashes, soon to be loosed upon them. War dogs. He'd rather fight lions. *They* knew fear. The dogs had had it bred out of them.

"We have to attack," he said. "Cimbria, Batavia! Beside me." He weighed the sword in his left hand, the javelin in his right. "*Now!*"

The world narrowed again. The last attack of the last battle—the one he'd never had a chance to fight at Actium. *Let this be the end to the slow carving away of my life. Oh goddess, hear me.*

The Germans at his sides never faltered.

The man who saw him coming flinched, ducked his head under the curve of his shield, and delayed his death a while longer. Anazâr sent his javelin into the right eye of the man standing behind him.

Shields rang. A woman screamed in pain somewhere, and then a man, and then a voice so agonized it was barely human, a sexless death rattle. Anazâr threw his sword from left hand to right—struck out again and again and again, steel seeking skin, throat, any chink in armor or shield.

He'd broken through the line. The pole of the standard was almost close enough to touch. And gods, *there were still more men.* Three advanced on him, closing in from all sides. Number enough to take down even the most skilled gladiator, even one such as Cyrenaicus. As the moment of his death approached, he felt a curious distance, time slowing even further from a stagger to a trickle. All the lives he'd lived, and the man named Cyrenaicus would die holding them.

The foremost Greek toppled to his knees. An arrow sprouted from the back of neck, just under his helmet.

"Die, Roman dogs!" screamed Rhakshna. She appeared to float above the far wall like a goddess of the air.

The two Greeks turned toward her. Anazâr took out the leg of the first with a single sword thrust. Another of Rhakshna's arrows slammed into the other, the last of Anazâr's opponents, the last of the men he'd thought would finally deliver him from his worthless sorry life.

And then she aimed for the rest.

He fell back into his own skin, felt the warm sun beating down on his shoulders, heard the crowd's chant resounding all throughout this holy space.

*The crowd's chant.*

AMAZONAE. AMAZONAE. AMAZONAE.

The last red crest fell to the sand.

Anazâr unseated the pole with shaking arms and lowered it to the ground. "Take the standard," he croaked to the women who now filled the central space of the fort. "We must present it to the crowd and beg for mercy. For having changed the story."

"Yes," said Venatrix. "Soon. We're taking his head, just now. It's the way of our people."

The Gauls were crouched on the ground surrounding a single Greek body. Anazâr didn't need their confirmation that it was the old trainer. Of course it was. He didn't stop them. Maybe before, he would have chastised them or called them away from their barbarian practice when under the watchful eyes of Rome, but he felt no such urge now. Instead, he turned his back on their work and listened to the sound of the hacking sword as it tore inexpertly through skin and sinew and bone.

When it was done, though, he still persuaded them to leave it behind.

As they left the fort to face the crowd, he looked behind, only once. He felt no kinship with Orpheus, only simple morbid curiosity. He'd never seen the man's face.

Resting there in a darkened circle of blood that seeped from the ragged neck, he looked much the same as any other man without a body. All that selfish petty evil, that specter of rape and violence, that taunting voice . . . extinguished forever. It made him think of Felix: *We're all the same. Bags of bones and blood and brilliance.* He didn't see the "brilliant" part, but then, he never had.

That was why he needed Felix.

As they marched out into the open arena and turned to face the roar of the crowd, arms upraised, sun baking the blood on their faces and bodies, broken but *standing*, Anazâr couldn't help but search the stands for Felix.

Held up by her sisters, Rhakshna, with a silent proud tilt of her chin, raised the standard.

And Anazâr wasn't sure what he wished for more: that Felix was out there somewhere, watching, or that he wasn't.

# CHAPTER 15

The crowd spared them.

But that didn't mean Marianus would.

For now, they sat huddled together in some dark holding cell, miles away from the sun and Rome's warm admiration. Rhakshna, Batavia, and Verecunda had been taken to the same doctors that treated the most famed gladiators. If they died tonight, it probably wouldn't be because of their wounds.

Without the strange spirit of battle in him, Anazâr's body shook, reminding him of the fever that sometimes followed on the heels of a wound and often took men's lives with it.

Cassia, filthy with moat water but somehow looking healthier and more whole than she ever had before, wrapped her arm around Amanikhabale's shoulder and finished her story. "Everyone was calling out, fire! Fire! Save the gold, run for the aedile, drag out the babies and—by the gods, it was chaos. The men who usually guarded me were on the other side of the insula. And then Felix—he wore a Phrygian cap and a false beard, but I could tell him by his eyes—grabbed my arm and we ran into the night. He'd raised the alarm as a ruse. Said he'd gotten an odd message to come the day after the games, but he'd come a day before instead because he wasn't such a fool as his brother thought. He took me to another insula."

The plan had been to send a letter to Felix according to the instructions of Marianus . . . and work out a way of imparting *another* message, hidden in some code, to come armed and wary. Marianus and Aelia must have simply sent the note themselves, bypassing Amanikhabale. And Felix, of course, had not trusted it.

"I was supposed to just stay in hiding and preserve my life, but I couldn't, I just couldn't. I had to come here, even when Felix told me you were only set to perform a comic act with dwarves. Now I'm glad I did. You could have all died!" She set her chin, which threatened to wobble with the onset of tears, and allowed herself to be gathered forehead to forehead against Amanikhabale.

"We were meant to," said Anazâr. "And we may, still. Cassia's disobedience and my own may have doomed us all."

*I should have let them die in the arena. Better there than the cross.*

He hadn't thought it through, at the time. All he'd seen was their blood. Atalanta, who'd never rise again. And after his intervention, too: Cheruscia, Nemesis. He hadn't seen her die in battle, but she wasn't here now and wasn't with the surgeons either, which left only one possibility. Her body, borne out of the arena along with the other corpses. Along with the headless body of their former trainer.

How long until Anazâr and the surviving gladiatrices were fated to follow?

Cassia had come. Was Felix here, too? Anazâr prayed he wasn't. He may have been able to trick his way to freeing Cassia, but there was no way he could be so lucky twice. Especially not here.

"Damn good show!"

Anazâr jumped to his feet and looked through the bars. Egnatius stood on the outside, escorting a troop of dwarves. The games' organizers must have found them new opponents for the comic act. Which meant it was nearly twilight. Not long, now, until he and his gladiatrices faced Marianus's wrath.

One of the dwarves gave him a thumbs up. "I thought you were going to be dog meat, but you really pulled through. That was brilliant with the bow and arrows. Completely against the rules and somebody's going to get whipped for it, but *brilliant.*"

Anazâr should have been flattered by the compliment or nervous about the warning. But all he could think about was . . . what if Egnatius wasn't here to congratulate him? Did he have a message to pass? News from Felix? A good-bye? A plan?

The dwarves passed on.

"Well," said Egnatius, lingering behind, "this is an interesting development. The aedile and the praetor have been in consultations since the match. There've been priests consulted. Entrails read. End result: it's not unacceptable to let you leave the grounds alive. Even Cyrenaicus. Even the one who punched out one of our archers. Congratulations!"

"Is our dear master pleased with our resounding victory?" asked Amanikhabale.

"You've certainly made him a lot of money, and that pleases most every man. He received a full fee, plus special prizes, and offers to buy you as bodyguards for outrageous sums. Which he accepted."

"Fortune truly smiles upon him!" the Aethiopian said.

Egnatius's face darkened. "Except, that is, for you, and the murderess beside you, and Cyrenaicus. You'll be going back to his house, in shackles. Guards!"

Two guards shoved Anazâr down the rickety ladder that led to the dim, cool pit of the Marianus cellar. He'd been down here before: it was where he'd slept on that very first night, a lifetime ago. He understood why he was being sent here now. Not to sleep, not this time. It was because it was surrounded on all sides by earth, muffling any sound, and far from the ears of passersby.

"On your knees, slave," growled a soldier. His silver breastplate shone from the shadows, a pale moon falling down upon Anazâr.

The soldier kicked his feet out from under him. He hit the earth cursing, "You're not my equal. Not for bravery, not for anything, not fit to lick my feet, you fucking toad born from shit—"

A boot to his stomach took the rest of his words. The soldier cinched his shackled hands and ankles together behind his back. "I won't kill you. That's what you want, I imagine. Won't be as easy as all that. Not unless your master says so, and I don't suspect he will." He flicked his eyes to the edge of the room, and Anazâr realized that Marianus was here, too. Watching, just out of Anazâr's field of vision. Silently approving of the soldier's treatment of him. So much for the compassionate patriarch he'd tricked himself into believing in.

The ladder creaked again. The soldier rose, ascended through a beam of light, pulled up the ladder, and closed the cellar door behind him. No escape.

Anazâr wheezed for breath until the bruised knot in his stomach finally untied itself, and the musty air flowed freely into his lungs. The cellar grew brighter as his eyes adjusted to the lamplight. He balanced, painfully, on spread knees, his arms stretched down and bound behind him, his throat and stomach bared.

Two more forms lay not far away, bound like him and fallen to their sides, with heavy burlap sacks tied over their heads.

"Amanikhabale? Cassia?" he gasped.

A muffled howl. Weak thrashing.

"You were magnificent," said Marianus, rising from where he'd been sitting on an overturned bolt of cloth, next to Aelia. *Always next to her. Shackling her, and unaware.* "I really would have liked to sell you. I thought about cutting your tongue out and doing just that, since you'd still fetch a handsome price after today, but the Aethiopian corrupts everything she touches. I can't trust you not to write."

He wanted to curse and rage and rage and *live*. But the fire had gone out in him. The last door he'd ever pass through had just closed above.

"Call the soldier back to kill him, dear," said Aelia, her sweet tone at odds with the grim, chill meaning of her words. "I'd like to be done with this business."

"Yes, I'll make sure it's done," said Marianus, gently. "But first, where is Felix?"

No answer from Aelia. She tucked an errant curl back into her upswept hair, seeming to give neither of them any notice.

Marianus reached out, snatching Anazâr's face between thumb and fingers. "Where. Is. Felix?" he repeated, growling now. Oh, he was asking Anazâr.

"I don't know," Anazâr replied, truthfully. "If he's half as smart as he thinks he is, long gone now, to Egypt or Greece or—"

"No. You do *not* play this game with me. I've heard a single slit to the eyeball—"

"Lucius. *Please.* He'll be more forthcoming if you start with the women."

"Oh," said Marianus. "I suppose you're right. As always, darling." He drew a little knife from his sleeve, like one used for paring fruit.

Anazâr's stomach flipped. His head whipped to Cassia and Amanikhabale, both hunched and shivering under their hoods. It took all the power in his body not to wail and rattle against his shackles. But no, it wouldn't help, would only goad Marianus into further cruelty. *Protect them.* Even if it meant turning the knife on himself.

"Why do you call her darling?" he gasped before he'd even had the chance to think it through. "It's me you fuck, while she's out spreading her legs for your brother. You should put *me* in that pretty stola and sit me somewhere nice and ornamental while you cut out *her* tongue."

Marianus rounded on him, but he wasn't angry, he was *grinning*. "How very transparent, Cyrenaicus. But I suppose nobody buys a gladiator for his wit." He studied his knife briefly. "Well then, considering all your plotting, it's clear you know these little bitches better than I do. Who should I start with, then?"

*Amanikhabale,* his ruthless gladiator's mind supplied. *She's weathered torture before and come out whole on the other side. Cassia's too weak to bear it.*

He couldn't choose. *He couldn't.* Maybe if he just clamped his mouth shut, Marianus would return to him with his knife. But he knew it wasn't true. Marianus wouldn't be manipulated so easily. He'd cut both and gauge Anazâr's reaction for himself.

"I can't!" Anazâr jerked in his bonds, shaking his head in exaggerated tearful frustration. "Please! Mercy, Dominus." Weakness drew violence like no other quality. Some men could not suffer seeing a wounded, writhing thing without wanting to stamp it out. *The last game. The last door.*

"Mercy? Tell me where my fucking brother is, and maybe then I'll show them mercy. The mercy of a quick death, anyway."

"Not for them, Dominus. For me. I've seen a man c-crucified. *Mercy.*" He lowered his head in imitation of a kicked dog. His spine screamed in agony and he yanked his neck back up again, into a pose equally animal and vulnerable.

"Your old master did say you were a coward. I didn't believe him, before." Finally, Marianus turned, touching the point of his knife to the pad of his forefinger, twisting it in thought. "I suppose I'll have to now. Very well then, say I show you mercy. What will you show *me* in return?"

Anazâr gulped air in genuine relief. Amanikhabale and Cassia both spared, for now at least.

Except he had nothing to offer. He could only forestall. Delay. And even that couldn't last forever. What was he hoping to accomplish, here? They'd all be tortured and die regardless. He *was* a coward, trying so desperately to goad Marianus into killing him first. It wouldn't save Amanikhabale and Cassia's lives, only save himself having to witness their torture.

The blade of the knife bit into the flesh of his left cheek. "Speak, slave."

"Anything, Dominus. Let the women go, and I'll tell you anything. I . . . Felix. He's my lover. We arranged to meet. I'll tell you where he is."

"He's right here."

*Felix.*

Anazâr looked up, unable to believe that the voice really could be—

But it was. Felix, standing half-hidden in shadow, his face looming over Aelia's shoulder, his hand clasping hard on the junction of her neck and collarbone. He didn't look to Anazâr, just stared, boring holes into his brother's eyes.

"Drop the knife, brother," he commanded.

The knife fell, hitting the packed earth with a delicate sound.

*He loves me beyond all measure.* Aelia's words. Her truth. His own truth.

*Felix.*

"Felix!" Anazâr shouted. "She's reaching for her—"

Aelia slid the hairpin into her fist and twisted in one fluid motion. The jeweled end flashed gold and pink and then—

*Red.*

Blood. Felix's blood, gushing out dark from where the hairpin had sunk into his eye socket.

"Felix!"

Felix clutched his face.

Fell.

Went still.

"Felix!"

Anazâr's whole body bucked against the iron of the chains. He was shouting, but he couldn't hear the words, just felt them searing up his throat, ripping his tongue in half. The chains didn't break. They never would. He didn't understand how he could have ever tricked himself into believing otherwise.

Felix was dead.

Hot tears streaked his face and he didn't care. He was tired of bearing his slave's burden with noble, quiet dignity. All he'd worked and strived for, and what had it gotten him? He cast aside the last of his hope of freedom. Gave in to the weight of the chains. Let them anchor him to the dirt.

And wept.

The point of Marianus's knife touched the underside of Anazâr's chin, tipping his face until they were eye to eye. Or would be, anyway, if Anazâr could bring himself to look at Marianus as he once had. As it was, even though his face was raised, his eyelids sank to hood his swimming vision. All he could see was a dark shadow creeping across the dirt floor.

"So you really were lovers, then," Marianus said, his voice vibrating with tight-reined anger. "Shame heaped on shame heaped on shame, Cyrenaicus. To think I once treasured you so dearly, and now here you are, cowering and sniveling for my cocksucking brother. At least now I'll be rid of both of you."

A trailing pink vision. Aelia's stola. A gentling woman's hand, stroking her dear husband's neck.

"Don't be so hasty, Lucius," she murmured, her voice a sweet, harmonious force. "We'll need to set the scene of Felix's terrible murder. A quarrel between a Roman citizen and his gladiator lover, *tsk tsk*. Well. A barbarian can't be expected to suppress his urges forever, can he?"

Marianus's expression darkened, the heat of his anger extinguished by the calculating coldness of their plot. "Of course."

"Good man." She smiled as her husband rose to standing, unfazed by the blood that welled in the wake of his knife as it cut up Anazâr's chin. She even unflinchingly pried the dripping thing out of Marianus's hand, wiping it clean on Anazâr's filthy tunic before stowing it neatly away in the folds of her stola. "Not your own blade, dear. Use this, instead."

From those same gentle silk folds, she produced another knife. Bigger, more worn than the one Marianus carried, and not even remotely ornamental. Secreted from the kitchen at some point, perhaps.

The one she'd intended Anazâr to kill her husband with before her plans were spoiled.

Now, she pressed it into Marianus's palm and closed his fingers around it. "Have the gladiator kneel next to your brother's body and slit his wretched throat with this. Once he's dead, we'll unshackle him and put the knife in his hand. Lay them both out in the pool of his blood." She paused, casting her gaze about the room like a hunting lioness. "And if the Aethiopian bitch knows what's good for her, she'll be sure to tell the whole lurid story of their affair—culminating in a truly tragic murder-suicide, of course—when she submits to torture later tonight. You do want to live, don't you, Aethiopian? Or shall I have this whole sorry household of slaves killed, and give testimony to the investigator myself?"

*Say yes,* Anazâr inwardly begged. *Say yes, and let this horrible blood sacrifice end with me.*

A long, unbearable silence, as dark and yawning as the unknown of the afterlife.

Amanikhabale spoke. Her voice trembled, but still rang clear and bright, even muffled as it was by the fabric of the hood. "Yes, Domina. For Cassia's life, I'll tell the most sordid tale Rome has ever heard."

If Aelia or Marianus reacted with surprise to the terms of Amanikhabale's bargain, Anazâr did not hear.

To die.

To follow Felix into death.

That would be fitting. That would be the pleasing fulfillment of an incomplete pattern.

 CHAPTER 16

Facedown in blood-soaked dirt, a dead Roman of the army of Octavianus flung over his back. Actium. Those were the siege months. The hungry months.

*The sortie had failed. The enemy's supply lines were too well-defended, and the cavalry had been caught between two lines of spearmen closing like the pincers of a monstrous crab. He'd been knocked off his horse, kicked in the head by another—*

*Anizgul lay beside him. A sword slash had burst one eye, laid his cheek open down to bone and tendons. The other eye intact, death-glassed.*

*Anazâr waited for the soldiers of Octavianus to come and send him to join his friend. A quick stab between the shoulder blades, that would be a fitting end. But their Latin shouts receded. So he rolled the corpse off his back, crawled from the mud, and ran for the trees.*

I'll mourn you later, friend, *he told Anizgul in his mind. The crushing weight of guilt fell upon him. It seemed like there was never a proper time to mourn. The count of the dead was ever climbing, unceasing. So why was he still alive?*

Anazâr wouldn't move under his own power, so Marianus hooked him under the arms and dragged him to where Felix's body lay.

"Don't make this hard on yourself, Cyrenaicus," Marianus said, grunting with the effort. "Lie down." And when Anazâr *still* didn't move, shouted, "Lie down, damn you!"

Felix's body was facedown, one arm at his side, the other fallen draped over his head, as if he were merely sleeping. There was so little blood, Anazâr could almost trick himself into thinking so. He wished he could reach out, touch him one last time, brush the hair from his brow or close his glassy remaining eye, make his pose a little more dignified or *something*. But he couldn't, chained as he was, so he knelt and waited for Marianus's impatience to turn to blows.

It didn't take long.

"I've had enough of this, you bastard fucking—" a punishing weight slammed into Anazâr's back between his shoulder blades

"—slave! Lie down! Lie down!" Over and over again, a hot, thudding pain not nearly as sharp as a whip, broader and duller but *deeper*, sinking into bone and muscle. Certainly not Aelia's kitchen knife. A candleholder, perhaps. *You can't kill me with that,* he almost said to Marianus, in scorn, or in pleading for something faster—he wasn't sure which one. The pain filled him, a constellation of agony: screaming back, bruised knees, wracked arms. And worst of all, the loss and the grief for the light in the world that had just gone out.

He should really just let himself fall. Perhaps, if he aimed right, he'd be able to land close enough to Felix that they could touch. Shoulder-to-shoulder, at least, or with their heads bent to each other's like strolling lovers.

"Lie down!"

If it didn't hurt so badly, it would seem absurd, the way Marianus screamed and flailed and beat him. His pampered master's body, so unused to labor, must be a mess of sweat and nerves by now. *Good.* Anazâr didn't need to seek out a final victory in his master's humiliation and discomfort, but he thought maybe Felix would appreciate it.

"Oh for Jupiter's sake, Lucius. You're making a fool of yourself now. Don't you see all he's doing is getting you worked up? He's obviously not going to do what you say, so would you *please* just put that bloody thing down, pick up the damn knife, and finish him? We'll have the women lay him out properly once he's dead."

"Sorry," said Marianus. "You're right, of course." The candleholder hit the ground with a heavy thud.

Anazâr sank into the throbbing, rhythmic pain of his bruises, letting them rock him like the waves of the ocean. Easing him down to death.

"The knife . . ." Marianus said, and there was cold terror in his voice, but it didn't make any sense, because surely Marianus was not the sort of man who balked at putting an animal to death?

Anazâr forced himself to open his eyes and look.

Felix's hand was wrapped around the hilt of the discarded kitchen knife, the arm that had been lying at his side now extended over his head to grasp it.

*Felix has the knife.*

*Felix is alive.*

Anazâr threw his bound body forward, barreling into Marianus's legs and taking them both to the ground in a pile of limbs and chains and toga. They rolled. Marianus straddled his bucking chest, and then came an open-handed slap across his face, then a punch, then another. But Anazâr was done accepting Marianus's abuse. He'd fight. He'd fight to the fucking death. Blood blinded his right eye. Spots enclosed on the vision of his right.

Aelia screamed.

No more blows came. Above him, Marianus swayed, held upright only by the arm draped over his shoulder and braced across his chest. Felix's arm, capturing his brother in a one-armed embrace.

No, not an embrace.

Stabbing him in the chest from behind.

The knife was lodged deep in Marianus's left chest. Blood cascaded down his chin, dappling the soiled white of his toga. A mortal wound. A quicker death than Marianus deserved. His body jerked and twitched and finally slumped forward over Felix's arm, head lolling only for a moment before Felix pushed him like a sack of wheat onto his side on the dirt floor.

"Anazâr," said Felix, rushing to kneel at Anazâr's side. Marianus's body was a misshapen lump in the background. "Oh, Anazâr."

Anazâr didn't even care that Felix was saying his name where others could hear it. Didn't care at all. He let the spell of it bring them both back to life.

Because Felix *was* alive. The hairpin was gone, leaving his one eye a bulging, bloodied mess, but it obviously had missed the killing angle. Blood was streaked across one cheek, finger marks from where he'd tried to wipe his face. But he was alive. Alive and whole and the eye would heal and all would be well.

"I love you," said Anazâr, and even though it came out a weak croak, he'd never said anything with such power or conviction or meaning.

"Of course you do," Felix replied, "I just saved your life." He smiled, the expression somewhat grim and horrible, considering the state of his face, and then he turned. "Aelia! Get me the fucking keys for these shackles, or so help me gods, I'll give your hairpin back to you in the same way it was delivered to me."

But Aelia didn't answer. Instead, she stood in the space where the ladder to the cellar was raised and lowered, peering to the ceiling.

"Help!" she shrieked. "Help! Help! Alexandros! Lower the ladder! Send the guards! Felix has gone mad! He killed Lucius!"

*The guards.*

Anazâr looked to Felix, smiling when Felix reached out and finally cupped his face in one soft hand.

*I'll die touching you. That's all I ever asked.*

"Alexandros! Alexandros?"

At last, a beam of light fell. The perfect shadowed outline of Alexandros's silhouetted head sketched itself across the floor. "Yes, Domina?" he asked, as calmly as if she'd been requesting wine.

"Lower the ladder! Your master is dead! Send the guards, damn you, man!"

"Oh apologies, mistress. I sent them away. I assumed you wouldn't want them sniffing around while you and your husband carried out your various misdeeds. It appears I was wrong? That the tables have turned? Oh, how tragic. *Felix!* Are you still alive down there?"

"I am indeed!" Felix called back cheerfully.

"And Cyrenaicus? The Aethiopian? And the murderess?"

"All alive, all alive." Felix grinned, turned to Anazâr, and winked his good eye. He stood, leaving Anazâr on the floor, to stroll to Aelia's side.

"What is going on, here? Alexandros, you lower that ladder right now, or I'll have all of you crucified." Without the hairpin, Aelia's hair had fallen, drooping lopsided over one half of her face. Her stola was torn, in the struggle perhaps. When she saw Felix's approach, she screamed and stumbled backward, drawing Marianus's pathetic little blade in her own defense. "Don't you come near me, Felix, you mad fucking dog!" She managed to get one frantic swipe through the air before she tripped over the hem of her skirts and the knife fell away. "Alexandros!"

But Alexandros's head-shaped shadow had disappeared from view.

"The key," said Felix, evenly.

Aelia's cries of "Alexandros! Alexandros!" diminished in volume until, at last, she barely whispered his name. She backed into a corner of the cellar, near the neatly stacked amphorae, and put her hands over her face.

Footsteps sounded above. Alexandros reappeared. A key fell through the opening in the ceiling; Felix snatched it up and scrambled to unlock Anazâr's shackles with it.

"The women first," said Anazâr, twisting his wrists in their bonds. He could bear them long enough to see the women freed, at least. Felix nodded, moving to where Amanikhabale and Cassia still lay prone in the dirt.

Cassia sobbed with relief when the hood was removed from her head. When the chains were removed, she and Amanikhabale fell into each other's arms. Their reunion seemed doomed, impossible, as if Fortune's wheel had carried them high only to crush them underneath at the next turn.

But the wheel didn't turn.

He believed it when Felix undid his shackles. Anazâr stood and then immediately fell again, his knees giving out. Felix sat him atop the overturned bolt of cloth and stroked his hair in absent affection.

They'd really survived. Really won free. Except . . .

Aelia, who'd gone again to stand in the shaft of light, still twisting, face contorting, crumbling to ruin as surely as in a Greek tragedy.

"Is everyone unchained?" Alexandros called down.

"Yes, sir!" Felix replied. He gave a soldier's salute, even though there was no way Alexandros could see the gesture.

"Very good then! All right, Domina, I'm going to lower the ladder now."

"*Finally!*" Aelia snarled. "I'll have you whipped for this!"

Alexandros was unperturbed. "But first, we need to have a little discussion. Namely, I have two very interesting letters here, forged by our Aethiopian friend. Skilled hands, this woman has. I don't know *why* you put them to waste by making her a gladiatrix." He paused for breath, then regained his original line of thought. "*Anyway*. Two letters. Both from dearly departed Marianus, of course, both spelling out his intent to kill Felix, who'd discovered his conspiracy to support the traitor Cornelius Gallus in a bid against the Emperor Augustus—excuse me, Emperor and Son of the Divine Caesar, Augustus. Except one suggests a third co-conspirator, a woman . . . now hmm, who would that be?"

"Alexandros," Aelia said, smoothing her voice to its usual controlled sweetness and demure tone. "Alexandros. Let's not speak of these letters again. You lower the ladder, we go together to find the guards and tell them Felix had the gladiator kill his brother. You'll have to be tortured for your testimony to that effect, of course, but when it's all over and Felix is executed and the gladiator is crucified, I'll have my new husband free you. As a reward for your many years of *loyal* service."

"Counteroffer," Alexandros replied. "You free my daughter in my stead. Oh, but no, I suppose you *can't*. Well then, I guess the original deal still stands. So tell me, Aelia, just how loyal are *you* to your traitor husband?"

Aelia set her chin, her composure regained, and Anazâr knew she'd lost. "I take Lucullus with me. I leave the name Marianus and this cursed house to Felix, seek a new marriage, and our paths never cross again. Those are my terms."

"Felix, is that agreeable?" asked Alexandros.

"I get to be a hero of Rome? I get to keep my house and my man and my family coffers?"

*My man.*

Anazâr's heart was full to bursting.

"I'll volunteer to testify," Amanikhabale put in. She hobbled forward, an arm thrown protectively around Cassia's trembling, slumped shoulders. "I don't mind being tortured so much. Will you promise you'll keep me and Cassia as slaves of your house, Felix? Not gladiatrices? You won't sell us?"

Felix turned to Anazâr, tilting his head in question.

His first decision as paterfamilias of the Marianus house, and he turned to Anazâr.

Anazâr nodded.

"You three planned the whole thing," said Anazâr, later, after the physician had left them alone. "You and Amanikhabale and Alexandros."

Felix prodded at the bandage covering his eye, seemingly dissatisfied with its presence there. "I had half a plan at best. I did what I could. Did you think I'd just let my brother and his wife play me like a game piece? Stand by and watch them gamble your life just the same?" He lowered his voice. "The problem was, Alexandros wouldn't commit. He doesn't hate me, but he doesn't trust me either. She never really wrote those letters. I advanced the possibility with Alexandros, that was all. I'd hoped to use them for blackmail. The Aethiopian had no idea; I've had no contact with her this last month, but Alexandros must have known she'd feign full knowledge. The thing is, he writes half my brother's letters anyway; he doesn't need the Aethiopian to forge the letter he's showing the praetor now—the one that doesn't implicate Aelia, that is, because if nothing else, he's a man of his word."

"So this could all still fall apart." Anazâr walked away from the couch where Felix sat, went to the doorway, listened at the curtain. A praetor was out there in the peristyle, with a full retinue and scribes to take official witness. Pain still chased all over Anazâr's upper body. That Felix was alive and relatively whole was a fact that floated at the edges of his comprehension, far too new and tenuous to celebrate.

"Yes. At worst, they'll arrest me, and take you and Cassia and every slave in the household to the real specialists, the ones with racks. B-but—" he stuttered. Took a deep breath. "But if we can get through the night, get the official version of events established with the praetor, we'll do well. Everyone has something to gain. Aelia wants to leave this household *with* Lucullus. Amanikhabale wants a position within the Marianus house for herself and her lover. Alexandros I tried to offer freedom—"

"I doubt he wants that," said Anazâr.

"No. He wants me to adopt his grandson. That's Alexandros the Youngest. A great big strapping lad, apparently. Who knows, I could have met him at the baths one day—ha!—so he's not exactly someone I'd think of *adopting*, but I doubt there'll be any uncomfortableness, since he's just going to keep on working in the same cloth-shop business along with his ex-father, but with equestrian status, so with any luck his *own* sons will probably turn into a pack of backstabbing blackguards like the rest of the Marianii. I did, however, wish to discuss another addition to our household with you . . ."

A scream sounded from the direction of the peristyle. Anazâr's hurt-laden skin crawled, and he had to remind himself to breathe.

"We need to make sure the physician stays for them," said Felix, who had gone serious very quickly.

"Where's papa?" asked Lucullus as Aelia swung him into her arms. She was already dressed in black, her pale cheeks marked neatly with ashes.

"Papa is dead and gone to join his ancestors," she said. "We're going to your grandfather's house now. Say good-bye."

"Good-bye, house!" said Lucullus. His sleep-confused face fell slack again and he settled in against her shoulder, returning to his dreams. He had no real understanding of death.

Perhaps Aelia would tell Lucullus in the days to come, when he kept begging for papa, that he would have a new father soon.

Felix stepped forward as if to say good-bye, but halted himself. Anazâr remained standing by the wall, under the shadows where the torchlight didn't fall.

Aelia's slave helped her and Lucullus into the litter. "I'll see you at the funeral, Felix. You and I and Alexandros can discuss the unwinding of certain business dealings at that point." She spoke without rancor, and without looking in their direction. Her arm parted the curtain to give the signal for departure, and she was aloft and gone, floating over the threshold into the midnight street, her slaves and guards filing behind her, heads lowered, cheeks marked with ash.

"Well, I suppose that's it," said Felix. "They're all gone." He turned to Anazâr. Reached out a hand, and Anazâr took it in his own, with some concern, because Felix—so calm during the excruciating tension of this evening, *gods*, how he'd been a champion under the eyes of the lawgivers—was trembling as violently as a reed in a windstorm. "And Lucius Marianus—and Lucius Marianus..."

"He's dead," said Anazâr. "You killed him."

"Why, yes, I did," said Felix, and fainted.

 CHAPTER 17

## The month of Julius.

Felix's hair still smelled of the smoke from the pyre, and there was a light dusting of gray ash in his eyebrows. His right eye socket displayed all the alarming colors of the sunset.

"*Water*," he croaked.

Anazâr wanted to go to him, but he would only put himself in the way. Already, Alexandros had motioned for a kitchen boy, who darted into the atrium and placed a glass pitcher of cool water in Felix's hands.

"It was a long walk from the outskirts of Rome," said Felix after he'd drained half the pitcher. "And rather lonely, too. Only the hired mourners for company. No business partners, no clients, no cousins. Nobody to appreciate my speech, which I think was rather finely written considering I'm the one who saw him dead."

"It's the name of Cornelius Gallus," said Alexandros, referring to the forged letter that had sealed all their fates. "Anyone associated with the man is shunned, even in death." Alexandros seemed in much better condition than Felix, although the bandages on his left hand gave witness to the legal procedure of last week.

"They're burning Gallus's poetry, I've heard. Such a shame." He shook his head, a small rueful smile on his lips. If he felt grief or sorrow after the day, he didn't show it. But then, Felix was a cypher at the best of times, prone to treating serious matters lightly and light ones with overexaggerated gravity. "Well, I suppose I'd better get with the rest of Rome and denounce his traitorous lines." He handed the pitcher back to the boy. "I'm for bed."

Anazâr watched him limp into the back of the house.

He waited as the house fell into some semblance of a normal nighttime pattern around him. He hadn't left its walls since the day Marianus had died, and was unsure of what to do with himself either without or within.

He waited. And then he followed Felix.

"I'm here," he called at the curtain. Felix wouldn't sleep in Lucius Marianus's old room, the one with the door. He'd kept his pallet in one of the small rooms to the right of the peristyle garden.

"Anazâr," said Felix. "Can you . . ." The exhaustion in his voice was as thick as cold honey.

"Of course." Anazâr took off his sandals to go lie down beside him.

"Don't go," mumbled Felix, eyes closed. The whole bed around him smelled of smoke, now, and Anazâr made a mental note to have it cleaned come morning. And then he erased the note, because Alexandros would be the one to have it taken care of.

"I won't go," he promised.

He lay there awake, Felix wrapped sleeping in his arms, and knew that for the first time he had a choice. Tomorrow, they'd go to the magistrate and fulfill the promise Felix had made, unprompted, when he'd woken from his faint.

*I'll free you.*

It finally dawned on him. If he wished to leave, tomorrow, he'd be free to. He could walk or find a horse, and return to the lands he came from, or pick a direction and just keep *going* until he found a place where the TMQF was as meaningless and ornamental as Rhakshna's chevrons.

*Don't go.*

Had Felix meant from his bed tonight, or from his life entirely?

And come tomorrow, how would Anazâr answer?

"If I do this for you, will you get up?" asked Anazâr, a little wearily.

"I'm already up, am I not?" Felix grinned, teeth shining in the gray early morning light. He gestured lewdly to his erection, which pointed quite energetically to his navel.

"Out of *bed*," Anazâr elaborated, giving that fat little cock a rough warning squeeze.

Which didn't serve as much of a warning at all, of course. Instead Felix sighed in relief and lifted his hips. "Do I really have to?" His decadent, sleepy whine seemed at odds with the enthusiastic pumping of his hips as he fucked Anazâr's fist.

"You're the master of this house now. Unless you want your family to fall to ruin, and take all of *us* with you, you're going to have to take on a few distasteful responsibilities. Among them is getting up early."

"I'm a creature of pleasure, Anazâr. I can't help my nature any more than that Sarmatian ball-crusher can help hers. What say you—we sell the domus and move to something a little smaller and secluded, where I can write. Just the two of us, oh and of course we'll take one or two slaves—"

Anazâr abruptly stopped his ministrations. "And what of the others? We *all* depend on you."

"Don't say 'we' like that when your freedom's all but secured. You're already a freedman in my eyes." He groaned, flung himself on his back and pulled the sheet over his eyes to block out the light.

"Your eyes don't hold sway over Roman law, if you haven't noticed. And even freed, I'd still have a responsibility to other slaves. Only a heartless man forgets that bond." He pulled the blanket away.

"I've heard freedmen make some of the harshest owners," said Felix. "I'm glad that won't be true of you. However inconvenient your morality proves with regards to my inherent love of leisure."

Anazâr gripped him by the hips, rolling him onto his hands and knees, and slid one hand down between his legs, from hole to cock in a single teasing stroke. "There are pleasures better than lazing about talking about radish rape. And you'll have them, if you please me."

Back arched, ass thrusting upward, Felix trilled with pleasure. "Do tell me more—"

"Lucius Marianus Felix! Your clients *continue* to wait!" barked Alexandros from just outside the curtain.

"The circling hounds of Cocytus! Damn them all," groaned Felix. But he rose to his feet and stumbled for his under-tunic.

"You'll make a good businessman," Anazâr said, sitting up. "I have faith in you. You'll talk circles around all those other fools and double the Marianus wealth in no time."

"Unlikely," said Felix, the word muffled as he wriggled the tunic over his head and down onto his lithe body, a movement that stirred Anazâr toward desires they'd never be able to consummate in the time remaining. He sighed. Felix, however, smiled enigmatically and rushed forward to press a quick little peck of a kiss on his chin.

"I won't beat around the bush," said the client first in line. It was a short and ragged line, compared to the last one Anazâr had seen in the Marianus atrium, but it was a line nonetheless. "Your brother said he'd loan me some money to expand my shop. Never got around to it." He worked his eyebrows in a hopeful motion.

"Alexandros, is there any reason not to lend it?" asked Felix. His toga folds crisp and properly placed, he looked fairly respectable from where Anazâr stood as bodyguard. Which showed, however, his good side, the one with the undamaged eye.

"Yes, Dominus. Two reasons, in fact." Alexandros lowered his voice. "One, we do not have the money." He raised it again. "Two, he has not repaid the last one we gave him."

"Oh dear," said Felix. "No, no, no, this won't do at all. Go away for a while, would you please?"

The man hung his head and left.

The next man had a complicated legal problem involving his wife's ex-husband suing to recover her dowry. Felix promised to bring it to the attention of the Marianus family lawyer. Then there was a woman, a widow named Tullia, who owned a bakery that supplied the Marianus textile factory with bread, complaining that the factory manager was shortchanging her. Felix again promised to look into the matter.

A thin young man in an equestrian toga came next, carrying a scroll and smiling in a somewhat unctuous manner. "I'm working on a book of poetry," he said. "Since you're a patron now, Felix, I was hoping you could—"

"Just because we had sex once doesn't mean I'm going to throw money at you. Well, perhaps if you were a whore I would. Are you a whore?"

Alexandros looked to Anazâr and lifted an eyebrow. Anazâr was helpless to do anything but shrug.

Felix, whose face was turning an alarming shade of red, didn't wait for an answer. "And anyway, your verse is more inept than your handjobs, if that's even possible. So apparently, even if you were a whore, I *still* wouldn't throw money at you. Begone, before I set my gladiator on you!"

*My gladiator.* Anazâr schooled his features into something neutral, suppressing the strong urge to pull some kind of face.

"You're just jealous," muttered the man over his shoulder as he made quickly for the exit.

The next man was Quintus. "I come here for my salary every week," he said. "You give me—I mean, your late brother gave me—"

"Alexandros," moaned Felix. "Take care of this." He looked around, as if searching for another exit unclogged by clients. Looking at the room now, it seemed there were far more of them than Anazâr had originally noted. He was beginning to understand the root of Felix's overwhelmed frustration. "I have an appointment with the magistrate. Ana— I mean *Cyrenaicus* and I must be off!"

"I'll follow you," said Quintus.

"Piss on that!"

"You don't want me and my cousins to follow you? I mean, that's sort of our job, when we're not guarding warehouses." He frowned.

"Yes, I suppose I need a fucking *retinue* now. Of course. Well, come on then."

The clients fell into line behind him. When they'd exited the front door, Anazâr saw Felix pick up the pace of his stride, as if he could outrun them, but his "retinue" just matched his speed, bustling along in anxious, needy silence. Would their desperation outweigh their inevitable revulsion at Felix's manner? Anazâr wasn't sure. For the sake of the household he hoped so.

"Is this man your natural son or brother?" asked the magistrate, in the chanting tone of a ritual. Solemn, ancient, and one of his eyes held a milky cloud, forming a weird mirror of Felix's youth and darkly bruised, swollen socket.

"No," said Felix.

"What is his purpose of manumission?"

"To be my bodyguard."

Felix's lawyer shook his head violently. They'd met him at the magistrate's office; he'd rushed Felix immediately into a corner for a private consultation.

"Sorry," said Felix. "I meant, he's going to be one of my managers. Right."

"We shall proceed, then. Cyrenaicus, step forward. Who will argue for the freedom of this unjustly enslaved man?"

Was there such a thing as justly enslaved? But those were the words of this ritual, this strange mock trial, this script that when read to the last letter would magically culminate in his improbable freedom.

"I will so argue," said the magistrate's lictor, and raised a stick. "I declare his status as freedman." The ceremony, at that moment of mock threat, became real to him, embodied, visceral. When the rod of vindicta touched him, he would be a freedman. And more than that, a Roman citizen.

"Does the lawful master contest the restoration of liberty?"

"No," said Felix, very firmly, but the magistrate wasn't listening; another lictor was whispering into his ear.

Anazâr heard. Heard the conviction in Felix's voice, heard Felix's pure uncomplicated belief that Anazâr should be free. Free to stay or leave. Free to love him, purely by choice.

*He is not your master.*

His love for Felix had *always* been a choice. And now, as then, he'd choose to love him. Choose to stay.

"There appears to be a complication," rasped the magistrate. "Lictor, return the vindicta."

*No. No no no.*

Felix's face showed the grief Anazâr could not allow himself.

"Are you all right?" asked Felix.

Anazâr leaned against the gate to the street. Clients waited outside; he couldn't let himself be seen like this. "Yes. I just need to catch my breath. Really, I'm all right."

"I'm so sorry. I thought we could get through it without the fucking *complication*. I struck it out of my mind that *Lucullus* is your master, and it doesn't matter if I'm the boy's real father, as far as the law's concerned I'm just your master's guardian, and there's a matter of filing a declaration in front of the proper witnesses, and I *hate* the law, I absolutely despise it, the courts and the magistrates and the whole rotten sanctimonious lot of them—"

Anazâr took a deep breath, straightened, and grabbed Felix's flailing wrist. He'd been slashing at the air like a swordsman. "I said, I'm all right. I trust you. You'll have full ownership when Aelia remarries. Until then, I trust you—I trust you not to sell me, even if you grow tired of me."

"I'll *never* grow tired of you." Perhaps that was the wrong thing for Anazâr to say, because even Felix's good eye looked raw and red now.

"Well, fine, but if you did, I know you wouldn't cast me aside. And you wouldn't . . ." *Whip me. Beat me. Humiliate me. Send me to the cross.* "I trust you to take care of me, Felix. I don't crave a master in my life, but if I did, it would be you."

"But I don't want this. I want *you*, but I don't want—"

"Calm yourself. We've come too far, risen too high. *Together*."

Felix blinked, and pain followed, written all over his face. But he calmed. "Damn, it hurts," he said, and dabbed a handkerchief at the corner of his wounded eye. "Though every time the pain strikes, I remember what a miracle it is I'm still alive."

"Oh, come off it. I remember learning in gladiator training, if you shove a thin spike in someone's eye, you're supposed to wiggle it back and forth. Otherwise, it's too unreliable as a killing stroke. Though I forgot the lesson in the cellar that night."

"Aren't we a fine pair of soldiers," said Felix, smiling crookedly, the way Anazâr loved.

"Lucius Marianus Felix!" called the lawyer, walking toward them from a far corner of the courtyard. "I've got some good news for you. You and your *freedman*. Come back with me."

"Does the lawful guardian acting in the best interests of the lawful master contest the restoration of liberty?"

"No," said Felix, very firmly. Again.

The lictor brought the rod down. Tapped Anazâr somewhat anticlimactically on the head.

"In concordance with the model of the ancients and the will of the people, I declare this man restored into liberty by Quiritian law." The magistrate gestured to Felix.

Felix grasped Anazâr by the shoulders and turned him around in a circle. Anazâr felt perilously light, as if he could float into the air without Felix's touch anchoring him to the earth.

"Walk forward in freedom, Lucius Marianus Cyrenaicus," said the magistrate. "And have your name entered onto the rolls. We are done here."

"Will you stay?" asked Felix as they walked away from the magistrate's office, leaving their tumultuous past somewhere within its halls and rooms. "With me?"

"As long as I can stand you," Anazâr replied. "So maybe stop letting your former lovers into the house. And don't leave any more fruit pits lying around in our bed. And wake up in the morning without my needing to cajole you."

"Can I still play the game where I try to use as many innuendos around Alexandros as I can manage without him noticing?"

"He always notices."

Several days later, after searching Felix's various haunts around the domus to no avail, Anazâr found the man in an office closet, searching through accounting scrolls. Alexandros was peering over one shoulder, keeping him on task, perhaps, or answering his questions about the minutiae of running household and business.

Felix had been true to his word about taking his new position of paterfamilias with due gravity, and that fact pleased Anazâr immensely, even if Felix occupied the role with far more complaining than seemed strictly necessary.

"Anazâr!" he greeted cheerfully upon looking up, squinting, from his rolls. "Just the man I wanted to see. We've been going over the future running of the family affairs."

"Oh?" Anazâr moved to his side, opposite Alexandros. He'd spent the afternoon wandering the streets, trying to come to grips with the feeling of walking them as a free man. He'd had to produce proof of his citizenship to two guards, which had been nerve-wracking but ultimately painless. His dread of that experience, however, had been easily balanced by the satisfaction he got from buying pastries at a street stall with his own money. He placed one before Felix now.

"How did you know I was hungry? Brilliant man." Felix grinned up at him, mouth begging for a kiss.

*Later.*

"Well, tell me what you've decided, then."

Felix nodded studiously. "Well, to start with, we're slightly rich, at the moment at least. The payment on the gladiatrices went through. Don't worry, they won't be returning to the arena. Some eccentric old codger of a senator with far too much money on his hands purchased them as bodyguards for his diplomatic travels. Supposedly to drive fear into the hearts of potential enemies when they see that even the women of Rome are fierce fighters. That or I think he may have something of a fetish, but I'm hardly one to judge."

*With that little box of pleasures you've gifted to me, kept under the bed? No, you are not.*

"Of course, there's a slew of debts to be paid—most of them mine, I'm sorry to say—and an array of business partners who've closed accounts for fear of scandal, but I still think we'll come out on the other side with a little more than we started with. I've also decided, with Alexandros's advice, to pay you a regular salary for your services as a bodyguard, which will leave Quintus and his fellows spread less thinly so they can focus on the warehouses."

"Thank you," said Anazâr, too stunned by the news to be more eloquent. "It goes without saying that I'd lay down my life for yours, Dominus." After gaining his freedom, the word had become something like a term of affection. Felix proved spectacularly enjoyable to serve, most days.

"Well, I'd prefer if you didn't, but it *is* technically a part of the job description, so..." Felix waved a hand dismissively. "And anyway. By the end of this week, I hope to have an appointment to adopt Alexandros's grandson, as we'd agreed, but I wanted to discuss something else with you, too. Do you remember the night... well, *the* night?"

*The night you saved my life and killed your brother? The night we fought for and won our freedom?*

"Yes," he said, and left it at that.

"Well, on that night I mentioned a further addition to our household. I've been speaking with the old woman Dara—you remember her, as well?—and she says the girl Litis has made good steps toward recovery, such that she can stand the sight of men again. I'd like to... well, that is... I'm *going* to adopt her. I've seen her housed and provided for thus far, but I think she deserves more than the hovel she's been living in, considering the sacrifice her mother made, and all because of the feud with my brother. I'd like to take her into our family, not as a slave, but as a daughter. It's hardly ever done for girls, but the lawyer says the adoption would be recognized. I'd have her raised and educated here, with Dara as her maid. *You* obviously wouldn't have to think of Litis as a daughter, but I—"

Alexandros be damned. Anazâr surged forward, capturing Felix's mouth in a kiss. Once the shock had worn off, Felix laughed against his lips, pulling back with a teasing little bite.

"You approve, then?"

"Gods, yes," Anazâr replied.

The sunlight hit the garden with such brilliance that the flowers seemed to glow around the edges with their own light. A blue-winged butterfly made its rounds from vine to vine, swooping and skipping through the bright air.

In the shadow of the colonnade, Amanikhabale rested. She wore a sleeveless tunic without a shawl now that the languid summer heat had arrived.

There were new scars on her back, mixed with the old ones.

Anazâr sat down beside her.

"Cassia told me you'd changed your mind," he said. "That both of you want freedom, and you will not stay. I'd hoped to continue our lessons, but I—well, I wish you well, wherever you decide to go."

She kept her eyes on the dance of the butterfly. "Opportunity presents itself. I've been in contact with one of my countrymen. An ivory merchant. He's old, and he wishes to return to Adulis before he dies. He'll marry me, and I'll be his nursemaid on the journey and until the end. His heir afterward."

Anazâr remembered her swift action in the arena, and how she'd kept Rhakshna from bleeding to her death. She'd saved them all, even barely wielding her sword. That she had such medical training surprised him; that she had kept it secret did not.

"I always thought I'd live and die in the mother of cities," said Cassia, who came walking toward them bearing water. "But she's told me such tales of Adulis! The soaring obelisks, the silk flags streaming over the port, the spices from far India sold cheap as salt. Sunrise over the Red Sea." She sat down and passed the water to Amanikhabale. "I'll be leaving my shame behind. And my daughter. I trust my sister to raise her, but Cyrenaicus, will you— Don't tell her I'm still alive, but . . ."

"I'll look in on her," he promised. A silence fell. They were used to departures without farewells, but this time, the air cried out for words, and he had so few of them.

At least he had his name to give.

"My name is Lucius Marianus Cyrenaicus now," he said. "But I was never from Cyrenaica. I was born deeper in the western desert, and named Anazâr of the free people, the Amazigh."

Amanikhabale smiled. "I'm no Nubian warrior queen, so I'm leaving that name behind when I walk through these gates. My name is Si'we of Adulis in Aksum. Hail and farewell, Anazâr."

"Hail and farewell."

# EPILOGUE

### The month of December. Emperor and Son of the Divine Caesar Augustus and Titus Statilius Taurus being consuls. Year 728 from the Founding of the City.

The northern sky was a roiling mass of dark gray clouds. Anazâr sighed and burrowed his hands deeper into the folds of his cloak. His thoughts drifted south, down to the warm shores of the Red Sea. "I hope it doesn't snow," he said.

"No!" said Lucia Mariana, and scrunched up her face in grave displeasure. "But I *want* it to snow. It used to snow all the time, in the mountains where I was born. We'd take wooden boards and slide on it."

"Did you!" said Anazâr. "It never snowed where I came from. And I've only seen snow once since I've been here."

"How can you say you don't like it, then?" She reached out and he took her small hand in his own, letting her lead him from the open air of the garden back toward the office.

"I suppose you're right."

"Of course I am."

Anazâr laughed at her smug, self-satisfied tone. "You sound more and more like Felix every day," he told her. "I'm starting to worry."

Speaking of Felix, they found him sitting behind his desk, half hidden by a mound of precariously stacked scrolls. A small brazier sat by his feet, giving off a comfortable warmth. He seemed half asleep.

Still holding Anazâr's hand, Lucia dropped her other hand onto her hip, every line of her body radiating impatient womanly disapproval. "Papa. Felix."

Felix's head snapped up, big gray eyes blinking back sleepiness. The scar on his eyelid became nearly invisible. "Oh, my, is it that time? I told Alexandros to . . ." He looked around the room, seemingly forgetting his train of thought. He looked a little like he'd forgotten where he even was. "After all . . . So . . ."

"I don't mind missing a lesson, but Big Man needs all the help he can get, don't you think?"

Anazâr looked down at her, feigning a wounded look, but it was true. Litis-now-Lucia had only joined the household a scant few months before, and had arrived just as unlearned as Anazâr, but she'd quickly surpassed him in nearly every subject. *Especially* reading, which Felix was inordinately pleased and proud to find she had quite a knack for.

After her arrival, each passing day found their house more and more filled with poetry, until Anazâr felt he was breathing words instead of air.

"Very well," said Felix. "Tablets!" And then, when he noticed there was no one running to answer his beck and call, rose in search of them himself.

Anazâr and Lucia sat cross-legged on the rug, close enough to the brazier to keep their fingers warm. Felix soon tossed them wax tablets, each with a stylus neatly slotted into the corner. "Sappho in Latin?" asked Anazâr, hoping Felix would answer in the affirmative. He liked the simple language, the shorter lines, the marvelous power of the images.

"No, something a little more philosophical, I think. We don't want Lucia getting bored." Which was true, because unoccupied, she could become quite the terror, like a tiny meddling Amanikhabale but with Rhakshna's fierce temper. "*The Nature of Things*, by Lucretius. I don't have it all memorized—I'm not *that* bloody brilliant—but I know quite a few passages by heart. Attend! *Nor can motions that bring death prevail forever, nor eternally entomb the welfare of the world; Nor, on the contrary, can motions that give birth to things and growth keep them forever created.*"

"Too long!" cried Lucia when he paused for air. Felix paid her no mind. He had a wonderful voice for recitation, even though Anazâr had to agree the lines were long and unwieldy. He forced himself not to drift off on them like a boat on the black sea of sleep, Felix's voice in his sails.

Tonight. He'd have Felix recite some lines for him tonight, when they were in bed together, until his dreams were filled with whispers.

"Thus the long war is everlasting waged, with equal strife, between the principles of things; Now here, now there, the vital forces of the world prevail, or fall. Mingled with funeral cries are the bewildered wails of infants coming to the shores of light." Felix took a deep breath and returned to his normal register. "Start with 'nor can motions.' N—"

The light from the garden dimmed as clouds rolled overhead.

Anazâr remembered the winter night he'd stolen the horse and ridden for his freedom. Remembered snowfall the next day, and the tracks left behind for the slave catchers, and the cold and the hunger and the bone-gnawing loneliness. The only snow he'd ever seen.

Lucia was right. For all he'd witnessed of the world, all the suffering and tragedy and misery, there seemed a wealth of unimaginable happiness and beauty just beyond the edge of his experience. Awaiting him.

*So let the snow fall.*

He traced the perfect circle of an O, looked up to Felix, and smiled.

# GLOSSARY

**Adulis**: A Red Sea trading port in modern-day Eritrea (see Authors' Note).

**Aethiopia**: A term used by the Romans for regions and peoples south of Egypt (see Authors' Note).

**Africa Proconsularis**: A Mediterranean coastal area encompassing modern-day Tunisia and part of Libya. Formerly Carthaginian territory that by Augustus's time was under the dominion of Rome.

**Aksum**: An ancient kingdom on the Horn of Africa (see Authors' Note).

**Amazigh**: The ethnic name for a people of Northwest Africa, also known as "Berbers" today (see Authors' Note).

**Atrium**: The open-ceilinged central court that formed the heart of the Roman home and held a pool to collect rainwater. Romans received guests and clients formally there.

**Bithynia**: A Hellenistic region in modern-day Turkey. Bithynia was a key Roman province.

**Calidarium**: A room in the Roman bathhouse where hot baths were taken. This was the hottest, steamiest room in the bathhouse progression.

**Cinaedus**: An effeminate or flamboyant man who didn't conform to Roman standards of sexuality and masculinity; also used to refer to a man who takes on a passive role in anal sex.

**Cyrenaica**: A city in modern-day eastern Libya.

**Damnati**: (singular: damnatus) Criminals sentenced to the arena to die or become gladiators.

**Denarius**: (plural: denarii) In Roman currency, the denarius was the most common coin, made of silver.

**Domus**: The city home of a wealthy Roman.

**Eques**: (plural: equites) The equestrian order was the next-highest rank after plebeians. Originally, it was linked to cavalry service in the military, but by Augustus's time, the association with cavalry and horsemanship was no longer strong. Members of the equestrian order were required to maintain a certain level of wealth or become unenrolled.

**Flagrum**: A scourge with sharp pieces of metal attached to each strand of the whip. Punishment by flagrum was intended to mutilate and kill.

**Frigidarium**: The cold room of the Roman bathhouse, which contained either a small cool dipping pool or a swimming pool.

**Galli**: (singular: Gallus) An order of eunuch worshippers of the Phrygian goddess Cybele. After voluntarily castrating themselves, the Galli adopted the dress and mannerisms of women.

**Gaul**: A region of Western Europe that would later encompass modern-day France and Belgium, as well as parts of Northern Italy and Western Germany. By the time of *Mark of the Gladiator*, parts of Germany were under Roman rule (see Authors' Note).

**Genii**: (singular: genius) An important animist religious/spiritual concept for ancient Romans. People, places and things could all have guiding spirits, referred to as their genius.

**Gladiatrix**: (plural: gladiatrices) A female gladiator.

**Hades**: The ancient Greek god of the underworld. The term is also used to refer to Hades's domain—in other words, the land of the dead.

**Insula**: Literally "island," but also used to describe the many apartment buildings in Rome, which were as heavily populated as small islands. All but the wealthiest Romans lived in insulae of varying quality. They reached as high as nine stories.

**Lanista**: The head of a gladiator troupe. Generally a disreputable and lowborn profession, although nobles could own gladiators and hire lanistae with no loss to reputation.

**Ludus**: A gladiator school.

**Murmillo**: A type of gladiator. Murmillos had distinctive heavy crested helmets and fought with large shields and straight swords.

**Numidians**: People of the old Numidian Empire in Northern Africa west of Carthage (roughly modern-day Algeria). The Numidian Empire flourished in the second century BCE, though by the first century BCE, it was under Roman rule.

**Ornatrix**: A hairdresser, beautician, and cosmetologist to Roman women.

**Parthia**: A region of modern-day northeastern Iran. Under the Arsacid rulers of the time, the Parthian Empire stretched from Mesopotamia into Central Asia.

**Paterfamilias**: The head of the Roman household. Not merely the father, this man was the absolute ruler of his house and all the people in it, including his adult sons or brothers as well as women, children, and slaves.

**Peculium**: A slave's money and property, which was under control of his or her master but could eventually be used to purchase their freedom.

**Peristylium** (also: peristyle) Large Roman houses had an open area both in front (the atrium) and in back (the peristylium). The peristyle was a more private area mostly devoted to a garden. The division between the two open areas contained a room called the tablinium, which commanded the house and served as the study for the head of the household.

**Pharmacopola**: A sometimes derogatory term for a seller of medicines.

**Phrygia**: A Hellenistic region in modern-day Turkey. The King Midas of legend was a Phrygian.

**Plebeian**: The lowest and most common division of Roman citizen, neither noble nor patrician. However, many plebeians were extremely rich and influential. Certain political posts were reserved for plebeians. By Augustus's time, people of plebeian descent could even become senators.

**Sarmatian**: A group of central Asian horse nomads with a warlike reputation (see Authors' Note).

**Senator**: A political and class position. The senatorial order ranked above the equestrian order. Although the original Roman senate had only patrician members, by the time of Augustus there were also plebeian senators.

**Serica**: A land in central Asia that the Romans believed silk came from.

**Tepidarium**: A room in the Roman bathhouse where warm baths were taken.

**Thraex**: A type of gladiator whose armor and weapons were based on those of Thracian. The thraex fought with a curved sword and small rectangular shield.

**TMQF**: *Tene me quia fugio*. Literally, "Halt me, for I am a runaway." One of several potential messages tattooed on slaves in order to mark their status and decrease their chances of escape.

**Vindicta**: The act of recompense or redress under Roman law. Also refers to a special rod used in the ceremony of manumission.

# AUTHORS' NOTE

### DATES

*Mark of the Gladiator* is set in Rome, 26 BCE. It's been five years since Augustus defeated Marcus Antonius (also commonly known as Marc Antony) at the Battle of Actium, and Rome is transitioning from republic to empire. There are still two elected consuls every year... but now Augustus is always one of them, and the other is always one of his closest supporters. Augustus himself will eventually become deified in his own right, by Senate vote, but for now, he's known as the son of the divine Julius Caesar.

Roman historians told dates mainly by who was consul that year, a maddening system in light of the fact that many consuls had the same names because they came from the same families. The secondary dating system was based on years from the founding of the city. According to this notation, 26 BCE was 728 years after founding.

### POETRY

The Romans based much of their literature on Greek sources; educated Romans studied Greek literature in the original and in translation. In the comic dinner scene when Felix snatches up a ladle, he's declaiming from Homer's *Iliad*, in Latin.

Cornelius Gallus is a real figure who was a famous poet before he became governor of Egypt. Contemporaries like Virgil and Horace spoke of him as a literary god. But he fell into disgrace, was stripped of his position by the Emperor Augustus, and killed himself in 26 BCE. Today, only a few lines of his poetry survive.

Sextus Propertius was a young rising star in 26 BCE. He published his second book of elegies around this year, and it's from that book that Felix's "don't hate me because I love too much" lines are taken. He wrote four books of elegies in all.

Lucretius's *On the Nature of Things*, the one Anazâr's new family uses for writing practice, came out a generation earlier, in 50 BCE, and was a major influence on later Latin poets.

Catullus, a poet of the same generation as Lucretius, is not mentioned in the text, but he did write a poem threatening to rape a literary rival with a radish. Roman poetry spanned a very wide range of subject matter.

All the translations featured here are part of the public domain.

## ETHNICITY

The Roman world centered around the Mediterranean, and Northern Africa was an integral part of it. Romans used many geographical terms for this area, some of which have quite different meanings today. Libya might mean any part of Africa west of Egypt. Aethiopia might mean any region south of Egypt. The Romans also used the word "Aethiopian" to describe anyone with dark skin.

Anazâr's people were politically part of the old Numidian empire, which spanned much of modern-day Algeria and Tunisia before being subsumed into the Roman Empire. Today they're commonly named "Berbers," which comes from the same word family as "barbarians" and is often considered offensive by the modern-day people, who refer to themselves as Amazigh people, or in the plural as Imazighen. Retired soccer player Zinedine Zidane is probably the most famous person worldwide of this ethnicity.

Nubia, directly south of Egypt, overlapped with modern-day Sudan. At the time of the story, the Roman Empire was engaged in a border war with the kingdom of Kush in Nubia. The Kushite queen Amanirenas successfully defended these borders. Our "Aethiopian" character, however, is most definitely not from Nubia, but from the Red Sea coast area that became modern-day northern Ethiopia and Eritrea. In that region, the kingdom of Aksum was a rising power, competing with Kush for trade with Egypt and also trading with India via sea routes.

The Gauls in modern-day France and Switzerland had already been conquered by Julius Caesar in his campaigns of 58 to 50 BCE, resulting in the massive enslavement referred to above. A generation later, there were still intermittent rebellions of Gallic tribes. Roman border wars with Germanic tribes had been going on for a century by this time, and would continue on for centuries longer.

The Sarmatians were central Asian horse nomads notorious for their warlike tendencies. The Greek historian Herodotus claimed that Sarmatian women were not allowed to marry until they had killed a man in battle. Archaeologists have since backed up some of the legends with physical evidence: many Sarmatian tombs include women buried with their armor and weapons. The closest people to the ancient Sarmatians are the modern-day Ossetians in Russia and Georgia.

# ACKNOWLEDGMENTS

This book could not have been written without many online historical resources. Chief among them is the Perseus Digital Project at http://www.perseus.tufts.edu/hopper.

## ALSO BY HEIDI BELLEAU AND VIOLETTA VANE

The Druid Stone
The War at the End of the World
Hawaiian Gothic
"Salting the Earth," a short story in the anthology Like it or Not
Cruce de Caminos
Harm Reduction
The Saturnalia Effect

## ALSO BY HEIDI BELLEAU

Bookended
The Flesh Cartel, with Rachel Haimowitz

# ABOUT THE AUTHORS

Violetta Vane grew up a drifter and a third culture kid who eventually put down roots in the Southeast US, although her heart lives somewhere along the Pacific coast of Mexico. She's worked in restaurants, strip clubs, academia, and the corporate world and studied everything from the philosophy of science, to queer theory, to medieval Spanish literature. She has a faintly checkered past, a cinematic imagination, and a passion for stories that make readers shiver, sweat, and think.

Heidi Belleau was born and raised in small-town New Brunswick, Canada. She now lives in the rugged oil-patch frontier of Northern BC with her husband, an Irish ex-pat whose long work hours in the trades leave her plenty of quiet time to write. She has a degree in history from Simon Fraser University with a concentration in British and Irish studies; much of her work centered on popular culture, oral folklore, and sexuality, but she was known to perplex her professors with non-ironic papers on the historical roots of modern romance novel tropes. (Ask her about Highlanders!) Her writing reflects everything she loves: diverse casts of characters, a sense of history and place, equal parts witty and filthy dialogue, the occasional mythological twist, and most of all, love—in all its weird and wonderful forms.

Please visit violettavane.com and/or heidibelleau.com to find free short stories, book extras, and news.

# Enjoyed this book?
# Visit RiptidePublishing.com
# to read three other exciting
# Warriors of Rome titles!

*The Left Hand of Calvus*
ISBN: 978-1-937551-61-2

*The City War*
ISBN: 978-1-937551-56-8

*He Is Wothy*
ISBN: 978-1-937551-54-4